Ride

to the

Altar

Linda W. Yezak

Ride to the Altar
Linda W. Yezak

Copyright © 2018
Linda W. Yezak

Cover design by Indie Cover Design –
www.indiecoverdesign.com.

Images from Big Stock Photo:
"Warm, Glowing, Southern Sunset" by Simeon D

"Lovely Couple Waiting St. Valentine's Day" by
Yacobchuk

Printed in the United States of America

Published by Canopy Books of Texas

ISBN: 978-0-9973336-6-4

Dedicated

to everyone who wanted to know what happened to Talon's first love, Janet, and why Patricia never seemed to talk to her mother. Thanks to your notes and comments, I developed the plot for Book Three of the Circle Bar Ranch series. I hope this answers your questions!

If you are offering your gift at the altar, and there remember that your brother or sister has something against you, leave your gift there in front of the altar. First go and be reconciled to them, then come and offer your gift. (Matthew 5:23-24, NIV)

Chapter One

A handshake is the initial measure of a man. The grip provides the best and the worst first impressions. Impossible through Skype, so Talon Carlson determined to use the alternative: steady, eye-to-eye contact.

He scrubbed his hands down his jean-clad thighs. Funny how he could propose to Patricia Talbert in an arena of seventy-five thousand avid bull-riding fans, yet he shook like a wobble-kneed colt in front of the blank computer screen. But he was just old fashioned enough to want to do this the right way.

He poked a button, Skype connected, and Patricia's father, Dale McAllister, appeared on the monitor. At six o'clock in the morning eastern time, the U.S. Senator from New York wore a suit and tie and looked ready for his Monday commute to DC. The somber attire complemented his authoritarian expression. Gunmetal-gray hair held silver wisps at the temples, and dark eyes bore an intensity matching his profession—or matching a father who was meeting his only daughter's fiancé for the first time. Didn't matter that the daughter was over thirty and the new owner of a two-thousand-acre ranch in Texas.

"It's nice to finally meet you, sir," Talon said. "I've heard a lot about you."

"Believe me, I've heard a lot about you too." Mr. McAllister's voice sounded deep, gruff. Intimidating.

"Yes, sir. I'm sure you have." He gulped. "Sorry that we have to meet like this. We intended to fly to New York—"

"Yes, Patty told me. No need to apologize. I understand you have a responsibility to your church, and performing funeral ceremonies is part of it." The senator offered a sympathetic nod. "Sorry for your loss."

"Thank you." The funeral had been for one of the most beloved women in the county, Beth Griffith. Her husband, Griff, had asked Talon personally to perform the eulogy. As a bullfighter, Griff had saved Talon's hide more than once, so there had been no question that Talon would say yes, even if it meant missing their flight to New York.

Mr. McAllister leaned back, though the distance between his face and the monitor didn't lessen the effect of his scrutiny. "I understand you have something to ask me."

"Yes, sir," Talon squeaked, then cleared his throat. He tried again, clasping his hands between his knees to stop their shaking. "Mr. McAllister, I love your daughter, and she loves me. I'd like your permission to marry her. Your permission and your blessing."

Pat's father tapped his fingers together. "You know she's been married before."

"Yes, sir. I know."

"You know she was hurt."

"Pretty badly, yes."

"I never did like that boy."

Nothing Talon could say to that. Since the older man's gaze seemed distant, best to just wait him out. He would never hurt Pat the way Kent Talbert had, but proof accompanies action. Mr. McAllister would know the kind of stuff Talon was made of as time went on. His saying so now wouldn't be convincing.

"Sometimes I think if he hadn't died, heaven help me, I would've killed him myself." The senator focused on him again. "You know what was wrong with him?"

Besides the fact he was a no-good, opportunistic, cheatin' womanizer, no. "Got my thoughts. What do you think?"

"He was a city boy. City folks—especially rich city folks—have different ideas from those of us raised on farms and ranches. Different priorities."

This seemed strange from a man who divided his time between DC and New York, but Talon nodded. "Yes, sir." After all, Mr. McAllister had been raised on a ranch, and it was his brother, Jake, who'd willed this one to Pat.

"I want a man for Patty who would make her happiness his top priority."

"As it should be."

"Are you that man?"

He straightened in his seat. "Mr. McAllister, I don't fall in love easily. Only once before in my life, and she died before we could get married. I love your daughter. I have a lot of respect for her. She's a good woman, and I'm honored she agreed to be my wife. I'll do everything in my power to assure her happiness and well-being."

The senator rubbed his jaw, pensively eyeing Talon through the monitor. "Patty told me about your first fiancée. What was her name?"

"Janet Parsons."

"Losing her was pretty rough on you."

"Yes, sir." About killed him. Took him years to get over her death, an experience made worse because he'd been a suspect in her murder. "Not something I care to repeat."

"I don't imagine. But if you loved that deeply once, you can do it again. You've been given a second chance, son. That doesn't happen often."

"No sir, it doesn't. I've been mighty blessed."

"I want you to continue to consider Patty a blessing in your life. That's what she is, and she deserves to be honored as such."

Talon didn't need to be told.

"She's old enough to make up her own mind about who she'll marry, but I appreciate your asking me. That means something." He sat quietly a moment, his face inscrutable, then he nodded. "I'm going to trust you with my little girl, young man. Don't let me down."

Talon released his breath. "I won't, sir."

"Call me Dale."

The grin started in Talon's heart, then burst forth on his lips. "I won't let you down ... Dale."

"Good. Welcome to the family. We'll let the women handle all the details." He shifted in his seat, making the leather squeak. "Is Patty around? I'd like to talk to her."

"I'm sure she's close by. I'll get her."

As Talon rose from his chair, the senator said, "Nice speaking with you, son."

"And with you, sir—Dale."

As he strode to the door to find Pat, he allowed himself a full-fledged grin. That hadn't been too bad. The hard part had been reading the man. Her father bore two expressions— stern and not so stern. Probably a requirement for being a senator. But then, he'd called Talon son and said to call him Dale. Good start.

When he opened the door, Pat stumbled through it. She caught her balance with a hand against the doorframe. Standing in the hallway with a crimson blush accentuating her sheepish expression, she looked adorable.

He chuckled. "Were you able to hear good enough?"

She scowled and swatted his arm. "Did it go all right? What did he say?"

"He said he wanted to talk to you."

"Okay, but what did he say about your proposal?"

"He said—"

"Talon!" One of the ranch hands, Chance Davis, burst through the front door and caught sight of them in the hall. "We've got more cows down."

"Ours or Griff's? How many this time?" Talon reached for his coat and hat on the rack by the door and headed out with Chance. They couldn't afford to keep losing cattle. They'd already stretched themselves too thin.

Patricia started to follow the men out to the cold late-October morning, but her father barked her name from the computer. She did an about-face and returned to the office.

The news about the animals had rattled thoughts of her dad right out of her mind. Every dead cow was money out of their account. How many had they lost this time?

She settled in the swivel chair Talon had abandoned at her cluttered desk and tried to offer her father a smile. "Hi, Daddy."

"Hi, baby. What was that I heard about dead cows?"

She shot a breath through her teeth. "We've lost a few recently, and we don't have a clue what's killing them."

"I heard Talon say something about them being Griff's. Maybe that won't hurt your herd."

"Griff's cows are our cows. He had to sell off his cattle and several acres of land to pay his late wife's medical bills." Broke her heart to think of it. After the funeral, the whole county had pitched in to help, but it wasn't quite enough. He'd still had to sell some of his assets. "We bought a quarter of the herd and about five hundred acres that join the ranch to the north."

Her dad frowned. "I didn't realize the Circle Bar was flush enough to make that kind of purchase."

She swept her fingers through her hair. They were okay for the most part, but the point was to winter the herd, then sell them in the spring to recoup some of their investment. Impossible if the cattle kept dying.

But how could she tell her father they could lose a substantial amount of money? How could she admit that the decision to put the Circle Bar in such a financial predicament had been her own? Oh, as foreman—and her fiancé—Talon had agreed, but the ultimate decision was hers. Her first major move as a ranch owner could cost her the spread.

She shook her head. They'd pull through. They had to.

"We're good. It's a little tight, but come spring we'll be better." She lightened her voice with an uncertain optimism. "Spring calving will help the bank account."

"I'm sure it will. Best time of the year." He slapped his chair arms and began to push himself up. "I'll get your mom. I know she's chompin' at the bit to talk to you."

"Don't, Daddy. Not right now. I want to check on the cattle and see what's happening."

He lowered himself to his seat again. "I understand, and I'll cover for you this time. But you will have to talk to her someday, Patty."

Not if she could help it. "I'm not ready yet. After the stunt she pulled, it may be a while."

"What stunt?"

"Don't act like you don't know. She sent Aunt Adele here to break us up."

He winced. "Yes, I know. That was wrong of her. But this has been going on for a while. You need to settle it." He held her gaze with an intensity he rarely used with her. "If you're willing to throw away a relationship with your mother because your feelings got hurt, how will you ever make a marriage work?"

"Ouch, Dad." There was more to it than that, but she didn't want to explain to him. Not now. She'd grown antsy to check the herd, and the last thing she wanted to discuss was her on-going feud with her mother. "I'll talk to her, but not right now."

"Fine. I'll have her call you later in the week. Will that work?"

"That'll work." Especially if she could be anywhere but here when the call came. "Gotta go, Daddy. Love you."

She disconnected before he could speak again. She had other things to worry about than her meddling mother.

Grabbing her jacket on the way, she ran down the porch steps and out to the old farm truck. After a couple of tries, the engine cranked, and she headed southwest where they'd pastured Griff's herd. That acreage held two ponds and the finest grass on the ranch. But with winter closing in, they'd had to supplement the hay with a high-protein feed.

The truck bounced and rattled over a rise. From there, the valley spread before her, and she spotted the headlights toward the south, where the guys rounded up the herd. She drove down the side of the hill until her headlights landed on Talon. He trotted Bodine toward her, then dismounted and walked the horse to her pickup.

She peered at him in the predawn grayness. "What's happening?"

"Three more down." He leaned against the window frame, worry lines etched in his face. "That's eight total. I don't know what happened. Pretty anxious to hear what the vet says."

Saturday, when he found the first group of dead cows—five that time—he loaded one of the carcasses to take to Zach Crampton, the large-animal vet. Zach had promised a report early this week, but he hadn't delivered yet.

"We should keep them separate from our own brand," she said, "at least until we know what's getting to them."

"That's the plan, but we're moving them again. Front pasture this time. Maybe we can keep a better eye on them."

Beyond her windshield, Chance Davis and Buster Milligan, another one of the longtime ranch hands, flanked the herd. Chance drove the four-wheeler, its light beams bouncing crazily over the rough terrain. Buster rode one of the horses, whooping and flinging his arm to drive the cattle northward, tracking the direction from which she'd just come. The senior hand, Frank Simmons, pushed the herd from behind with his pickup. Hard to believe that out of a herd that size, eight dead cows could threaten their bottom line so severely, but over the past year, as she learned contemporary ranching techniques, she'd really stretched the budget to make the ranch as efficient and modern as possible. Every cow was important, especially if it was pregnant. And as far as she knew, they hadn't lost eight head. They'd lost sixteen.

She asked, "Have you heard whether any of the other ranchers are losing Griff's cattle?"

"No, but maybe Zach has or someone at the Co-op. Chance and I are going to order range cubes for the new storage bin this morning. I'll ask around while we're there."

"Good."

She shook her head. If losing a few head could hurt them financially, losing the herd would be devastating.

Chapter Two

By the time Talon and Chance entered the Co-op Feed Store that morning, Talon already felt wrung out. He'd called the vet before they left, knowing it was too soon to get a report. The wait would be interminable, but at least the doctor had given him one answer. None of the other ranchers in the area had lost cattle. Good news for everyone else.

Chance forced Talon's mind to the task at hand. "About time we get a feed bin high enough to drive under. That'll sure make the mornings easier. How'd you talk Pat into it?"

"It was her idea. She figured if we wanted to increase the herd and the acreage, we needed better storage. Pulling a lever to fill the hopper will be better than heftin' feed bags."

"Yep." Chance headed back to the equine section with a "catch you in a bit" tossed over his shoulder.

Talon stayed his course and threaded his way through the aisles, past the veterinary pharmaceuticals, fertilizers, and tractor parts, all with different sharp odors vying for his attention. At the order desk in the back of the store, he rapped his knuckles on the faded laminate countertop. Both men on the other side turned toward him. Bart Nelson grinned.

Colton Royder scowled.

"You take this guy," he said to Bart. "I'll be in back."

Bart waved him off, then turned to Talon. "Good to see ya, man. What can I do for you?"

Talon nodded toward Colton's retreating back. "He working here now?"

"Yeah, we took him on last week." Bart leaned toward him on the counter, resting his forearms on the surface, and glanced around before speaking in a low voice. "Ben Kilgore fired him. He was on rocky ground anyway after the way he acted in March during that bull-riding event y'all were in."

"Ben said he was a good hand."

"He also said the boy's got a temper."

"Truth in that. What is it about the kid's temperament made y'all hire him?"

Bart shrugged. "He's the boss-man's nephew. What're ya goin' to do?"

"Put up with him, I guess."

Bart raised his eyes heavenward and nodded. "Now, what can I do for you?"

"Bought a new storage bin for feed. Reckon you can get a truck out, fill it up?"

"Sure. What you want in it? How much?"

Talon gave him the weight requirement and the brand of range cubes they used.

Bart nodded. "We can deliver it tomorrow. That soon enough?"

"Sounds like a plan."

As Bart crossed over to the desktop computer, Talon reached for his wallet. "How much do I owe you?"

"Nothing yet. We'll bill you after the first delivery."

"Great. Thanks." He started to leave but then turned back. "You heard anything about Griff Griffith's cattle dying?"

"No, no one's said a word to me if they've lost any. Didn't you buy some from him?"

"A sizeable number of them, yeah. And we've lost a few."

Bart winced. "I haven't heard about that happenin' any-where else. Most folks are like you, ordering more cubes than usual to feed their extra cattle."

"Maybe the vet'll give us an answer soon."

Talon wandered away from the counter and searched for Chance in the equine section but caught sight of Colton instead. Just what he needed, having to confront that arrogant kid every time he came in. He'd beaten Colton—and everyone else—in that last event, enough that he could hang up his spurs like Pat wanted and not regret it. Colton had carried on about losing, but by then, no one cared. Talon slipped an engagement ring on Pat's finger in front of the entire crowd at the stadium, then strutted off with her on his arm and a whopper of a check in his hip pocket.

After that, Colton was just a flea on a dog.

Talon found Chance at the back wall, near the harnesses and lead ropes. When he approached, Chance pointed at the community bulletin board. "Marc Travis is selling a couple of his Quarter Horses."

A dun and a strawberry roan posed in an image fringed with several copies of Marc's phone number, ready to rip off the page. Both horses seemed young and healthy.

"He trains them right," Talon said. "You thinking of getting one?"

"Nope. I was thinking about Pat. Didn't she say once that she wanted to teach kids how to ride?"

"I think she meant for English saddle riding. Show jumping and such, like she used to do." He stroked his jaw. "Wonder if she could use Quarter Horses for that."

"She jumps Tandy, and he's a Quarter Horse."

"So she does..." What had happened to her dream? She hadn't mentioned it since she first moved into the ranch house last year. Had she been too busy helping him chase his dreams to chase her own?

He tore Marc's number from the bottom of the page and stuffed it into his shirt pocket. "Ready to head for the ranch? Got all that fence work waiting on us."

Chance groaned. "Let's stop by the house first."

"I reckon the fence can wait a bit."

Thirty minutes later, they parked at the building site sitting on the acreage Pat had carved out for them from a corner of the Circle Bar. The wedding present held the double purpose of getting Chance and Marie out of the ranch's main house while still keeping them near enough that Pat wouldn't miss her best friend.

Talon released a low whistle. Despite the construction clutter on the grounds, the outside of the house was inviting, with its wraparound porch, three dormers, and a chimney on either end stretching to the sky. Chance and Marie had opted for an off-white brick with maroon trim and a darker maroon metal roof.

"It's coming along."

"Yeah." Chance killed the engine and stared at it with pride. "The electrician came out last week, so the crew will start putting the drywall up today."

He climbed from the pickup and headed for the house, with Talon trailing. They entered a skeletal, two-by-four world that echoed with the loud pops of nail guns and the high-pitched whine of a table saw. Electrical wires nested between the studs and hung from the ceiling, waiting to power a home.

A balding, brawny guy of sixty operated the table saw. He caught sight of Chance and turned off the machine, then lifted his safety glasses to his forehead. "Comin' right along, doncha think?"

"Yep." Chance followed the foreman deeper into the forest of two-by-fours.

Talon felt a slight twinge of envy as he looked around. Chance had it made. He married Marie—Pat's best friend from New York—just a few months after they'd met, and now they were moving on with their lives together. Thanks to her past life with that lout of a husband of hers, Pat wanted to move a bit more slowly. If she'd only set a date.

Nearby, two men worked together hanging drywall; the younger one held it against the frame, and the older one shot nails into it, fastening it to the studs. When the older one finished, he turned to give instructions to the other, and Talon got a better view of him. Justin Anthony. He sported a slight bump in his nose, evidence it had been broken, and he was thinner than Talon remembered, but it was definitely him.

Talon approached him and extended his hand. "Hey, man, haven't seen you in years. How's it going?"

Justin shook with him. "Tolerable. Heckuva lot better now that I don't ride them bulls."

"I hear ya." Talon nodded toward the drywall. "You're doing this now?"

He shot a thumb toward the foreman, who was returning with Chance at his heels. "Working for my old man. I figure I'll take over the company someday. Not as exciting as the rodeo circuit, but it's safer. Pays better."

"That's what counts."

Chance slapped Talon on the back. "Ready?"

"Reckon so. That fence won't build itself." Before they reached the door, Talon turned back to Justin. "Close as you are to the house, you ought to come on up and see us sometime."

Justin eyed him with his brow furrowed. "Oh, you can count on it."

His tone made the hair on the back of Talon's neck stand up—or maybe it was the chill from the open door. Either way, he shook it off. "See ya soon."

In the ranch office, the computer chimed with a Skype alert. Patricia scowled at it. Maybe hooking up the account hadn't been such a great idea after all. Given one more moment, she would've been on her way to the lawyer's office to sign the papers on the land they'd bought from Griff. She could still pretend she hadn't heard and continue with her plans, but she'd promised Daddy. No point putting it off.

She sighed and poked a key to connect. "Good morning, Mama."

"Good morning, darling. I'm so happy for you." Natalie McAllister's tone oozed a syrupy sweetness, along with a suspicious hint of spider-and-fly. "Talon seems like a fine man. Your father was quite impressed."

Patricia fisted her hands in her lap, preparing for the other Prada pump to hit the oriental rug in her parents' Manhattan condo. "But?"

"But nothing, dear. Your father approves of him, and your aunt Adele is particularly fond of him. She told me how much you two seem to love each other and how happy you are at the ranch. I can see why you'd hate to leave it."

"I have no intention of leaving it."

"Of course not, dear. I didn't think that you did." She sighed. "Will there ever come a time when we can have a conversation without suspicion and barbs?"

They hadn't yet. But maybe Mama truly was happy for her. Who knew? Who could tell? Still, offering the benefit of the doubt would help avoid the confrontation Patricia had been ducking for over a year. "You're right. I'm sorry."

Mom waved the apology aside. "So, have you set a date? We really need to start planning."

"Actually, we haven't decided anything yet. We've been too busy lately to give it much thought."

"Perfect. You remember the Redbury, don't you?" She disappeared from the screen, and a picture of an elegant, golden-hued room replaced her. The area featured muted, recessed lighting, mirrored pillars, and ornate doors and windows. The image shifted to another one of the same room, decked out with tables and chairs draped in champagne-colored covers. Flowers and candles adorned the tables, and bows accentuated each chair back. "This would be a perfect place to hold the wedding and reception. If we book it now, we could grab the next available date. You know how long the waiting list—"

"Mama, I'm not sure I want to get married in New York. My life is here now."

"Oh nonsense. Of course you'll get married here. Now, what about this place?" The images shifted to a more modern venue, all brass and glass and beautiful views. "This is the Skylark. See those windows? All that natural light? Wouldn't it be wonderful to have the Hudson River as a backdrop to your wedding?"

Patricia huffed. "You're not listening to me. Would you come back onscreen please?"

"Of course, dear." Her mother reappeared, complete with sweet smiles and innocence. "What did you want to say?"

"What I've been saying all along. I live here now. In Texas. All my friends are here. If I have another large ceremony—and I'm not saying I will—it'll be here, at the ranch, like Marie and Chance's wedding."

"But what about your friends here?"

"I have no friends there." Other than Marie, all her New York friends had turned out to be like Kent: two-faced opportunistic users. She'd discovered this the hard way at considerable emotional cost. "Aside from you and Daddy, there is no one in New York I want to see."

Her mother sniffed. "You talk as if you're never coming back."

"I'll visit, of course, but this is my home."

"You'll visit?" Her eyes brightened. "If you come soon enough, we can at least shop for your gown. Bridesmaid dresses too. Wouldn't you like that? And maybe we can visit the different venues, just to see. What could it hurt?"

She swallowed a sigh. Maybe Mom was trying to get along. But it felt more like she was trying to take control of a union she'd disapproved of a few months before. Disapproved enough to send Adele Cameron to Texas to sabotage it.

But maybe she was trying. "I'll think about it."

"Please do. I'm anxious to see you. It's been too long."

True. She hadn't been back since helping with Daddy's election campaign last year. "I will, but no promises, okay? We really have our hands full right now."

"As long as you'll think about it. Hope to hear from you soon. I love you."

"Love you too, Mom." She disconnected and released a breath. She'd fulfilled a promise to her dad and refused to make promises to her mom. Now, maybe she could put them both off a while longer.

Aunt Adele strolled into the room. "Everything okay?"

"How much did you hear?"

Her aunt settled into a brown leather chair across from her desk. Despite the deceitfulness that brought her here, Patricia was glad she had come. Spending several months on the ranch had been healthy for her.

"I didn't hear much," she said. "Just you trying to get out of a visit with your mother."

Heat rose to her cheeks. "We're busy around here. A lot of work to be done."

"A lot of work that the men handled themselves before you came along and can still handle themselves. This shouldn't stop you from returning to the City for a few days."

"Mom wants us to get married in Manhattan." Funny how enthusiastic she'd seemed about their wedding, considering she didn't want Patricia to marry a cowboy. "What has she said about Talon? Has she really changed her mind about him?"

"You sound more worried about her than you did your father."

"Daddy grew up on a ranch. I knew we'd get his blessing. But Mom ..." She was harder to read.

Her aunt leaned forward. "Honey, why don't you let the men handle this business."

Patricia raised a brow. "This is the twenty-first century. Women handle business these days."

She scowled. "Don't get smart. I know you can, but you need a break, and a trip to Manhattan would be just the ticket. We could fly out together. I'd enjoy being home again." She cocked her head and peered at Patricia from the corner of her eye. "Besides, you can't hide from your mother forever."

Oh, but she could try.

Chapter Three

A t the coffee bar of the Quad-B—Boots, Buckles, and Bibles Boutique—Patricia put money in the jar for her espresso and sat at a small table to watch Marie Davis assemble a display of Christian magnets. Marriage had settled the former runway model, who had always been on the lookout for a fun time. These days, Chance gave her all the fun she needed. Their relationship was good for her, not to mention her relationship with God. She'd grown in Him so much and so quickly she almost didn't resemble the woman Patricia had known and loved for years.

But then, Patricia had changed a lot too. The big three combination of God, the Circle Bar, and a cowboy named Talon kept her happy these days. Now, if she could only figure out what was happening to the herd—and how to avoid a trip to Manhattan and how to plan her wedding and—

"Get your papers signed?" Marie glanced at her from the display case.

She patted her purse. "Signed, sealed, and delivered. The Farm and Ranch Credit Bureau and the Circle Bar will be engaged in business for the next thirty years."

Marie snorted. "The Bureau is getting a lot of business from the ranch, when you include our house loan." She stopped fussing with the magnets. "Chance said the ranch has lost some cattle. That's gotta hurt financially, right? Cut the bottom line?"

"It certainly doesn't help." Patricia blew on her coffee and took a tentative sip. "The guys took one of the cows to the vet to autopsy—well, necropsy. That's the right term for dead cattle. Anyway, maybe it'll turn out to be nothing." Although losing eight cows didn't seem minor. Still, what she knew about cattle wouldn't fill a thimble.

"I hope it's nothing, or at least something that can be easily solved. The Quad-B's doing okay, but I don't think it could support Chance and me if something happened to the ranch." She finished with the display and made room for it on the glass counter. "You have a lot of people depending on you for their livelihoods, and that includes us."

Patricia lowered her cup to the table. Everyone on the ranch, a total of eight people who had made the Circle Bar their home, depended on her. Buying more land and cattle, upgrading the ranch with the equipment it needed, had seemed the right decisions at the time. But maybe she'd been wrong to do so much at once.

If the ranch kept losing cattle, losing her investment, the results would be far worse than simply letting the others down. They'd all struggle financially. Maybe even hunt for other jobs, other homes. Buster and Frank had dedicated most of their adult lives to the Circle Bar. Jorge "Chef" Garcia and his wife, Consuela—their handyman and cook-slash-housekeeper— owned a property nearby, but they had worked on the ranch for over thirty years. They were family.

Talon and Chance had grown up there.

She sank lower in her seat. What had she done?

"Aw, honey, I'm sorry." Marie gave her shoulders a squeeze. "I shouldn't have said that. Everything will be fine. You'll see."

"I hope you're right." Though the rock in the pit of her stomach said otherwise.

The shop door opened with a chime and a cold gust of wind. Katie Pierson entered, shivering in her puffy ski jacket. "I swear, the temperature dropped ten degrees since I left for lunch. October never can figure out how cold it wants to be. Tomorrow it's supposed to reach the seventies." She shrugged out of her coat and glimpsed Patricia. "Oh hey, Pat. If you two are heading to Betsy's for her meatloaf special, you'd better hurry. She's almost out."

Marie wrinkled her nose. "How can you eat that stuff?"

"Just like Ma used to make." Katie waggled her elegant brows and headed to the back to hang up her jacket. When she returned, she leaned against the counter. "What's new out your way, Pat? Heard talk in the diner about y'all losing cattle."

"Word gets around fast, doesn't it?"

She shrugged. "Numbers like we're talking do. Half a herd in a week tends to draw attention. Any idea what's happening to them?"

"We're hoping the vet can tell us. And it's not half a herd." Not yet anyway. "We've lost eight cows. Apparently, someone's been exaggerating."

The door opened again, and a couple of young women, bundled to their noses, bustled inside. If the temperature dropped below sixty in Texas, the locals yanked out their heavy coats. This barely passed as sweater weather in New York.

Katie pushed away from the counter. "If Zach Crampton is your vet, you're in good hands." She strode to the customers and asked if she could show them something.

Patricia pushed aside her tepid espresso and looked at Marie. "Do you want to brave the so-called cold weather and go out to lunch?"

Marie pressed her hand against her stomach. "Not really. I've been queasy all morning, and the thought of Betsy's meatloaf only made it worse."

"What's wrong?"

"No clue. Must have been something I ate at breakfast. Usually I love Consuela's sausage and egg burritos, but maybe they didn't agree with me today."

"I'm sorry about that, but I'm glad you want to skip lunch. I'm not anxious to meet the town gossips." She stood and draped her purse strap over her shoulder. "I want to head back to the ranch."

Not that she could do anything, but if another cow had fallen, she didn't want to be in town when she heard about it.

This made her crazy. They'd pastured cattle all over that ranch without an ounce of trouble. Surely it was something unique to Griff's cows, but what? If only Zach would call. The pressure of waiting kept her insides knotted.

That evening, Talon slipped his arm around Pat's shoulders and enjoyed her warmth as she snuggled against him on the couch. They hadn't bothered turning on the TV. Nothing to watch anyway. A fire blazed in the hearth, a lamp added a soft glow, and they were alone. He had all the entertainment he needed.

A log snapped in the fireplace, sending red embers up the flue. Yellow and blue flames danced around the wood, mesmerizing him. Soon the stress of finding dead cattle oozed from his body.

After a few moments, Pat stirred. "Buster gave you the final head count, didn't he? Did we lose any more?"

"No, thank the good Lord. They seem content in the front pasture." He rested his legs on the coffee table, angling them so his boots didn't scar the wood. "Maybe it was all a fluke."

"That many cows?"

"We'll know for sure later in the week, but that's what I'm hoping." He snugged her closer. He didn't want to ruin this evening discussing ranch matters. "Heard you talked to your mother today. How'd that go?"

She wrinkled her nose—sure sign of a distasteful subject. "She wants me to come to New York to shop for a wedding gown. Aunt Adele is no help. She's practically setting up the arrangements."

"It's not a bad thought." It would take her mind off the problems here. "Maybe you should go."

"Oh no. You too?" She scowled. "I thought you'd be on my side."

"What can I say? It'll make your mother happy. And if you tell her it was my idea, you'd win me some brownie points."

"You may need brownie points, but you'll have to earn them after we get this mess with the cattle straightened up. Besides, I can't leave with everything unsettled here. I'd go crazy not knowing."

"Which is why God invented Skype." Not his favorite form of communication, but effective enough if she couldn't be here with him. "Your mother was really excited about us flying up last month, and I know the change of plans disappointed her. Maybe this will smooth her feathers."

She cocked a brow. "You know she wants us to get married in Manhattan."

He barked out a laugh. "No. Not in the plans. Maybe while you're there, you can convince her to come here for a while."

"Oh, please no. Don't you remember what it was like when Aunt Adele first moved in? Having my mother here would be tons worse. And having the two of them together—in the same house with Consuela?" She shuddered. "Wars have started over less."

"Those old gals will have to learn to get along. If your mother wants to see her grandbabies, she'll need to come here sometime." There was more to it, this business between Pat and her mother. Pat seemed to keep some grudge simmering below the surface. Whatever it was, he wanted it resolved before they got married. He'd like to enter into a relationship with his in-laws with a clean slate, without the tension between them and their daughter. "What's the deal between you and your mom, anyway? You always seem angry with her."

She emitted a light snort. "Don't you remember why Aunt Adele came? Don't you know who sent her? If Mama had her way, I'd be back under her thumb in Manhattan."

"Yeah, but I don't remember you being on the best of terms with her even before Adele got here." He shifted to get a better look at her. "Did something happen between you two before you got here?"

"We have a whole history of happenings between us." She leaned against him, making herself comfortable with him as her pillow. Not that he minded. "I don't want to talk about it tonight."

"Okay, then let's talk about babies—the ones your mother is likely to fly all the way to Texas to see." Dreaming about their future always served as better fodder for conversation. Having a family with this woman would fulfill him more than anything he'd ever imagined. "How many do you want?"

She sighed a soft, contented breath that warmed his heart. "Let's start with four and see how it goes from there."

"Four at once?"

"Good heavens, no. We can space them apart a couple of years each."

"I think that's a good plan." He got up to put another log on the fire, then turned his back to the heat, facing Pat. Her honey-colored hair curled on her shoulders, and wisps brushed her cheeks. Long lashes fringed sage-green eyes that looked at him with a warm glow of love.

Her father needn't worry. He could never forget what a blessing she was.

Thoughts best saved for marriage entered his head, and he shoved them aside for a safer topic. "So, what should we name these four little rug-rats we're planning to have?"

"We're getting ahead of ourselves, aren't we?" She crossed over to him and wrapped her arms around his waist. A smile played along her lips. "We don't even have our wedding date, and you want to discuss kids' names?"

"Cart before the horse." He gave her a small peck on those lovely lips. "I'll stink at helping you plan the wedding, you know. I don't know the first thing about all that fluffery. Which is why you should go to your mom's and work it out with her. As long as we don't have to get married in Manhattan."

"Like I said, I'm not leaving. Not until things are settled here." Her gentle features turned serious. "Do you think something could've been wrong with the cows before we got them?"

"I don't know. Every rancher in the county pitched in when Beth got so bad. It's not like they were ever neglected."

"But no one else has had any trouble."

That was the kicker.

He stepped away from her and rubbed the tension from the back of his neck.

"Maybe they just haven't had trouble yet." She emphasized *yet*.

Hope that theirs wouldn't be the only ranch in this mess brought a deep stab of guilt. He didn't want to wish misfortune on the others, but surely, this problem wasn't unique to the Circle Bar.

He drew her into his arms again. "Until we hear from Zach, anything I say would be speculation. We'll just have to be patient."

He rested his chin on the top of her head and smirked. Patience wasn't a strong suit for either of them.

Patricia rolled to her side and pulled the covers up over her shoulder. "Father, I don't know what to do about all this," she whispered. "I'm in over my head."

She'd invested so much into the ranch—much of last year's earnings plus her own money. The balance on their account sat at an all-time low, as far as she could tell from the records, but that hadn't bothered her when she figured in the sale of the extra cattle. Now, with cows dying, she'd have a hard time recouping the investment. Until the balance started climbing again, she'd have to sacrifice a few things, not the least of which were the trappings of a formal wedding.

Mama would be only too glad to help her, if she could fly to New York, but that costly of a trip was out of the question. Besides, anything her mother "helped" with, she insisted on controlling, and that was one of the multitude of things Patricia didn't miss about living in the City.

No, her days of being careless with her funds were over. They'd have to put off the wedding until they could afford it. They hadn't really taken the time to discuss plans, but this would be Talon's first—and last—wedding. Though she'd already had a huge event and she'd be fine with something simpler this time, she wanted their wedding to be special for him. Whatever *special* meant to him. He might want something simple too, or he might want to invite the entire congregation and everyone he knew on the rodeo circuit. Who knew? With everything going on, she couldn't bring herself to discuss it. Besides, she couldn't afford an extravagant affair, and asking her parents to fund another one for her was out of the question, even if Mama promised on her life not to control it. They'd just have to wait.

She reached over and caressed the pillow that would one day cradle his head. Maybe it wouldn't be too long of a wait.

Chapter Four

With a leathered fist, Talon ratcheted the wire stretcher until the line pulled taut enough to play a tune, then wrapped the loose end tightly around one of the corner posts they'd spent yesterday planting. He yanked the hammer from his hip pocket and a fencing staple from between his lips and secured the wire.

Buster Milligan stretched out the second line of barbed wire to him, then glanced down the ranch road. "Someone's coming."

A dull silver tanker with the green Co-op emblem kicked up a dust cloud. "That'll be our range cubes for the storage bin."

"Our lives are about to get a bit easier."

"Funny thing to say while we're working the fence line."

"I said *a bit* easier," Buster drawled. "Heaven forbid fences should ever build themselves. We'd get downright lazy."

Chance rode toward them on the four-wheeler and pulled up beside Talon. "That's Colton Royder driving the rig."

Talon groaned. "And we were having such a nice day." He yanked a glove off with his teeth, then pulled off the other with his bared hand.

Chance twisted on his seat and glanced back at the rig. "Want me to handle it?"

"Tempting as that sounds, I reckon I'll have to do business with him from now on, like it or not. Guess I ought to get used to it." He shoved his gloves into his jacket pocket, then handed the hammer to Chance, motioning with it toward the ATV. "Trade with me."

"Yeah. Like that's a fair trade." He climbed off the vehicle and nabbed the hammer.

"No reason for you to have all the fun," Talon said as he straddled the seat.

Buster nodded toward the tanker. "Go easy on the boy."

Talon snorted. "I'll try."

He rode down to meet the Co-op rig. Colton glowered from the driver's seat. That kid could sure hold a grudge.

Talon waved for him to follow and led the way back to the new storage bin sitting high on a metal frame. Colton pulled the tanker beside the bin and positioned the auger arm over the top. Talon could have left him to his job—would have, had it been anyone else. But, just in case, he killed the engine of his four-wheeler and settled in with his hands on his knees.

Before long, he could hear the range cubes hitting the bin's metal floor even over the rumbling of the diesel truck's idling. Seemed silly that the noise would give him a thrill, but having this convenience was more proof that Pat intended to bring the ranch into the twenty-first century. Of course, the new computer, along with its livestock-management program, was the first clue she'd been serious. For a city girl, she'd learned this business fast. Since her father had been raised on a ranch, she might have been familiar with things before she came. The rest she learned by jumping in and getting her hands dirty. What an incredible woman.

The sound of the cubes muffled as the bin filled. Colton dropped from the rig's cab and strutted stone-faced toward Talon with a clipboard in his hand. Talon had no intention of feeding the kid's temper.

Colton thrust the clipboard and a pen at him. "You gotta sign this."

Talon accepted the paperwork. "Great day, isn't it?"

The kid grunted.

He signed the form, snapped out the customer copy, and handed back the pen and clipboard. "You know, Colton, you ought to smile more. Adds years to your life. Gives you a bright disposition. Shoot, you may even learn to like it."

"You done with me?"

He grinned. "Oh, I reckon I've been done with you awhile."

So much for not feeding his temper. But to Colton's credit, he turned and walked away.

Talon stayed put until the big rig circled back to the ranch road and headed toward the gate.

Patricia stood in the kitchen, peeling carrots and potatoes into a newspaper she'd lined into one side of the double sink. A garbage disposal would be great, but it would also clog up the septic system.

Wearing a bibbed apron over a pressed, long-sleeved blouse, Aunt Adele browned stew meat. Consuela hummed tunelessly and whipped together a cornbread batter. Working in the kitchen with a bunch of women was nice, but Patricia missed having Marie there.

Consuela reached around her and moved the faucet to the other side of the sink to wash her hands. "You're quiet. What's wrong with you? You sick?"

"She's worried about going to New York," Aunt Adele answered over her shoulder, then eyed Patricia. "It's not like Natalie can force you to get married there. Just visit for a couple of weeks. How bad can it be?"

"She's already shopping for a wedding venue. You know how devious she is. She'll have me agreeing to the Redbury before I realize what hit me."

Consuela grabbed a kitchen towel. "Why would you want to get married in New York?"

Patricia aimed her glare at Aunt Adele. "I don't."

"Good." Consuela plopped the towel beside Patricia, then returned to her batter to ladle it into muffin tins. "Get married here, like Marie. Big wedding, like hers. Lots of people, lots of food."

Patricia grimaced. If she had her way, the wedding wouldn't be anywhere near as big as Marie's. It all depended on Talon, of course, but surely, he'd agree with her about the size. "Maybe something smaller, more intimate. The people here, a few from the church, Mama and Daddy. Twenty, tops."

"That would be much easier than Marie's." She leaned closer. "I will bake a cake. You like my cakes, *si*?"

"*Si. Muy bueno.*"

The older woman patted her cheek. "See? You learn Spanish."

Aunt Adele shifted from the stove. "You can get married here, but that doesn't mean you shouldn't visit your mother. We'll go together, and if Natalie pulls any of her tricks, I'll step in."

Patricia had run out of arguments. Even Talon thought she should go. She was fighting a losing battle. "I'll hold you to that."

"Good." Aunt Adele laid down her spoon. "Now, when do you want to leave?"

"First things first. I want to know what's killing the cattle. Right now, that's all I'm really thinking of. I'm not going until I know everything here will be okay."

"Yes, dear, but we don't want to risk getting snowed in. The sooner we leave, the better."

"I know." Patricia wadded the peelings in newspaper and threw them away. "I guess we should go before the end of the month or early next."

That didn't give her much time. November was a week and a half away. If they heard from the vet before then, and if they were able to fix the problem at minimal cost—and if the vet didn't cost too much ...

What was she thinking? She couldn't afford to fly to New York. Well, maybe she could if she booked a bargain-priced time, like eleven at night or two in the morning. Got seats near the tail of the plane. No more first class for her. Cut-rate all the way.

Consuela brought the cutting board to the countertop between the sink and stove and grabbed a carrot to chop. "Is it pretty in New York?"

"This time of year it is," Patricia answered. It would be worth flying with her knees in her chest to see her home state in autumn. "The leaves are changing colors, just like here, but the reds are more vibrant. Central Park is gorgeous in October."

"It would be great if we could go at Thanksgiving and see Macy's parade. Or at Christmas," Aunt Adele said with a wistful tone. "Christmas is magical."

"Oh, it is. With all the lights and decorations. You go to bed after Thanksgiving and wake up to a whole different world."

"It sounds exciting," Consuela's voice held a dreamy, wishful hint.

Patricia elbowed her. "You should come. Really, Consuela, you'd love it. I mean, we do need to get back before the snow, but I wish you'd come."

Her brown cheeks flushed as she shrugged away the thought. "Who would take care of everyone here? Who would cook? Clean? Wash clothes? Have you seen how much laundry these men bring in every week?"

"Surely, we could come up with something. You deserve a vacation. What about Marie?"

Consuela shook her head. "She works. She won't have time to do everything."

Patricia dried her hands and leaned against the counter. There was only one way to do this. She fought back the grin threatening to stretch her lips. "Okay, what about this? Chef makes breakfast, Marie makes dinner, and the guys can scrounge for leftovers at lunch."

Consuela frowned. "That won't work. Men need food—and what about their clothes?"

Patricia held up a finger. "It would work fine if we were gone for only two or three days."

"That's hardly worth the trip," Aunt Adele grumbled. "Surely, you can spare your mother more time than that."

"But if we stayed two weeks, Consuela couldn't come."

"Then stay for a week. Could we do that? One week?"

"Five days?"

Aunt Adele nodded. "Okay, five days."

Bingo. If they flew out at some ridiculously late time on the first day and flew back at an equally ridiculous time early on the fifth day, she'd have only three full days to fend off Mama's tricks and barbs.

She turned to Consuela. "Could you do that?"

Excitement lit her dark-brown eyes. "Let me talk to Chef."

"Miz Pat?" Frank called as he entered the house, then he poked his head into the kitchen. "I think you need to come out here for a bit."

"What is it?"

"The doc's here."

"The vet?" He'd come in person? She pushed away from the counter and followed Frank. This was it. At last they'd get some answers. But a band tightened around her chest. What kind of answers would they be? Would all this finally come to an end?

She let the screen door slam behind her and matched Frank's stride across the lawn.

Several vehicles sat in front of the barn. Beside them, a group of men huddled with Talon. They turned to her as she approached. Talon took her by the elbow and guided her toward a lanky man with a shock of dark hair hanging over his brow. His electric blue eyes peered at her through wire-rimmed glasses.

"Pat, this is Zach Crampton, our vet."

She shook his hand. "Nice to meet you. Did you find out what happened to our cows?"

"Yes'm, I did." He slipped off his glasses and wiped them with his shirt. "Not good news, I'm afraid."

Talk about a slow drawl. Patricia wanted to drag the words from his throat. She jammed her hands into her hip pockets. "What did you find?"

"The cattle were poisoned. Cyanide."

"Cyanide?" The word punched the wind out of her. She looked up at Talon. "Who would do such a thing?"

"Maybe no one." The vet slipped his wire-rims back on and swept his hand toward three other men. "These guys here are from the Agriculture Extension Service. They'll take samples from that back pasture, see if they can figure out where the cows came into contact with the poison."

"Could be the hay," one of the agents said. "Had a case around Austin where a rancher lost fifteen out of eighteen head to hydrogen cyanide, or prussic acid poisoning as it's called. The drought we've been having can mess with the chemical compound of some of the forage grasses, resulting in high concentrations of cyanide. Prussic poisoning is odd at this time of year, but we'll test for it."

Compared to thinking someone had murdered her cattle, this seemed much better. "So, it's likely nobody is poisoning them deliberately. That's a relief."

"It may not be deliberate, but the results are the same." Zach turned to Talon. "You haven't lost any more, have you?"

"No, not since we moved them to the front. Even those that were droopy seem to be doing better now."

"Well, good. That's good." He stared off into the distance with a pondering gaze and a maddening slowness to share his thoughts, then asked, "Did y'all bury the others?"

"No. We had them carted off, disposed of properly."

"Well, good. That's good." He shoved his hand out at Talon, then nodded at everyone else. "Reckon y'all don't need me anymore, but if you do, you know how to reach me."

Once he left, the Ag agent turned to Talon. "Mind showing us which pasture the cattle were in?"

"I will," Frank said. "Best we take the pickup."

The men stopped by their vehicle, then loaded some supplies into Frank's truck. Talon watched, but he didn't seem to be seeing them.

She touched his arm. "What's wrong? I thought you'd feel better once we had an answer."

He shook his head. "This isn't good news."

"It's better than my initial thought when he said they were poisoned. I thought someone was targeting us for some reason."

Frank cranked the pickup, and the diesel roared to life. As he drove away, Talon said, "It depends. Along with the range cubes, the cattle are foraging on this summer's grass and hay from the barn. If the grass is poisoning them, that's an easy fix. We'll just disc it under and feed them hay. But if it's the hay ... "

She followed his gaze to the pole barn out beyond the stables. They'd filled it, ground to rooftop, with huge, round bales intended to get the herd through the winter. Her heart sank.

Chapter Five

❝You didn't have to come with me." Talon sat in the passenger seat with his forearm resting along the pickup's open window and his legs stretched as far as possible in front of him. "It's a waste of an afternoon."

"Beats working the fence," Chance answered. "After the news you got this morning about the prussic poisoning, I figured you could use the company."

"Appreciate it."

With Chance driving, towing the eighteen-foot trailer to the Rocking T Ranch, Talon had nothing to do but ride and stew. Blasted shame to buy hay when they had a barn full of it, but until the Ag guys confirmed that it hadn't killed the cattle, he wouldn't touch it again.

"Good thing the Travises have some hay to sell," Chance said. "Seems like everyone else has a tight clamp on it. Expecting a rough winter, I guess."

"I have to admit I tried Marc's place first. Didn't talk to the others."

Chance cocked a brow at him. "Killing two birds with one stone?"

"Doesn't hurt to take a peek at those horses he's been showing off." He had some funds left from his win in Houston earlier in the year. If he could jaw Marc's price down, he'd get Pat the roan as a wedding present, start her off in her new career as a riding instructor.

After the vet left this morning, Talon told her how much the hay would cost. She'd winced. Lately, her shoulders seemed to sag under the weight of her responsibilities, and no amount of reassurances from him seemed to help. Granted, his reassurances hadn't been all that convincing.

Chance turned the rig at the Rocking T and drove over the cattle guard. Healthy cattle grazed lazily on both sides of the ranch road. Ahead, the long metal arms of a heavy-duty walker held the lead ropes of a couple of Quarter Horses and encouraged them to keep their pace as it turned in circles like a merry-go-round. Sunlight highlighted the coat of the strawberry roan, making it shine until the horse trotted into the shadow of the stables. Pat would like that one. Fine-looking animal.

He caught sight of Marc near the horse paddock and motioned to Chance. "Let me off here."

Chance eased to a stop. Talon jumped from the truck and strode toward the paddock.

Marc greeted him with an easy smile, then his expression shifted to concern. "Rumor has it you've been having some trouble at your place. Hate to hear it."

"Thanks. Hope to get it settled soon." He nodded at the roan. "She's a beauty."

"Yeah, her mom was Popsicle. Won the cutting horse futurity in Fort Worth a few years ago."

"Great blood lines. What did you name her?"

A flush crept up the trainer's tanned neck. "Cherry Berry. Madison named her."

As if she'd heard her name over the creaking of the horse walker and the noise of truck engines, little Madison bounded from the shadows. In tiny red boots and blue jeans, she darted toward her daddy and wrapped her arms around his leg.

He scooped her up. "Maddie, this is Mr. Carlson, our preacher. Remember him from church?"

Cottony-blond curls, barely contained by a red ribbon, bounced as she nodded.

Talon grinned at her. "Howdy, Miss Madison. You're getting mighty big. How old are you now?"

She popped her thumb in her mouth and tucked her chin into the neck of her pink fleece jacket. Red splotches colored each cheek, and darkly lashed lids dropped over her cobalt-blue eyes. Spitting image of her mother. Talon wanted a little one just like her, with Pat's honey-colored hair and sage-green eyes.

Madison shifted and hid her face in Marc's shoulder. He chuckled as he rubbed her back. "She's four and usually not this shy. She got up too early this morning. I bet she needs a nap."

"No." She pushed against him and scrambled to get down.

He laughed as he released her. "I guess she told me."

"She's a cutie." Maybe he and Pat could get married next week and start trying to create a little one like that of their own.

He brought the subject back around to horses, Cherry Berry in particular, and tossed out a casual question about the purchase price. Marc quoted a figure, and Talon nodded as if it was a sensible number. Probably was for a horse of that caliber. Sure would chew through his winnings.

"Interested?" Marc asked.

"Definitely. But interest ain't ability." He'd have to wait until things back at the ranch looked a little sunnier. "I may have to think on it awhile."

"I understand, what with the way things are going at the Circle Bar. But don't study it too long. Maddie gets more attached to that horse every day. I'll either have to sell her or make up my mind to keep her to maintain the peace."

Chance drove toward them, the trailer loaded with enough hay to do them for the week. With Marc at his side, Talon strode over to meet the truck. "I'll sit down with pen and paper this week and let you know. That price firm?"

He shoved his hands in his hip pockets and stared at the ground as they walked. When they reached the pickup, he met Talon's gaze. "Tell ya what, preacher. Come up with your best offer, and I'll see what I can do."

"I appreciate it." Talon extended his hand to shake on the deal. "I'll get back with you as soon as I can. Don't want Maddie undercutting my sale."

Chance flicked a wave at Marc as Talon climbed inside, then eased the truck out to the ranch road. "Looks like that was a profitable meeting."

"Not too bad." Talon caught a glimpse of Maddie by the stables, offering a timid wave. He waved back. Yep, he wanted one just like her. At least one. "Marc's a good man. Price is steep though."

"You plan to make an offer?"

"Soon as I can figure one that won't insult him."

As he turned on the main road, Chance said, "We upset some folks back there."

"Today? What did we do?"

"No, not today. Earlier this year. Seems some of the Rocking T crew bet a whoppin' sum on Colton to win the bull- riding event."

Talon chuckled. "That's downright sad, isn't it?"

"Must've been rough. Aaron Tillman told me Brennan lost a massive chunk of change betting against you. What'd you ever do to him?"

"Brennan Roberts shadows Colton everywhere he goes. I don't have to do anything but breathe to earn his attitude."

"He has it in for you. Wasn't too friendly with me, either."

Brennan had probably put himself in financial trouble making a fool's bet and didn't have anyone to blame but Chance and him. Heaven forbid he should take responsibility for his own lame choices. At twenty-five, he was certainly old enough.

Talon shook his head. "Nothing you can do for a guy like that but pray for him."

"Yeah," Chance said. "Celebrating the fact he got what was coming to him probably isn't the Christian way."

"Probably not." But the thought held a certain appeal.

Patricia brushed Tandy's broad back, and the old Quarter Horse nodded his approval.

"You like that, don't you?" She scratched behind his ear, then brushed from his shoulder to his hoof, working off the dust and grass burs he'd picked up during their ride.

She couldn't stay away from the herd, even though they seemed better in the front pasture. She'd ridden up behind one cow sitting on her chest. Patricia's heart almost stopped until she rounded the cow and discovered her placidly chewing her cud.

Outside the horse barn, the rumble of the pickup and trailer announced the guys' return. Before long, Talon joined her as she was braiding Tandy's tail. He kissed her neck just behind her ear and sent a sensuous chill skittering down her spine. That man sure knew how to announce his presence.

He put his arms around her from behind, leaving her hands free to continue their work. "You turning him into one of your show horses?"

"He would be a good one, but no. I'm just keeping busy. Everything happening here has me antsy. And my head is full of questions. This relaxes me."

Talon shifted and leaned against the stall gate. "What questions?"

She frowned. This kind of thing wasn't the stuff Daddy's stories had been made of when he tucked her into bed at night. Everything he told her about ranching seemed fun and romantic. But cattle dying? Prussic poisoning? Not topics he broached. Her questions stemmed from her ignorance, which embarrassed her. But this wasn't the time to pretend to know it all. Besides, Talon knew her better than that.

She tucked the braid and secured it, then turned to him, resting her arm across Tandy's rump. "There's something I don't understand. If the drought caused the chemical compound of the forage grass to become poisonous, then why isn't the grass in the front pasture poisonous too? Or the grass where our own brand is pastured?"

Talon rubbed his jaw. "You've got a point. You'd think we'd have dead cattle all over the ranch. It's all the same kind of—"

"Talon, Patricia, come quickly," Aunt Adele called from the porch. "The agriculture agent is on the phone."

They left the stable and joined Frank, Buster, and Chance, all heading for the house.

Patricia led the way to the office down the hall and sat at her desk. Talon stood behind her. Frank and Aunt Adele took the chairs in front of the desk, with Buster and Chance standing behind them. Worry and anticipation etched each face.

Patricia put the phone on speaker. "Hello? This is Patricia Talbert."

"Yes'm. Hello. This is Ed Elliott, county extension agent. How ya doin', ma'am?"

These Texans and their proper manners would be the death of her. New Yorker would've come to the point. But niceties ruled in Texas. "I'm fine, thank you."

Talon leaned over her shoulder and spoke toward the phone. "Hey, Ed. If I'd known I would hear from you this fast, I would've waited to buy hay."

"Sorry 'bout that, but our first test told us what we needed to know. I would've called sooner, but we had to double-check our findings."

"You have something for us, then." Patricia's nerves coiled.

"Yes'm. This isn't the kind of news I like to give over the phone, or any other way for that matter. It is poison, like we guessed, but it's localized."

"Localized?"

"Heavily concentrated in a particular area in that pasture."

Talon rested his hand on Patricia's shoulder. "That explains why the other cattle haven't been affected."

"Yes," she answered, then spoke toward the phone. "But what happened? Why is that one place bad?"

The line was quiet for a long minute, then Ed cleared his throat. "Ma'am, that patch was salted with a good amount of potassium cyanide—not hydrogen cyanide, like we talked about before. Potassium cyanide. You'd use it as a poison against rats and pests. But you wouldn't disseminate it like that. The quantity was too heavy for that small of an area. Someone targeted your animals."

"Targeted ..." She stared at the phone and tried to process the news. What she'd been most afraid of turned out to be true. But that was insane. Who would poison their cows?

"Is the rest of the forage okay?" Talon asked. "Did you test other areas in that pasture?"

"Yeah, it seems fine outside that one area."

"What about the hay? Did you test the hay?"

"We checked everything, including the pond back there. The hay's fine, but the water tested positive."

"Oh no," Patricia's head was reeling. "Someone poisoned the pond?"

"Yes, but it's diluted. The test showed only trace amounts. The water'll be fine."

Frank rose from his seat and edged closer to the desk. "Ed, you said it was localized in that area. Can you show me where it's at?"

"Sure. I'll bring a satellite image and pinpoint it for you."

"That'll work."

"We appreciate it, Ed," Patricia added. "Thank you for your time."

"You're welcome, ma'am. Sorry it wasn't better news."

After she disconnected the call, she glanced around at the others. Buster's gray brows were drawn tight, and Chance's lips formed a straight line. Even Aunt Adele's expression matched the shocked numbness Patricia felt.

"Who could be doing this?" she asked. "Who could possibly hate us that much?"

Frank returned to his seat. "You reckon this is Colton's doing?"

"The kid's all bluff and bluster. He wouldn't do this." Talon leaned against the desk with his arms crossed. "For all we know, it was Brennan Roberts and the others from the Rocking T. Chance found out they lost a bundle betting on Colton."

Patricia peered up at him. "But it could be Colton. You beat him badly in that competition, right out there on national television. The stakes were high with that monster of a check. Colton's been pretty hateful ever since he lost."

He smirked. "He's always been hateful."

Frank stroked his bushy mustache. "Yeah, but maybe the boy's flipped his lid or something. He's always had a short fuse, but he ain't never been so bad that Ben had to fire him. And now he's workin' at the Co-op. No tellin' what kind of chemicals he can order up there."

Talon nodded. "Yeah, you have a point."

"Or maybe it's all of them," Chance said. "Animals are meaner in a pack."

The other guys nodded in agreement, and Patricia said, "Don't you think we should tell the sheriff about them?"

"What if we're wrong? I mean, Colton's a jerk, sure, but he's never done anything remotely like this before. The others have worked at the Rockin' T for a long time. They could lose their jobs. And we could be causing trouble for them unnecessarily. Serious trouble."

"Or we could be stoppin' him before he gets worse," Buster argued. "I reckon Sheriff Brewer can check him out without causin' a raucous. And if he ain't the culprit, no one'll ever know Brewer'd been snooping."

Talon held his hands up in surrender. "All right, all right. I'll talk to him. See what he thinks."

Aunt Adele caught Patricia's eye. "The good news is it's localized. Maybe it's an easy fix."

"Maybe." Patricia rubbed her temples. The bad news gave her a headache.

Chapter Six

In the purple haze of predawn, Talon yawned as he worked the last pasture of the morning. He'd been up late the previous night, still fuming over the loss of the cattle. The conversation with Sheriff Brewer had been a quick one. Talon and Pat couldn't tell him much, other than the pasture had been poisoned and they had a few suspects in mind. The sheriff had scratched some notes and promised to look into it, but Talon didn't expect much. They just didn't have anything to go on.

The bale on the spool at the back of his truck unrolled, and the cattle stretched out behind him, following the hay. He turned around and hit the button to release the range cubes from the hopper in the truck bed. He counted the herd during this second pass. They usually trotted out to meet the feed truck, so his count should've been close to accurate, but there were too many missing for his comfort. He followed his tracks along the unrolled hay once more, driving slower this time, and counted the brawny backs again.

Ten off.

His gut clenched as he headed toward one of the water tanks. They couldn't be missing that many cattle. Not again.

His gaze swept the pasture the width of the headlights in search of the animals, looking for cow-sized humps on the ground. When he angled beside the pond, he found them. First one. Then, farther out, three more. One or two more as he drove along and the headlights brightened the distance.

He stopped the truck and examined a few of the cows in its beams. They looked like the others had, but these bore the Circle Bar Ranch brand. Some of the ranch's best breeders lay on their sides and stared through dead, glazed eyes.

Talon leaned his head back and sucked in wavering breaths of air to slow his pounding heart.

What was happening here?

He jumped in his truck and headed to the house, kicking up rocks and scattering the live cattle. Inside, the smell of bacon and pancakes greeted him, and his stomach moaned. But instead of heading to the lights and laughter of the breakfast table, he slammed into the office and called the sheriff again, demanding Brewer come out as soon as possible. Then he called Zach, waking him in the early dawn, and asked him to come too.

Patricia stood in the doorway. She took one look at him and rushed into the room. "What is it? What's wrong?"

"We've lost more. Our own this time."

She fumbled behind her for the nearest chair and lowered herself into it. "How many?"

"I counted ten down in the west pasture."

Her jaw slackened and she gaped at him. "I don't understand any of this. Who would be targeting us? Why?"

Talon walked around to the front of the desk, shaking his head. "I don't know. I don't want to believe it's Colton. I've known him and his brother too long. He's always been a pain, but other than a scuffle or two, he's never done anything like this. But if it's him and that pack of coyotes he runs with, I'll string them up myself."

After Sheriff Brewer and the vet left, Patricia returned to her office and sat down at the computer. Knowing what to suspect this time, Zach didn't take long to confirm a diagnosis of poisoning. A hint of almond. Vivid, cherry-red color in the cows' mouths. Sure signs of cyanide. This time, he'd told Talon what signs to look for—dizziness, weakness, labored breathing—for an early warning that the cows had been poisoned. If Zach could arrive soon enough, he could perhaps save them from further loss.

But the best prevention would be to catch the guys doing this.

Patricia spent the remainder of the morning researching potassium cyanide. What she found made her shudder. Those poor cows. Death by the poison must be excruciating. And to think the Germans had used a variation of it in the gas chambers.

She shuddered again, then read farther down the page. Not all of its purposes were horrible. The compound was used in electroplating—no one did that around here that she knew of. Also in photography, but with digital photography, who bothered with it anymore?

That it was an agricultural fumigant and pest exterminator cast even more suspicion in Colton's direction. Working at the Co-op, he could get it easily. Then again, so could anyone else. She'd found it on Amazon. But who else had a motive?

With a shake of her head, she changed the direction of her research. Best to leave the investigation up to the sheriff—but her money was still on Colton Royder. Lord help her if she ever saw him again. She'd throttle the kid without an ounce of remorse. He'd face criminal charges for certain, but civil litigation would also be in his future. She'd sue him for every penny he had and then some.

She pored over the most recent stock report for the price per pound, then calculated what the dead cattle had cost them, and groaned. The loss of the cows alone—not including any calves they might have birthed in the spring—delivered a substantial blow. Maybe if she hadn't stretched their account so thin, they could have absorbed the loss. But not now.

She swiveled her chair to face the window. Currently, they had three good-sized cattle pastures: in the southwest, the west, and the north, just down from the outbuildings. These didn't include the land she'd bought from Griff or the acreage where they raised hay for harvesting. With two of the three main pastures out of use, how would that affect their grazing rotation schedule? Right now, the north pasture would have to hold both the ranch brand and Griff's cattle. Figure acreage required per head, and the land wouldn't support that many cows for long, especially this late in the year. They'd have to rely heavily on the hay bales long before Texas saw the worst of winter.

If the guys finished the fence soon, they could move the herd to Griff's land.

She closed her eyes and rubbed her temples. Talon and the guys would know what to do. Surely, they'd had to adjust the grazing rotation before. *Father God, please guide us.*

"I expected to see you searching for airline tickets on the internet."

She peeked at her aunt. "How can I leave when someone is attacking us?"

"And what can you do while you're here?" Aunt Adele walked behind the desk to massage Patricia's shoulders. "Talon told the sheriff who he suspects. I may not know the others, but from what I've seen of Colton, it's a good suspicion. Everything is in Sheriff Brewer's hands now."

"But what if it happens again?"

"What if it does? What can you do? Leave it to the men."

"The men don't own the ranch," she muttered. "I do. I ought to be here."

"True, the men don't own it, but they run it—and they've been running it far longer than you have." Aunt Adele leaned against the desk. "You need a break, Consuela needs a break, and I'm dying to check on my condo and spend time in the City."

Patricia slanted a look at her. "What? Dallas doesn't do it for you?"

She flipped her hand elegantly. "Dallas is a sweet little town, dear, but nothing compares to New York."

Sweet little town. Patricia had lived on the ranch almost two years now, and Dallas seemed too large. Huge. Who knew what New York would feel like?

"Sweetheart, you need to be with your mother. You haven't talked to her but once that I know of since I arrived.

I know it wasn't the brightest of plans for Natalie to send me here the way she did—"

"Don't put it all at her feet. You could have said no."

She held out her hands, imploring her to understand. "But it worked out, didn't it? We've come to accept your decision, so there's no longer any dispute. You've forgiven me for my foolishness, but you must forgive Natalie too. All she wants is what's best for you."

Patricia sighed. Part of her doubted that. Mama tended to do what was best for Daddy's image, and if she'd thought marrying her daughter to a cowboy fit the bill, she would have personally sent her to Texas long ago.

But the pain in Mama's eyes when she thought Patricia would never return to New York again seemed authentic. "Yes, I suppose we should go."

"Good!" Aunt Adele waved toward the computer. "Tap, tap! Let's hear those keys clicking! Maybe we can get there and back before the snow."

Patricia halfheartedly brought the computer back to life and searched for the cheapest tickets she could find from DFW to LaGuardia, especially since she'd be paying for Consuela too. The prices almost made her choke. Funny how she'd never thought twice about such expenses before.

As if reading her thoughts, Aunt Adele patted her arm. "Why don't we make this my treat?"

She almost balked, but caught herself. Until the ranch account had a better cushion, she'd take all the help she could get. She swallowed her pride and nodded. "Thank you. I appreciate it."

She purchased tickets to leave Tuesday—the day after Consuela's laundry day—and return the following Saturday. Her stomach flipped. Bridal gown shopping in Manhattan seemed discordant with what was happening here. She had a wedding to plan, but she also had a ranch to run, and that ranch was under attack. How could she possibly concentrate on gowns?

"How can I possibly concentrate on gowns?" she asked Talon. Rhetorically, of course. She didn't expect or want him to answer unless he would agree with her. Recent history had proven he wouldn't. Not this time.

She paced the front porch, her boots clomping on the floorboards. The evening was warm, and they'd extended their work hours to the last possible light. "Work" meaning moving the herd. While the other guys strung fence line, she pitched in and helped Frank drive the Circle Bar cattle from the west pasture to the north one where they'd put Griff's herd. Perhaps she'd feel the pain later, but for now, all she felt was anger. All that land out there, and they had to cram their cattle into one pasture. The area held many acres, so it wasn't like the cows were stuffed in like fish in a can, but—

"Do you want to marry me?" Talon stood from the old rocker and caught her by the shoulders.

"Of course I do. But I can't concentrate on it right now. We're losing a lot money. I've got us in such deep debt, I'm ruining everything. It'll get worse if we can't catch whoever is killing the cattle. How can I go to New York—"

He rested his fingers against her lips. His gentle touch effectively scattered her thoughts; she couldn't speak now if she wanted to. Her mouth still tingled after he removed his hand to slide it into hers.

"You aren't ruining anything. This isn't on you. We'll be okay, but your aunt is right." With a finger under her chin, he lifted her head. "The guys and I can handle the ranch, and there really isn't anything you can do about the jerk causing this. But only you can choose what gown you want to wear. What flowers you want. What color to smear across these luscious lips of yours."

He lowered his head and sought out those lips he'd been talking about, and she didn't make them too hard to find. She leaned into him, into his reassuring strength. He could handle this. The guys would be fine. The ranch would be fine.

As long as Talon held her, the entire world would be fine. Or not. In his arms, she found it difficult to care.

Her head was swimming the backstroke by the time he released her. She didn't want to open her eyes, didn't want to step back from his embrace. She would stagger dizzily. Every time he kissed her like that, she felt insanely drunk.

"What were we talking about?" he murmured.

"I don't know. Lipstick or some such foolishness."

He chuckled. "'Some such foolishness'? You've been hanging around Consuela too long."

Her eyes popped open. "Consuela! What if Chef says she can't go? I was counting on her to be a buffer between Mama and me. Someone on my side when Aunt Adele returns to her condo. Someone who understands that I don't want to get married in New York."

"Oh, he'll let her go. I wouldn't worry about that."

Footsteps approaching made them turn. Their faces grim, Frank and Buster climbed the porch steps to join them.

"Excuse us, Miz Pat, but we've been thinkin'." Frank twisted his hat in his hands in a show of anxiety she'd never seen in him before. He'd always been the calm one. "We got all the cattle in one place now—"

"Yeah, all right there together." Buster's bushy brows were drawn in a deep V, rippling his forehead with wrinkles. "Wouldn't take much to wipe out the whole herd."

Frank nodded. "Every attack has been at night, and by the time we find the cattle, they've been dead awhile."

"What are you suggesting?" Patricia asked, but Talon was already nodding as if he knew where they were heading with their comments.

"We have to keep watch over them," he said.

"You mean sit up with them all night?"

"There's no other way," Frank confirmed. "We got some prize bulls in that herd. It's bad enough losing the cows, but we can't lose them bulls too."

Talon nodded, his face somber. "Best put some coffee on," he suggested. "It's going to be a long night."

Chapter Seven

Marie's yawn proved too contagious for Patricia to resist. They seemed to be passing it back and forth like some horrid virus.

"I wonder how long this night-watch will last." Marie blinked several times and focused on the road. "I won't survive it. I only got two hours' sleep last night, and that was during Chance's watch. The whole time he was supposed to be sleeping, he was too restless. And if he don't sleep, I don't sleep."

"You sound like a ranch hand."

Marie shrugged and turned on the blacktop leading to her new home's construction site.

Patricia yawned again, and Marie snorted lightly. "What's your excuse?"

"I couldn't sleep after my shift," which had been early, meaning she'd been awake the entire night. She stretched the best she could in the small space Marie's car allowed. Since they came to Texas, she'd been driving around in pickups, so the midsize sedan felt cramped. "I drank a lot of coffee and watched old movies. And I kept wondering whether the guys would really shoot had someone shown up last night."

Marie darted a look her way. "They don't have guns, do they?"

"Talon strapped a shotgun to his saddle last night. He kept it in a scabbard. With all the wild things around here that could harm the guys or the animals, I suppose they all have shotguns."

Marie shuddered. "You don't think Texas ranchers are still wild-West enough to shoot first and ask questions later, do you?"

They were angry enough, but no. "I can't picture any of them actually shooting someone. Maybe they'd fire a warning shot into the air."

Marie pulled up to the front of the house, and Patricia gasped. She hadn't been out to see it in a while and didn't expected to find it this close to being finished. Even in its unfinished state, it was spectacular.

The sight apparently worked on Marie like a shot of caffeine. She scrambled from the car the moment she turned off the ignition. "C'mon. I'll show you around."

When they crossed the threshold, Patricia's jaw dropped. The drywall was up and prepped for painting, enabling her to see the layout of the house. The open-concept living space would catch the dawn, and the master bedroom would feature the sun setting on the distant hills. Although the kitchen remained incomplete, it would have plenty of storage space, and the square opening in the countertop indicated room for a professional, six-burner stove. Marie loved to cook, but Patricia hadn't realized how much.

After showing off the master bedroom and what would be a guest bedroom, Marie took her to another, tinier bedroom, and swept her hand like a game-show hostess. "And this will be the nursery."

"It's adorable." Patricia gave her a side-arm hug. "When do you think you'll be ready to have a little one sleeping in here?"

"In about six months."

Patricia gaped at her. "In six months? You're pregnant?"

With a broad grin and excitement shining from her eyes, she bobbed her head, making her bangs bounce.

Patricia squealed, grabbing her in a hug and rocking with her gleefully. "I can't believe it. Why didn't you tell me sooner?"

"We found out just this week, and with everything going on, I couldn't find a good time to tell you."

"So your queasiness in the mornings?"

Marie grinned. "Morning sickness. This was the first morning in a while I've been able to keep breakfast down."

A wiry man stepped into the room and offered Marie a broken-toothed smile. Around his neck, he wore a heavy gold chain supporting an unusual medallion that caught the light and Patricia's attention.

"I thought I heard someone in here."

"It's just us, Justin." She linked her arm with Patricia's and introduced her. "She owns the Circle Bar, which used to include our land here. But she gave us our acreage as a wedding present. Isn't she the greatest?"

"The greatest." Justin turned his smile to Patricia. With the broken tooth, a humped nose, and short, graying hair, he looked like an old boxer, but in truth, he couldn't have been much older than she.

She nodded toward his necklace. "That's a great chain. Love the pendant. I don't think I've ever seen anything like it before. Where did you get it?"

"Made it." He slipped it under his T-shirt and focused on Marie. "You plan to hang around and help today?"

She slapped at him. "You are such a kidder."

"You stay too long, we're likely to hand you a trowel."

"No, that's quite all right. We were just admiring your handiwork." She ushered Patricia to the door. "Continue on. Don't let us get in your way."

"Come on back this evening," he called. "It'll be all finished and ready for painting."

Marie tossed a wave over her shoulder and hustled Patricia through the house.

As they walked out to the car, Patricia asked, "Have you decided what color you want the nursery? Is the baby a boy or a girl?"

"We decided we wanted to be surprised." Marie unlocked the vehicle. "We can shop for the baby's room this afternoon, if you want."

"I'd love that." Patricia grinned. "When I get back from Manhattan, we may have to take you shopping for maternity clothes."

"You know me. That's my idea of fun."

Patricia peered back at the house, picking out the window of the baby's room. A baby. Just thinking of it made her giddy inside. And this was Marie's baby. Imagine how she'd feel if it were her own. Hers and Talon's. His dark hair, her green eyes. Or maybe it would be a brown-eyed blonde.

How soon after they married would he want to start having a family? Marie and Chance had been married only seven months, and by this time next year, their first would be a toddler. Judging from what Talon had said the other night, he'd want to start a family just as quickly.

The idea of having children with her cowboy preacher put wings on her heart and sent it flying despite her weariness. But they couldn't start a family until they were married.

Suddenly, the trip to New York to shop for wedding gowns didn't seem half bad.

Talon tightened the cross cable on the gate, then checked the gate's swing once more. This time it didn't scrape the ground.

The five hundred acres they'd bought from Griff bordered the backyards of the ranch house and the outbuildings. It had always been fenced, but the fence had been neglected. Wires down. Posts rotted and askew. The new fence would protect the house from the cattle, but with someone out there poisoning the herd, it didn't seem wise to move the cows up here. Too much land where they could roam unprotected. He needed to divide the land into two pastures. Make it more manageable.

Someone down on the ranch road honked the horn of an unfamiliar vehicle. Talon shaded his eyes, but couldn't make out the emblem on the side of the truck. Whoever it was seemed important, judging by the way Frank and Pat hustled toward him.

Talon climbed onto the four-wheeler and headed down. The nearer he got, the more visible the emblem became: Texas Agriculture Extension Service. Maybe now they'd know the extent of the damage. He stopped, switched off the engine, and joined them.

Ed Elliott leaned against the front fender of his truck, holding a rolled map. "Considering what's been going on out here, y'all got off pretty lucky."

"Lucky?" Frank eyed him. "You call losin' eighteen head lucky?"

Ed glanced at him. "I thought it was just eight."

"Lost another ten yesterday in the west pasture."

Ed scowled and uttered a mild oath. "I'll get the team out here again, get them to scour the acreage and see what they find. You got the cattle out of there?"

"Yep," Talon answered, "but what were you saying about us being lucky?"

"We tested all our samples and found potassium cyanide salted around a small area, maybe two or three acres of the pasture we were in Monday. The rest of the land seemed clean, but I'd stretch out about five extra acres all the way around it, just to be safe." He unrolled the aerial map on the hood of the truck and showed them the location. "This dot here represents where we found the highest concentration of the poison. The circle around it shows what we estimate to be a safe zone."

"How do we get rid of the poison?" Pat asked. "Should we burn the pasture?"

"I'm not sure I'd recommend that. Burning that much potassium cyanide could produce a toxic gas. I imagine it would quickly dissipate, but why risk working in poisonous fumes?"

"What's our alternative?"

"I'd get the volunteer fire department out here and water it down—dissolve it."

Frank scratched his jaw and studied the map. "The run-off would poison the pond back there, wouldn't it? Add to the trace amount you already found in it?"

"No, not necessarily. Enough water would dilute it until it's harmless." Ed rolled the map and handed it to Frank. "If it were me, I'd hose it down good, then disc the ground, turn all that old grass under so the cattle can't get to it again. Maybe not put them back out there until spring."

Frank nodded. "There's my job then. I'll get on the horn and call the fire department and hook the disc up to the tractor."

"Yes, sir. That's your best bet," Ed said. "I'll get my men out here again to go over that other area, see how much damage was done."

"How soon can they get here?" Talon asked.

Ed glanced at the sun, then checked his watch. "Early in the morning. That okay with you?"

No. He wanted them here now. This minute. And he wanted answers ten minutes after that. "Reckon it'll have to be."

Chapter Eight

The following Monday night, Patricia snuggled closer to Talon on the back-porch swing, seeking his warmth. The sun had set on yet another blissfully uneventful day, and the air had a nip to it. The temperatures this close to November caused even her Yankee blood to chill. Sometimes New York stayed warm until Halloween, but the weather this year promised to be cooler than normal. She'd altered her packing plans based on the lower temperatures forecasted for Manhattan.

They'd leave in October and come home in November. It might be only a few days, but it felt like a month. And the whole time she was gone, she'd be out of the loop here.

She didn't want to think about that. "Good job on the fence. Is it finished now?"

"That part of it is. It looks a mite better than it did before."

"Until you and the guys cleaned off the fence line, I didn't even know it was there. Funny how we could have crossed the boundary to be on Griff's property, but had to drive three miles to get to his house."

He squeezed her shoulders. "Still not used to these wide, open spaces, are you?"

"I'm getting there. But it is a shock to see how much property one person can own. Mom and Dad have a condo that's thirty-six hundred square feet, and it's considered huge in the City. It sits on top of several others and under several more." She shook her head. "Out here, we can go for days without seeing a neighbor."

"You talk as if you like it."

"Yes, I guess I do. I'll miss it here while I'm away."

"I'll miss you." He kissed her hair.

She turned up her face so her hair wouldn't be the only thing enjoying his kisses. How she dreaded leaving him for five days. Five whole days.

She ran her hand along his strong jaw and the rough stubble growing there. "Maybe I should stay home."

"You're already packed."

"I can always unpack."

He chuckled. "Maybe you should just get this over with. Get it settled. I don't want to go into our marriage with you still upset with your mother. Best to resolve whatever's bothering you so we can have a clean slate."

"Yeah, yeah. You're right. I know you're right." She tilted her head. "But if I'm also shopping for a wedding dress while I'm there, I need to know how big this shindig is going to be. You want a major event? All the family and friends?"

His eyes widened as if she'd caught him off guard, then he squinted at her. "Do you want a major event?"

"I've already done this once. I thought I'd let you decide. You're a pretty big man around here. Everyone loves and respects you. We could have a huge affair and invite everyone from three counties if you want."

He grimaced. "No. On my list of negatives, that ranks right up there with having the wedding in New York. Think small."

"Good, I was hoping you'd say that. I'll shop for something appropriate for a more intimate ceremony." She gave him an impish grin. "Want to come with me?"

"Oh yeah. You know I do. But somebody's gotta run the ranch."

All the lighthearted teasing drained right out of her. She owned the ranch, and leaving while things were crazy made her feel like she was shirking her responsibility. She should stay.

But Aunt Adele was right. The guys had been working here long before she inherited the spread, and they'd do fine without her. Talon had a point too. She should make an honest effort to reconcile with Mama.

But couldn't it wait until everything here settled down?

Who knew when that would be?

The bad case of indecisiveness she'd battled after Kent died threatened to relapse. She needed to go. They had plans and tickets, and Mama was expecting them. She couldn't back out now. Regardless of what was happening at the ranch.

"It's going to be okay, isn't it? Do you think whoever was killing our cattle has stopped now?" Stupid question. Why would he stop? Out of the kindness of his heart? But before she could step on that plane and be half a country away, she wanted some kind of reassurance. However flimsy.

"Nothing has happened since last week, right? And today's Monday, so I think we're good. We went through several days without an incident. Maybe us staying out with the herd is a deterrent." He smiled. "I reckon it's safe now."

His confident tone brought her the relief she sought. Or maybe she just wanted to believe it. "Good. I don't think I could take it if something happened while I was gone." She listened to the porch-swing chain squeak against its hooks in the ceiling, then sought Talon's eyes again. "Will you and the guys keep watching the herd at night?"

"A little while longer. Never hurts to be safe." He studied her. "You're still worried?"

"I'd feel better if we could pray about it before I left."

"Good plan." He straightened on the swing, sitting shoulder to shoulder with her, and took her hand. "Father God, we thank you for the few uneventful days you've given us, and we're asking you for many more. We pray that whoever was causing this trouble for us has had his fill of devilment now and will leave us alone. Please keep Pat, Consuela, and Adele safe while they travel. Give them a good trip and a safe return."

"And, Father, please keep Talon and the others safe here on the ranch while I'm away. Give them the strength they need to complete the jobs they have to do. Please, like Talon said, let the attack be over now." And let the jerk doing it be caught and strung up by the toenails.

"In the name of your Son, Jesus, we pray. Amen."

Talon waited for her to say amen in agreement, but Patricia hesitated. Maybe she shouldn't have wished revenge on the guy while they were still praying. Although she'd gladly bring the rope to the toenail-stringing party, God said vengeance belonged to Him.

She sighed. Obedience meant leaving it to Him and His timing.

And Thy will be done. "Amen."

Talon hugged her closer and kissed her one more time, long and lingering, then gave her a boost. "You'd better go get some rest. Y'all are leaving mighty early in the morning."

"That wasn't my choice, believe me. Once Aunt Adele volunteered to pay for the tickets, I lost all control of when we'd be leaving." She stood and gave him a hand up. Silly, really—like they were already an old married couple. She could picture them in their seventies helping each other to their feet.

She wasn't ready to leave him, though he had a point. Five came early on a good day, but a day full of traveling, when she was more accustomed to physical activity, would be a killer.

"You'll see us off in the morning?"

"Absolutely." He opened the back door for her and gave her a quick peck before she entered the kitchen. "I'll see you in the morning."

He closed her in, and she watched him through the window as he headed around the house toward the bunkhouse on the other side of the ranch road. She flipped off the kitchen light and strolled through the dining room to the den, where she switched off the lamps. If they could ever decide on a date, he wouldn't have to leave her at night, and they'd have their own nighttime ritual before climbing the stairs to their shared bedroom. Their shared bed.

She giggled quietly. She, Consuela, and Aunt Adele would return from New York this coming Saturday. Would the following Saturday be too soon to have a wedding?

Next morning, Frank loaded the women's suitcases into the bed of the four-door pickup, then gave Adele a hand to the front passenger seat. Consuela had already made herself at home in the backseat and was giving Chef last-minute reminders through the window. Everyone was waiting for Pat, but Talon couldn't release her yet. Five days felt like an eternity, and something in him—something human and faithless—felt afraid for her safety. But with everything happening around here, perhaps she'd be better off with her parents.

He kissed her one more time, then held her, breathing in the spicy-sweetness of her shampoo, memorizing how she felt in his arms, and reminding himself that his deception had been necessary.

She clung to him too, her cheek resting in the hollow of his shoulder, her face turned toward his neck. Was she memorizing him too? Would she forgive him once she realized what he'd done?

Too soon, she pulled away. "I guess I have to go."

His heart caught in his throat. "I guess so." He traced her lips with his fingertip and dove into the green pools of her eyes as if he'd never see them again. "I love you."

"I love you too." Her voice sounded small, choked. Leaving him was hard for her too.

He offered a grin. "Have fun."

She laughed with the wryness he'd aimed for with his comment. "I'll try."

He helped her to the back seat, blew a kiss at Consuela, and said to Frank, "Be careful driving to the airport. Dark as it is, maybe you won't have too much traffic."

"Ain't worried about the traffic 'round here," Frank grumbled. "Once we get there, it'll be bull's-loose crazy."

Adele placed a hand on his arm. "At least you won't be driving in Manhattan."

"Thank God for small favors."

As they drove away, Pat turned and waved. She might as well have reached out and pulled his heart through the back glass. She was taking it with her anyway.

He'd lied to her last night—a huge, bald-faced lie. No way was this attack on the ranch over. Whoever had targeted them wouldn't be satisfied with killing a few head of cows.

That was just the appetizer. Until they caught the guy, Talon felt better with the women off the ranch. He would've packed Marie along with them if he could have. They could call him sexist and lecture him all day on the strength and independence of modern-day women, then gripe about ranchers' old-fashioned notions until their pretty little faces turned blue, but at least they'd be safe.

If Pat found out he'd lied and why, she have his hide stretched out and drying in the Texas sun before he knew what hit him. He was marrying a little spit-fire.

Smiling to himself, he headed inside where Chef had made breakfast for a smaller crowd this morning. Buster, Chance, and a half-asleep Marie passed platters of hash browns, sausage, and scrambled eggs, while Chef took his place at the table.

Talon poured a mug of coffee in the kitchen, then returned to the dining room and sat in his usual seat. He scrubbed his face with both hands and yawned. Since Frank was driving the women to the airport this morning and Pat was one of the ones he was hauling, the number of hands available to guard the cattle last night had shrunk, making those left behind serve a longer shift. Talon had covered between two and five this morning, and since he hadn't fallen asleep until around midnight last night, he felt muddleheaded.

Buster studied him a moment, then scooped up some hash browns. With the loaded fork hovering over his plate, he asked, "You gonna make it through the day?"

"No choice. We've got too much to do." He eyed the breakfast spread. He preferred a few hours in the bunk over a big meal, but he'd better eat. Long day ahead.

He snagged the bowl of eggs and motioned for someone to pass the sausage. "Frank said the fire trucks will be here again sometime today to hose down that new spot the Ag agents mapped for us. But since he's running to Dallas, one of us'll have to show them where to go. But we still need to get a start on fencing off Griff's acreage into two pastures now that the papers are signed."

He'd probably always call it Griff's, though technically it would be the new north pasture.

Chef handed him the potatoes. "I can help. Put me where you want me."

"You and Chance can work the cattle."

He smiled. "*Bueno*. Much better'n working the fence."

"I wish there was something I could do to help," Marie said, earning a smile and an affectionate rub on the shoulder from Chance. "I guess the best I can do is go to work and stay out of the way."

She was right. Maybe she'd be safe while she worked in town, but what about at night? With Chance pulling a shift with the herd, she would be alone in the house. So far, the nutcase attacking them had concentrated on the herd, but who knew when he'd shift his focus.

Talon took a sip of his coffee, then cleared his throat. "About tonight. Chef, could you take the early shift with the herd? Buster, Frank, and I will work out the other shifts."

"That's fine."

"What about me?" Chance asked.

Talon flashed a glance at Marie, who was concentrating on her eggs. "You need to guard the house."

Aunt Adele's hands rested in her lap. She looked in her element inside the limo. "It's a shame Natalie couldn't meet us at the airport. I half expected her to greet us on the runway."

"The duties of a senator's wife are never ending," Patricia said. Her mother's absence would likely be the highlight of the day. A few moments of peace before Patricia had to put herself on guard against Mama's barbs suited her fine. She'd already had a long, emotional day, thanks to her ongoing internal debate over the wisdom of leaving the ranch before the danger had clearly passed. Talon's reassurance hadn't survived the long hours on the plane.

Consuela alternated between gaping out the limousine window beside her and cowering tight-fisted in her seat. After her first flight and her first trip to any city larger than Stephenville, she apparently didn't know how to feel about either.

"What do you think of Manhattan so far?" Patricia asked.

"It's loud and crowded and busy"— a car horn blared nearby, and she jumped—"and loud!"

Patricia agreed with her double assessment of loud. After all her time on the ranch, where the tractor made the most racket and traffic noise drifted from the distance, she no longer felt comfortable with all this commotion. The buildings seemed to close in on her; the overabundance of visual stimuli threatened to give her a headache. And she'd been raised here. Consuela's senses must've been saturated.

"The pulse of this city can't be beat." Aunt Adele wore the smile of the proud native New Yorker showing off her city. "It's vibrant and exciting, exuding a life of its own. There's no other place like it."

"That's true. While we're here, I hope we can show Consuela some of the highlights."

Aunt Adele tsked. "You're in such a hurry to get back to Texas you didn't leave us enough time for a decent tour of the city. And it's the wrong time of year. Too warm to see the skaters at Rockefeller Center and too early for the Macy's

Thanksgiving Day Parade or the Christmas displays at the stores."

"I know, but there are so many other things. Staten Island, Times Square, Central Park." Things she had hoped to see with Talon before their plans were changed. Now she was here and he was home, and ...

Was everything really okay? She shouldn't have left. It didn't feel right. Why would anyone kill a few cows, then stop suddenly? It didn't make sense regardless of what Talon had said.

She shook off the thoughts—again—and turned to Consuela. "Where would you like to go?"

Consuela pressed her hands into her lap. "To a bathroom."

"We're almost there. I can see the building from here."

"All I see from here are buildings."

True. The horizon was only as far as the next steel or granite structure. Nothing like the ranch. But, in defense of her home state, most of New York didn't bear the weight of this much concrete. It had its beautiful, rustic areas too.

Her parents' limo driver, Anthony, pulled into the circle drive in front of the enormous, modern tower of condos in which Patricia's parents lived. He parked, then came around to open the door for them.

Patricia thanked him and started to lead the way to the door, but Consuela stopped her. "Shouldn't I get our bags?"

"You're on vacation." Patricia slipped her arm around her. "It's your turn to be waited on."

"My turn." Grinning, Consuela straightened her shoulders and stood a little taller. "I'm on vacation."

They headed to the entrance, where the doorman greeted them. "Nice to see you again, Miss Patricia."

"Good to see you again too, George. Did my mother make it home?"

"Yes ma'am. She went up about an hour ago."

"Oh good, she's here." Aunt Adele ushered them into the lobby and toward the elevators. "I know you're anxious to see her."

Not really, and if the anxiety gnawing at her stomach grew any stronger, she might turn around and return to the airport. After their two-hour drive to the DFW Airport, three-hour flight, and extra forty-five-minute drive to Manhattan—not to mention all the time spent waiting on planes and luggage—all she really wanted were a quick meal and a nap. A long conversation with Talon would top her list, but since cell phones didn't work worth a flip on the ranch and he wasn't likely to catch the house phone, she'd have to be patient until he called her this evening.

What she *didn't* want was another civilized fight with Mom. If only Daddy could be home this week.

As the elevator doors opened, she latched arms with Consuela, who appeared as nervous as she felt. Maybe they could strengthen each other.

Mom met them before they reached her door and waved them into a condo that held all the homey warmth of a hotel room. The sterile whites and gray contrasts were once to Patricia's taste, but now she preferred the sunny colors and cushy furniture at the ranch house.

As soon as they were all inside, her mother wrapped her in a hug. A real hug. Not the light touch and air kisses she'd expected.

Patricia reluctantly returned the affection. What would come next? An assessment of her appearance after a year on the ranch? Instead of having golden skin from a salon spray, she wore an uneven tan from working in the sun. Instead of manicured nails and pampered hands, her cuticles were rough and palms calloused. Instead of the sleek look developed from exercises her workout coach tailored for her, her arms and legs bore the bulges of developing muscles. She didn't look like a bodybuilder by any means, but she had changed enough to be noticeable. Now she braced for the inevitable commentary from a mother who had no doubt noticed.

Instead, Mom released her and hugged Aunt Adele as thoroughly, then smiled at their companion. "You must be Consuela. Welcome to my home."

Consuela ducked her head in greeting and flashed a panicked glance at Patricia, who pointed to the powder room. Consuela bobbed her head one more time. "Excuse me, Señora."

As Consuela darted away, Mama directed them into the living area with its two walls of windows, open to a breathtaking view of the city skyline and the Hudson River in the distance. When Consuela rejoined them, the panorama made her gasp. "¡*Qué hermosa!*"

"It is beautiful, isn't it?" Patricia said. "We're not on the ranch anymore, are we?"

She slowly shook her head as she took in the cityscape. "Not everything is bigger in Texas."

Mama rubbed her hands together. "Are you hungry? Oscar made a light lunch for us—steak tacos in honor of Consuela and the others at the ranch."

Aunt Adele nodded. "I'll eat anything. I'm starved. But I hope while we're here, we'll have a meal or two that's less Western. Since Chef Gregory returned to New York, our meals have been more ... *rustic*."

Patricia smirked. Not one hour in Manhattan, and the full extent of Aunt Adele's snobbery had returned. She and Mama together would stretch her endurance.

Chapter Nine

Even through the monitor, Talon could see the fatigue in Pat's eyes, but the sight of her with her hair pulled back and her face cleansed of makeup erased his own exhaustion. Though he preferred to have her next to him to feel her warmth and steal a kiss or two dozen, this means of continuing their bedtime ritual wasn't bad. He could see her, hear her. Two of the five senses. That would have to do.

"It's quiet here," he said. "You don't have to worry about us. What about you? How's your mom?"

"Insufferable, as always."

"I don't believe that. The woman who gave birth to a miracle like you can't be all bad."

She waved his compliment aside. "She's not bad, really, just different from me. We've never had anything in common."

"Is that why there's so much friction between you two?"

"That's part of it, I suppose. And her sending Aunt Adele to Texas to be our chaperone certainly didn't help." She raised her gray-green eyes heavenward, then returned her attention to him. "Even when I fit in her world, we wanted different things. After Kent died, she wanted me to remarry, maintain my position in society. I just wanted to work and forget those years even happened. I had no intention of remarrying."

"I'm glad you do now."

The smile she gave him made him want to grab her through the monitor and yank her home. His arms felt empty, and his lips longed to taste hers. He stifled a groan. She'd been gone only a day. The next four would be miserable.

After they ended the connection, with promises to meet again at the same time the next evening, Talon grabbed his hat and headed outside.

Chance and Marie sat together on the rockers on the opposite side of the porch from the office window, offering him as much privacy as possible. They glanced at him as he stepped out.

Marie slipped a strand of raven hair behind her ear. "How does Consuela like New York?"

"I think she's a bit overwhelmed." He leaned against a porch rail. "Pat said her knuckles stayed white most of the day."

Chance nodded to the general direction of the front pasture. "Chef taking a shift out there seems strange while I'm sitting here like a lazy hound dog."

"It's the first time he and Consuela have been apart. This gives him something to do."

"Yeah, he'll go home so tired he won't have time to mope. He'll fall into bed, and we'll be lucky if he gets up early enough to feed us in the morning."

"That's what I'm hoping." Along with the assurance Marie wouldn't be alone in the house.

The fatigue he'd been fighting won the battle. He yawned and arched his aching back. "I'm going to get some shut-eye. Two o'clock comes fast."

He waved good-night to them as he walked down the steps and ambled over to the bunkhouse. In the not too distant future—he hoped—the sleeping arrangement would be different all the way around. Chance and Marie would have their own home, and he would move back into the main house. He and Pat would share the master suite. And maybe, not long after, they'd have a baby boy to keep them hopping. Talon could cuddle him while he was little and teach him to ride as he got older. By then, they'd have a little girl too.

By the time he slipped into the bunkhouse, he'd named baby number three and was daydreaming about baby number four. He didn't care if they had a set of boys or girls or a wonderful mixture of both as long as they all looked like Pat. A whole passel of little blonds with sage-green eyes would suit him fine.

From his recliner in front of the TV, Buster snored in opposite breaths from Frank's snorts emanating from his bunk. Everyone had driven themselves hard today. Frank had returned from the airport around noon and, after a quick lunch, draped his arthritic legs around Pat's horse Tandy. Buster and Talon had worked to subdivide Griff's land and get the fence started. The sooner they finished, the sooner they could move the herd out of that small pasture.

He stepped softly to his bunk and eased out of his boots. A shower would be great, but a few minutes' rest would be better.

By the time he opened his eyes again, the moon shone through the bunkhouse windows and illuminated Frank's empty bed. Judging from the silence, Buster wasn't inside either. The guys must've been shifting the guard. He still had a few hours before it was his turn.

When he rolled over, paper crumpled under his hand. The guys must've left him a note. He sat up and flipped on the bedside lamp to read the scratchy handwriting.

It's been almost nine years. Do you still miss her?
Do you think of her at all? I do. I think of her every
single day. You didn't deserve her.

What? Whose sick joke was this?

He flipped it over to the back. Blank.

The paper had been ripped from a college-lined spiral
notebook and folded into fourths. The torn ring perforations
on the left side gave it a careless, tattered look. Whoever
wrote this ignored the lines and used the entire page to scrawl
his message in bold, black ink.

Moving closer to the light, Talon read it again.

"Nine years." This wasn't about Pat. It was about Janet.

He shook his head slowly as he read it a third time. "You
didn't deserve her."

The paper crackled in his trembling hands. Who would
write this? What kind of revolting coward would write such
a thing?

He jerked his head toward the window. Was the guy still
around, lurking outside to sneer at his reaction?

Talon crushed the note in his right hand and charged to
the door. Scalding blood pumped through his veins as he
dashed outside and collided with a human mass—a sniveling,
cowardly—

He wadded the man's shirtfront in his left hand and drew
back his other fist—

"Talon! Hey, it's me!"

Frank's voice cut through his rage. He blinked, gave his head a quick shake. Frank stared at him as if he'd been mule-kicked in the head. Maybe he had.

He grabbed the older man's shoulders. "Did you see anyone out here? Did you see him?"

"See who?"

"There was someone here. Someone came into the bunkhouse." He raised the note, still clenched in his fist. "He left this."

Frank took the letter and tilted it toward the security lights so he could see it better. While he read, Talon jumped off the porch and searched around the steps and the yard. What the security lights didn't illuminate, the moon did with a blue glow. But nothing moved. Nothing seemed out of place. He darted back inside, grabbed his flashlight from its drawer, and headed out again.

"Ain't no one out here," Frank told him. "It's quiet. Whoever left this is long gone."

The cold air chilled the sweat trickling down Talon's back. Someone was out here. Didn't matter that Frank hadn't seen him; he could still be here. Waiting. Wanting to see the results of his evil. He might even be the one who killed Janet. And now, for some warped reason, he wanted to make Talon suffer for her death.

He flashed his light at every shadow around the pens, then headed for the barn to do the same. The horses shuffled in their stalls, snorting softly, but nothing else moved. Not in the tack room. Not near the feed supply. Not around the alfalfa bales.

Breathing in shallow huffs, he left the barn and cut across the yard to the main house. He aimed the beam at the porch and the bushes, down the rows of vegetables on the west side and around to the back porch, then through Adele's flower beds on the east side.

Nothing. No sign. Like some phantom had materialized and disappeared, leaving the note as the only evidence he'd been there at all.

Talon strode back to the bunkhouse. Frank had flicked on the porch light and perched on the rocker like a target for a madman. But that yellow cur could be anywhere by now. Besides, if he'd intended to kill somebody, it would be Talon—and he'd had the perfect opportunity already.

Frank held up the note and eyed Talon as he approached. "Reckon this is what all the commotion has been about?"

"Yeah. It has to be. Nothing else makes sense." Talon flopped onto the top porch step, still scanning the shadows. He flexed his fists and tried to regain control of his heart, his breathing. Closing his eyes, he drew in a deep breath of cold night air.

Janet, sweet Janet, with her chestnut hair and bright hazel eyes and infectious laugh that still echoed in his memory often enough to make his heart hurt. Somehow, all this centered around her.

With a groan and an audible cracking of his joints, Frank sat beside him. "It's been over eight years. Wonder why this is happenin' now. Where's this fella been all this time?"

"And who is he?" Talon took the note. Frank had tried to smooth out the wrinkles Talon made when he crushed it in his fist, but the creases remained, spider-webbing the message. The writing didn't look familiar, but no one he knew good enough to recognize their handwriting would've left this kind of note.

Frank yanked up a dried weed by the porch and started crumbling its leaves, releasing a musty scent to the chilly breeze. "What do you remember about that night? What happened?"

"You know what happened." And he didn't want to revisit it, not even in the relative safety of distance. It was a long time ago, and though it still hurt to think of it, the pain had eased some. Dulled considerably after he met Pat.

"Yep, but maybe your hindsight has grown a mite keener since then. Might be you'll remember something in the retellin' you ain't thought of before."

He squeezed his eyes shut again. Frank made sense, but his suggestion felt like a scalpel slicing open an old scar.

"Y'all were staying in some fancy hotel in Dallas," Frank said, as if he needed reminding. "The whole weddin' party had rooms there. So, why'd ya need to go to a grocery store? What did you need that room service couldn't bring you?"

"Flowers." Something silly. He'd insisted on buying flowers before he took her back to the hotel. It had been his feeble attempt at being romantic.

She'd told him that night would be the last time he would see her before the wedding, and he wanted to get her something that would keep him in her mind. Only place to get flowers at that time of night was a grocery store. He'd left her in the truck and started walking toward the store—

He jerked as the gunshot sounded in his memory as surely as if fired from beside him.

Frank steadied him with a hand on his shoulder. "What do you remember?"

"I can't do this." He erupted from the porch and paced in the yard. Dead grass prickled his bare feet.

The bullet had pierced the windshield of his old pickup and embedded in her skull. But he didn't know that. After he heard the shot, he didn't look toward the truck. He ducked. Turned to see where it came from. Then, from the corner of his eye, he saw movement.

Someone tossed the gun to him and drove away.

He'd caught the weapon by sheer reflex, then glanced back toward the truck. Janet had slumped to the side.

"This isn't helping." He quit pacing and faced Frank. "I don't remember anything I haven't already told everyone."

"I'll tell you what I remember." Frank struggled up from the step and leaned against the post. "Police said they found you sitting outside the pickup. You'd pulled Janet out and was holdin' her and wailin'. They said there was a gun on the passenger seat. Said witnesses in the parkin' lot saw you holdin' it." He came down to stand beside Talon. "Where'd it come from?"

"I've told you—I've told everyone. Some guy threw it at me."

"Okay, what'd he look like?"

"I don't know. It happened too fast. I caught a glimpse of him in his truck, throwing something at me, then he burned rubber getting away from there." He closed his eyes again and reached for the gun in his mind. A small caliber handgun of some sort. He'd studied it, turning it over in his hands, trying to force his brain to make sense out of what happened. That was when he looked back to see what the guy had shot at. The hole in his windshield was tiny. Hard to believe a bullet that small could pierce it and still have enough power to ...

He shook away the memory. "This is useless. Get your flashlight. Maybe we can find some tracks or something. The guy must've left some sign, some clue."

As he walked past, Frank grabbed his arm. "The guy's pickup. What did it look like?"

"I told you. I can't do this."

He jerked free from Frank's grasp, snagged his flashlight from the porch railing, and went inside. Stupid to think he could track the guy tonight. He hadn't seen footprints when he searched the first time, no crushed grass the size of a man's boot. He certainly wouldn't be able to find a trail along the gravel road. Whoever this guy was, he'd be back. Whatever his intentions, he hadn't fulfilled them with a few dead cows and a note.

He yanked on his boots. He wouldn't be sleeping anymore tonight. Might as well relieve Buster.

When Frank came in, Talon said, "Let's keep this just between us for now."

Frank stopped at his bunk. "You got to tell the others. They oughta know to be on the lookout for someone."

"Yeah, but if Chance tells Marie, she'll tell Pat. Same if Chef tells Consuela. I don't want her knowing yet. She'd be home on the next plane out of New York."

Frank squinted at him. "Haven't you learned your lesson about keeping her in the dark?"

"Yes, but this is different." He pointed at the note. "If this guy is angry about Janet, then he may target Pat. I have to keep her safe."

He hadn't been able to do the same for Janet.

Chapter Ten

P atricia sat down to a breakfast of avocado slices drizzled with a creamy jalapeño sauce, toasted wedges of a seed-riddled artisan bread, and a side of kiwi. Nothing like the sausage, grits, and eggs or the breakfast taquitos she'd get back home, but appropriate for the Manhattan setting.

Nudging the green fruit with her fork, Consuela leaned toward her and whispered, "What is this?"

"Chinese gooseberry," Mama answered. "Kiwi. You've heard of it, haven't you?"

"Heard of, never seen." Consuela watched Patricia cut a slice in half with her fork and slide the fruit in her mouth, then copied her. She took a tentative bite and grinned. "It's good."

"It is good," Patricia said, then squinted at her mother. "And green, like everything else on the plate. Has Chef Oscar lost his eye for color?"

"Don't blame Oscar, dear. It was my idea." Mama dabbed her lips with her napkin, then laid it beside her plate. "I've been thinking about the color scheme for your wedding. What do you think about green?"

Green? For her *wedding*? Her blood started sizzling through her veins; her tongue held an acerbic flavor.

She nudged the fruit. "The kiwi color is out." Then, she stabbed an avocado slice and held it up for scrutiny. "Perhaps this shade? Or maybe jalapeno green? Or maybe jade green, the color of jealousy and suspicion and bitterness"— the color wrapped around her heart the entire time she and Kent were married. "What about that shade of green, Mom?"

"Oh, don't be angry. I was just trying to help." She took a delicate bite of her toast and flicked the crumbs from her fingers to her plate. "You've given us such little time together I felt it necessary to plan ahead. I took the liberty of lining up several shops for us to visit. Anthony will bring the car around as soon as Adele gets here."

Consuela beamed. "I get to go shopping in New York City!"

At least one of them felt enthusiastic. Patricia didn't see the point. They hadn't set a date yet. Things were too busy, too unsettled, for her to be thinking of weddings now. Well, that wasn't entirely true. She thought of weddings in relation to the fact that after theirs, they'd finally live in the same house, which was far more important anyway.

But never, in all her imaginings, had she ever considered *green* an appropriate color for a wedding.

Aunt Adele floated in and gave everyone a cheery greeting. "I can't begin to tell you how wonderful it is to sleep in my own bed." She bent to kiss Patricia's cheek. "No offense, dear, but that mattress you have me on at the ranch is hard and lumpy."

She hadn't intended to be housing her aunt, but she'd been given no choice in the matter. "I'll see about getting you another."

"Don't bother, dear. You and Talon will be married soon, and I will no longer be needed." She glanced to the kitchen. "Is there any coffee left? Gregory made some for me this morning, but I feel the need for another cup."

Patricia slipped another half slice of kiwi into her mouth. Vivid green kiwi.

She'd better change her attitude toward shopping and take the idea more seriously, or she'd find herself saying yes to all her mother's suggestions just so she wouldn't have to decide. If she didn't stay alert, her bridesmaids would stroll down the aisle in dresses the color of salad. Besides, last night Talon said everything was quiet. Maybe the attack had ended. Still didn't make sense that whoever had been killing their cattle and poisoning the pastures would suddenly quit, but nothing had happened in several days. Maybe the sheriff had caught the guy.

Yes, that must've been it. The sheriff wasn't required to tell them they'd caught the perpetrator, was he? He probably would, out of courtesy, but was it required?

Maybe not. They'd probably find out in the crime section of the local paper.

Why couldn't she feel at ease about it? Why was her spirit restless? Something was wrong; she could feel it. She glanced at the clock. Eight in Texas. No one would be inside to answer if she called.

They absolutely must get a cell phone tower on the spread. Next time she came to New York to visit her parents, Talon should be with her, but if not . . .

They must get a tower.

Mama waved them out of the condo, anxious to go shopping. Patricia still couldn't summon the enthusiasm necessary to try on dresses all morning, much less the strength to perform the mental gymnastics required to hold a diplomatic battle with her mother the entire time. Not that she'd been diplomatic earlier.

At her wedding, Marie had worn a tea-length dress with pink Western boots and a Stetson with a veil. Had she been there, Mama would have no doubt made her disapproval known. Privately, of course. But Marie's choice would have suited Patricia perfectly.

Consuela caught her arm as they followed Mama and Aunt Adele through the lobby. "Señora McAllister told me to think about lunch and where I want to go."

"That's a daunting task. With every possible thing you could eat from every possible culture, you have a huge selection to choose from. Did you glance through the menus she gave you?"

"Si. Everything looks expensive."

"Don't worry about the cost. You're on vacation. We can go as fancy as you'd like."

"I don't want to go fancy. Your aunt's Chef Gregory gave us fancy while he was there. That was good, but it was enough. I want ..." She ducked her head and a flush reddened her dark cheeks. "I want a New York pizza. Real, you know? *Authentico*. Is that okay?"

Pizza! How long had it been since she'd had a good one? That stuff they served in Texas couldn't compare. "I know just the place. And you'll get to see Times Square while we're there."

She glanced at Consuela's feet. Sensible shoes as always. Good. She'd need them.

Mama led the way to the limo and, after a short drive, led the way again to the door of the ritziest bridal shop in the city. With the potential financial losses the ranch might endure this year, Patricia couldn't see spending such a ludicrous amount of money on bridesmaid dresses that would never be worn again. She'd had her big wedding. The results reeked.

"Mama, I thought you understood that I don't want an expensive affair."

"Of course, dear, but there's no harm in looking, is there? Besides, just because the event will be a small one, doesn't mean it can't be tasteful."

Patricia raised her eyes heavenward. What had she expected? A trip to a department store?

They entered a boutique that smelled of sandalwood and jasmine, with heavy undertones of elite money. Hairless manikins with thrust-out hips and elegantly uplifted arms modeled the latest in chic satin and Swarovski crystal beadwork. Around the walls, gowns hung on display beneath individual spotlights designed to emphasize their sparkle and gleam. Furniture was sparse and upholstered in muted tones of heather gray and winter wheat. The tufted, barrel-backed chairs arranged around side tables and the long, padded benches offered rest to those in wait of the bride to be. Rest, yes. But comfort? They seemed as prim and proper as the arch-browed woman who greeted them.

Patricia strolled along the walls, leaving the chat with the gown consultant to her mother, and scanned the bridal dresses. She loved beautiful gowns as much as the next fashionista. The question wasn't whether she'd find something she liked, but whether she could resist it.

She could. The determining factor was who would be wearing the dresses. Pregnant or not, Marie would look amazing in anything, and Katie had the perfect figure for many of these gowns, but not the temperament. The thought of her swimming through yards of material before she found where her head went made Patricia giggle, though she probably wasn't being fair. She loved Katie tremendously but hadn't been acquainted with her long enough to know how many weddings she'd been in and how many gowns she'd struggled into.

As she glanced through the dresses the store lady presented, she shook her head. "These really are too much. Too fancy, too sophisticated for what I want."

She turned to the others. "I want something simple. Maybe even Western, like Marie had at her wedding."

"I heard about Marie's wedding." Mama nodded toward her sister. Aunt Adele had been the only one from Patricia's family to come to Texas for the event. No telling what she'd reported back. "I don't think cowboy boots are appropriate."

"They are in Texas," Consuela mumbled. She fingered the fabric of the gown the consultant was holding, both awed by the material and disgusted with its extravagance. An attitude Patricia expected to see on everyone's face if she and Talon held the ceremony at the Cowboy Church.

She hadn't thought of that. Talon was the pastor of the Cowboy Church. Who would perform the ceremony—and where? Should they get married inside, in a traditional church? Or at the ranch, as Marie had? She needed more time to think this through.

"I don't even know when we're getting married or where." She waved the consultant aside with a thank you and retrieved her purse she'd left beside her mother on a padded bench. "This is premature and definitely not what I want."

Mama stood. "But are you at least getting ideas? You know how weddings are. So much to plan for. You can't leave everything to the last minute."

"Mother, I don't even know what the last minute is. We haven't had time to discuss what we want."

Aunt Adele rested a hand on her arm with a knowing look in her eye. "You and Talon really do need to decide, unless you want me living with you indefinitely."

"You know everything we've been through, how crazy it's been at the ranch. I thought you'd be on my side."

"Frankly, I'm on my side. I'm ready to move back home. The sooner you two get hitched, as they say in the South, the sooner I can get my life back."

"But I thought you liked it on the ranch."

"Not as much as I like it in the city." She gently brushed Patricia's hair from her eyes, a twinkle of humor shining from her own. "What did you think I'd do once I was no longer needed? Reside in your guest room forever?"

No. Oh, most definitely no.

"Let's go." Her mother took her by the elbow and aimed her toward the door. "I have one more place for you to see before we go to lunch." She twisted back toward Consuela, who followed. "Have you been thinking of where you'd like to go? What's on our menu today?"

"Pizza."

"I thought we'd take her to that little hole in the wall near Times Square," Patricia said. "You know the one. They have the best deep-dish pizza."

"I know the place. Good. Our next stop is on the way."

After they'd ridden a short distance, Mama asked Anthony to pull over. They circled the drive of another residential tower. She looped her purse over her arm. "Bear with me a few minutes. I promised a friend I'd take a look at this apartment and give her my opinion."

Anthony opened the door for her, but before she stepped out, she hesitated and looked back at them. "Would you like to come too? I'm sure she won't mind if all of us go up."

Like ducks waddling in a row, they followed her to a small, one-bedroom apartment. The furnished condo wasn't on the grand scale of her parents', but anyone would be lucky to have it. Ultramodern kitchen and bath, nice-sized living room with windows opened to a great cityscape. Union Square and some of New York's finest restaurants were within walking distance. The place seemed perfect for a young, upwardly mobile couple.

Mama stood in the living room with a finger on her chin and glanced toward the galley kitchen. "What do you think, Patricia? Does the kitchen look too small?"

"Consuela is a better one to ask. She spends much of her time in the kitchen."

Consuela's wide eyes could rival a full moon as she ran her palm over the granite counter. She opened the doors of the top-of-the-line refrigerator—far more space inside than the one at home—then tested the oven door. The dishwasher was considerably smaller than the one on the ranch, but whoever would live here probably wouldn't have eight hungry people to feed.

She opened one more appliance door, her puzzlement evident on her face. "What is this?"

"It's a wine fridge," Aunt Adele answered. "Nice size too. One could store quite a collection in there."

Consuela shrugged. "It would be better as a cabinet."

Ever practical. She might have loved the kitchen, but frills didn't impress her.

"What do you think? Isn't it perfect?" Her mother crossed the room to stand beside Patricia and slipped an arm around her waist. "This is a steal at one point eight million."

Consuela gasped. "That much for this little place? It could fit inside our living room."

"For the location, it's a good price," Patricia told her, then turned to her mother. "It's nice. Who do you have in mind for it?"

"You, dear." She gave Patricia's waist a squeeze. "I think this would be perfect for you and Talon."

Patricia gawked at her. "What on earth gave you the idea Talon would want to live in New York?" She stepped away from her mother's grasp and glared at Aunt Adele, whose brows had drawn. "Did you give her the impression we would live here?"

"No," her aunt and mother said in unison, then Mama took over. "I just thought maybe you two could treat the ranch as a getaway. Stop living such a harsh life. Don't you think—"

Patricia shot her hand up, palm facing her mother, halting her from uttering one more ludicrous statement. "I'll meet you back at the limo."

She turned toward the door, then stopped and motioned for Consuela to join her. "Better yet, we'll walk."

"But—"

"Don't speak, Mother. Not another word."

Chapter Eleven

Bart Nelson stood alone at the Co-op service desk, studying papers on a clipboard. Talon lengthened his stride to get to him before a customer did. Or before Colton returned from wherever he'd disappeared to. Colton and his buddies weren't old enough to shave when Janet died, so the jealousy angle didn't fit, but Talon still wanted to rule Colton out. Who knew what was in that kid's head?

Bart caught sight of him, and his smile of greeting drooped in a heartbeat. "You okay, man? You look like you went a few rounds at Jacob's ladder."

"Putting it lightly." He flattened his palms on the countertop. "Got a favor to ask of you, and I need you to keep it quiet."

Bart lowered the clipboard and leaned toward him. "Shoot."

"I need to know if anyone's ordered potassium cyanide for any reason in the past few months."

"I heard you lost more cattle. That the poisoning agent?"

Talon nodded. "High quantities in concentrated areas. The volunteer fire department has flooded a couple of places in the pastures. Supposed to help, but we're leery of putting the herd back out there."

"Can't say as I blame you." He brought the computer to life and tapped a few keys. "Nasty stuff if in the wrong hands, from what I understand. It'll do a good job on the creepy-crawlies, but we rarely get a call for it."

He kept shaking his head as he scrolled, and each shift from right to left tightened Talon's gut. Having Bart search this had been a longshot. Talon expected to drop Colton as a suspect, but he'd hoped someone else would rise to the top in his place. If Bart found nothing, he would have no clue where to turn next.

Bart rested his hands on either side of the keyboard. "Nothing, man."

Talon grimaced. "Thanks anyway."

"Let me know if something else crosses your mind. I want to help if I can."

"Thanks again."

Back to the drawing board—assuming he could find the drawing board. Foolish idea to think he could investigate on his own, but he needed to try. Needed to do something.

Sheriff Derrick Brewer hadn't uttered a word in over a week. Wouldn't hurt to check in. Fortunately he was in the office. It would've been more encouraging if he were out working on this case, but maybe he'd hit a dead end too.

As Talon entered the private office, Sheriff Brewer yanked his booted feet from his desktop and lowered his chair to all fours. He dropped the file he'd been studying and stretched across the desk to shake hands. "Good to see you. What brings you here?"

"Decided I'd check in. Learn anything new?"

"Nothing. Not one single thing." Brewer's frustration reflected his own. "With you being the preacher out there at the Cowboy Church, I expected the suspect list to be short. I never figured it'd be nonexistent. Once Colton and the guys from the Rocking T turned up clean, we expanded the investigation to include everyone we could find who bet against you during your last bull-riding event. That's the only motive that makes sense at this point, but we came up dry." He grinned. "You and Chance are pretty popular around here. Not many people bet against either of you."

Talon lowered his head and gave the back of his neck a good rub. He should've known the sheriff had already investigated Colton. The man excelled at his job, far better than Talon did at sleuthing. The idea of keeping the note to himself, of investigating it himself, bit the dust with the realization he didn't know what he was doing. Maybe Brewer would have better luck with it.

As he flopped down on a chair across from the sheriff's, he pulled the note from his shirt pocket and handed it over. "Somebody came in the bunkhouse last night and left this on my bed."

Sheriff Brewer massaged his temple as he read the short note, then flipped it over to its blank side. Talon had done the same, as if maybe—just maybe—the fool had signed the back.

Brewer read it again, then looked at him from under his brow. "Anyone see who left it?"

"Nope."

"Any idea what time it landed on your bed?"

"Sometime around midnight."

"Nobody heard him?"

"I figure I was the only one in the bunkhouse at the time. Probably happened when Frank and Buster were changing shifts with the cattle. Frank came in not long after I found it."

"He didn't see anyone?"

Talon shook his head. How could someone move around the ranch buildings so easily without being noticed? Had he tried to go inside the main house? Had he considered targeting Pat? The recurring thought made his stomach roil.

Sheriff Brewer punched a button on his phone and ordered his secretary to hunt down the Janet Parsons file.

The Janet Parsons file. She'd been reduced to a few pages in a manila folder.

Bile rose in his throat, and his hands became clammy. He scrubbed them down his thighs and swallowed several times. That one image of him holding her limp body against his own splashed over the good memories like a blood-red tide. He hadn't even been allowed out of jail to attend her funeral. By the time the authorities realized the prints on the bullet casings didn't match Talon's, she'd already been buried.

It took years for the sweet memories to return, a few at a time at first, as if to not overwhelm him. But eventually he could think about her without seeing her pale face illuminated by the dome light in the pickup. Without seeing the blood streaking her forehead and cheek.

Now that was all he could see.

"What we have here won't do us much good," Sheriff Brewer said. "We just kept inquiries and notes on collaborative efforts. Dallas PD has the big file. We'll have to make a request for it." He leaned back and crossed his arms over his protruding belly. "If I remember correctly, once they released you, they couldn't come up with another viable suspect."

"No. The prints on the bullets weren't in the system." He clamped his jaw until the pressure on his teeth threatened to cause a headache. He couldn't do this. He couldn't last night with Frank, and he couldn't now. He would implode if he didn't get out of here. "Do you need me anymore? I've got a ranch to run."

The sheriff gave him a strange look, then shrugged. "I reckon I know where to find you if I—"

Talon bolted from the room, taking long strides to the front door and the fresh air beyond. Outside, he propped his hands on his knees and panted like a whipped dog. He was in a free fall, a horrible nightmare, with a sweaty grip on sanity. His hand was slipping.

Oh, Father, help me!

If only he could take a deep breath, maybe the dizziness would subside. He couldn't black out in the middle of town. Gossips and speculators would have a ball with the news that the preacher passed out cold in front of the sheriff's office.

He clenched his eyes shut and focused on his breathing. At last, he forced in a lungful of air and shoved it out. A few more full breaths, and his heart settled down. After another moment of holding his knees, he managed to gain control of himself. He took a few shaky steps to his pickup and closed himself inside. If anyone but Sheriff Brewer had witnessed his meltdown, they'd had the decency to leave him alone.

He needed to hold himself together, needed to face his memories of Janet objectively. Whatever he could dredge up from that day might help solve the case and bring a stop to the attacks on the ranch. But Pat would return soon. How could they solve a case in three days that they hadn't solved in almost nine years?

He slammed his palms on the steering wheel. Why couldn't he think? Why couldn't he see something in his mind's eye that would give a clue worth pursuing?

Why did memories of Janet leave his stomach in knots and his heart aching as if he'd lost her only yesterday? He'd loved her. Of course he'd loved her. But he had Pat now. He loved and treasured her too. He must keep her safe. Must buy time to make sense of all this. How could he convince her to stay in New York?

The light was on under Consuela's bedroom door. Patricia rapped gently on the frame and entered at her bidding. Wrapped in a pink housecoat, she stood before a full-length mirror, vigorously brushing short hair that held more gray than Patricia had realized.

"What's wrong, *chica*?"

Patricia locked her hands behind back. "Have you talked to Chef yet?"

"Sure. Not long ago."

"Did he ... say anything?"

"Huh. When does he not say anything?" She placed the brush on the dresser, then sat on the foot of her bed and patted the space beside her. "Tell me what is wrong."

Patricia settled on the mattress. "I talked to Talon, and something seems off. Something's happening that he's not telling me."

"Something bad?"

"I don't know. I couldn't tell. Did Chef say anything to you?"

"Nothing to cause worry. What did Talon say?"

"Nothing really, but it seemed like he was hiding something. He tried to talk me into staying here longer."

"That won't work. I'm surprised you didn't buy a ticket home today." She studied Patricia, her expression holding a blend of concern and sympathy. "You okay now? Still mad?"

"Only when I think about it." Patricia stood and paced to the mirror and back. "Can you believe her? What on earth made her think Talon and I would live here? What gave her the idea the ranch was just a hobby to me—or him? It's his life. How could he leave it?"

"He couldn't, but your mother has no understanding." Consuela reached for Patricia's hand. "Or maybe it is you that has no understanding."

"What do you mean?"

"You are her *única niña*, no? Her only child? And now you are far away. What mama would want her baby so far from her?"

"But people grow up and move away. Fly the coop." She dropped to the bed again. "I have my own plans. I don't want to continue living hers."

"And a good mama wouldn't ask you to." Consuela patted her arm. "Señora Natalie is a good mama. She is just lonely for you. A woman misses her daughter. Sons move away, but daughters become special friends."

Friendship with her mother? If Mama wanted to develop a friendship, she'd gone about it the wrong way. Why couldn't she just respect Patricia's decision? If she would only try to see, try to understand ...

Of course, she could point the same accusing finger at herself. She'd done little to try to understand her mother's side of all this. But the only side Mama had presented was *don't marry a cowboy*, with *don't move to Texas* close on its heels.

Talon's song and dance tonight about her not leaving New York until they'd settled their differences rattled her even worse. They'd done considerably better since last spring's fiasco. He no longer kept secrets from her. He sought her out to discuss things far more often than he used to. Or at least it seemed that way. Was he hiding something now? Surely, he missed her as much as she missed him. Why would he want her to extend her visit?

He'd said things were still quiet on the ranch. Maybe the secret he kept was a surprise for her.

Could he be planning their wedding? It was a crazy thought, but she wouldn't put it past him. He'd be taking all the planning and decision-making burdens off her shoulders. It wouldn't take much to please her. At this point, she'd have the ceremony at DFW with the entire airport as witnesses. He probably tired of the wait just as she did. Maybe her idea of getting married the Saturday after she returned home wasn't that farfetched.

Chapter Twelve

"Good morning." Patricia approached her mother, who sat at the dining table with her coffee and newspaper. She kissed her cheek and gave her shoulders a squeeze before heading to the kitchen for her own cup of coffee.

"You seem to be in a good mood today. Did you rest well?"

"Extremely." She'd drifted to sleep daydreaming about what a Talon-planned wedding might look like. With Marie there to guide him, he'd undoubtedly come up with something amazing. She would have to call her friend tonight to get a hint. Talon had probably sworn her to secrecy, but girlfriend loyalty reigned supreme. Marie would tell her something useful, even if she kept the bulk of the plans concealed. Assuming, of course, that her crazy hunch was correct.

She sat at the table beside her mother. "Are we going shopping again today?"

Mama folded her paper and set it aside. "And have yet another emotional display? I think not."

Her mother's tone seemed snippy, but Patricia wouldn't bite—not today. Even Mama couldn't kill her mood. "So what are the plans?"

Consuela stepped into the room as Mama answered, "Since Consuela's time here is short, I thought we'd take her around to all the favorite tourist spots."

"I would like that." Consuela looked as excited as a child at Christmas. "Where will we go?"

Mama gave her an indulgent smile. "That's totally up to you."

Before long, they had a game plan and left early enough to accomplish most of it. During the day, as she carted them all over the city—or Anthony did—Mama behaved like a perfect hostess. By the time they got to Nathan's on Coney Island, Patricia had begun to relax. Maybe Mama had given up on her trickery to get her to move back to Manhattan.

Not likely, but at least today, maybe she'd let it drop.

Patricia nudged Consuela and pointed with her hotdog toward the huge wooden roller coaster, the biggest attraction on the island. "Want to go on the Cyclone?"

She shook her head and licked mustard off her lip. "You crazy, *muchacha*. I'm not going on that thing."

Mama stepped closer. "What would you like to do?"

Her cheeks reddened, and she shifted her glance between Patricia and her mother from beneath her lashes. The shy woman who stood here didn't match the fireball from the ranch. This side of her was endearing. She did so much for everyone else, always thinking of others. That anything would be done especially for her seemed alien to her, and with childlike joy, she showed how much she appreciated it.

"Could I—could we go to the beach? Can I put my feet in the ocean?"

"That's a wonderful idea," Mama said. "It's a beautiful day, and it's the off-season, so it won't be too crowded."

The moment they got to the shore, Consuela slipped off her shoes and marched straight to the water. Patricia wasn't far behind. She walked deep enough that the hems of her clamdiggers got damp. Each wave that tugged the sand from beneath her feet pulled away what remained of her stress. She could handle her mother, and if what Consuela had said about mother-daughter relationships was true, she could even sympathize with her. How nice it would be not to be on edge and leery all the time.

Mama waded closer and slipped her arm around Patricia's waist. "Don't you miss this? You're landlocked on the ranch, aren't you? Remember our trips to Maine for fresh lobster? Holidays on the Jersey shore?"

"Oh, Mother, stop." So much for the friendship idea or any thought that Mama had given up. "Do you have to ruin everything?"

Patricia turned away and waded back to shore. If they were to develop a relationship, God would have to show her how, because she flat wasn't seeing it. The woman was impossible.

"Honey, I'm sorry. I didn't mean to upset you again."

She whirled around, her quick motion splashing the water higher up her clothes. "Then why did you? We were having a great day. Why did you have to start in on me again?"

"What did I say? I just wanted to reminisce with you."

"It's never quite that simple, Mother. Every sentence you utter is wrapped in an ulterior motive."

Her mother sighed and allowed her hands to drop by her sides. "I didn't mean to bring it up today, but since you have accused me of it anyway, fine. It's true. You're moving miles away from everything you know. When the novelty of ranch life wears off, you'll regret your decision. I want you to have a backup plan. Someplace you can come home to."

Her father had said the same thing the year before, but nothing could be further from the truth. She loved the ranch and everyone on it. The life both challenged her and brought her peace. Every day was different. Each day brought something new, something *real*, unlike her life in New York.

"I'll never return here to live, and whether I return to visit depends on how quickly you can accept that fact." She stomped through the waves to the shore.

Consuela stood several feet away, holding a shell she ignored in favor of frowning at Patricia.

Great. Now she had two mothers, and both were upset with her. Was no one capable of seeing her side in this?

"I don't think I can take another day of this," Patricia told Talon that night.

He gave her a sympathetic look through the monitor. "I know, babe, but I don't want this hanging over us when we get married. She's your mother. What Consuela said makes sense. She's acting like this because she doesn't want you living half a country away. Can you blame her?"

"She can buy a first-class ticket without even blinking. You said it yourself. If she wants to see her grandchildren, she'll have to come to Texas once in a while." Mama hadn't been back to the Lone Star State since Daddy's parents died.

She propped her chin on her hand. "I'm beginning to think I'm adopted. Daddy was raised on a ranch and turned his back on it. Mama hates the idea of it entirely. And I can't imagine living anywhere else. It's like I've finally found where I belong. I wish Mama could understand."

"Maybe you can help her."

He looked and sounded weary—no small wonder considering it was nine o'clock his time. During normal days, the guys were up at least by five, and these weren't normal days. Were they still staying up all night with the herd?

"How's it going out there?" she asked. "Still cattle-sitting?"

"Yeah. We will for a while longer, I guess. I'll feel better when Sheriff Brewer catches this guy."

He hadn't? Then, why did the attacks on the ranch stop? It didn't make sense. "And there haven't been any more incidents?"

Talon rubbed his eyes. His dark hair matted against his scalp, as it always did after a long day under a hat. Even exhausted, he looked adorable. Her rugged, tender cowboy.

An ache spread from her heart to her throat. She needed to be in his arms right now.

"Things have been fairly quiet." He leaned on his forearms toward the computer, giving her a better view of his tired, bloodshot eyes. "Not much happening, but we did manage to rule out Colton. I just don't think he's behind all this."

He didn't *think?* "He's the most logical choice. How did you rule him out? Have you talked to the sheriff?"

"He doesn't believe it's Colton either. The sheriff even went so far as to ferret out everyone who bet against us during the last event and cleared them all."

"Great," she grumbled. "Where does that leave us now? Does he have any other ideas?"

"I think so, but he's not letting me in on it yet."

Someone tapped on the door, and Patricia groaned.

"Just a minute," she called, then refocused on Talon. "I guess I need to go. That may be Mama wanting to talk. I'm at the point where talking is useless. I'm ready to come home."

"You need to straighten this out with her. Maybe even reconnect with your dad too. Make them comfortable with the idea you're marrying a Texas cowboy. It's quiet around here. We can spare you for another week."

"Another week?" Goodness, he was a cool one. Not even a telltale sparkle in his eye that he was planning their wedding—if that was what he'd been doing. "Not unless you want a bald bride."

"What do you mean?"

"If I had to stay here that long, I'd pull my hair out."

Laughter erased some of the fatigue from his face. "You're nuts, you know that?"

"I try." She blew a kiss at the screen. "I love you."

"I love you. Try to make things right."

Closing the lid on her laptop made her heart hurt. Being this far away from him left her hollow inside. She'd barely survived these three days, but two whole weeks? With her mother?

He didn't know what he was asking.

She straightened her shoulders, fortifying herself for another round with the matriarch, but opened the door to a scowling Consuela instead.

She barged in and glared at Patricia with her arms crossed. "You need to be nice to your mama."

Patricia mimicked her stance. "All right. What's got your salsa boiling?"

"You don't boil salsa. You should learn to cook."

She raised a brow. The bargain was that Consuela would teach her how to cook when Aunt Adele moved out of her kitchen and away from the ranch. This trip to Manhattan proved to be the only time Aunt Adele had left since assuming her role as chaperone.

An irrelevant point. "You came in to argue about my cooking skills?"

"You don't have any," she muttered, then let her arms fall limp. "No. That is not why I'm here. Be nice to your mama. She is hurting too."

Patricia's stomach flopped. "Hurting? What did she say?"

"Nothing." Consuela sat on the edge of the bed. "But everything, if you know how to listen. She talks about you. She showed me pictures of you when you were growing up and when you rode horses in college. She showed me a scrapbook of everything you've ever done. She's proud of you."

Patricia hung her head. Mama had kept up with that scrapbook—every scrapbook—since Patricia was born, each one more elaborate as technology allowed. She'd designed the last one through an online service. It was neater than the others. Fancier. But not as personal.

"You are her baby. She misses you."

"I know. You've told me. Aunt Adele has too." She rubbed the tension from her brow. "But I wish she could understand that I can't live here."

"You need to talk to her, be nice to her. Maybe she will see your side." She squeezed Patricia's shoulder, then slipped out of the room.

Maybe they were right, Consuela, Talon, and Aunt Adele. Maybe if she could just get her mother to listen—not just hear her but *listen* for once—she could make her understand. She should try to be more understanding too. If

Mama really was worried about the distance, she could offer to come back to the City more often.

Tomorrow, she'd make an effort to be more understanding. Maybe she and Mama could sit and talk. Actually have a heart-to-heart. They'd never done that before.

She brought her fingers to her lips and gazed out the window at the headlights of the one-way traffic several floors below. A heart-to-heart with her mother. Could anything be more intimidating?

After a rough night, Patricia wobbled into the kitchen midmorning, just in time to see Aunt Adele sweep through the condo in a flurry, drawing Consuela right along with her. Aunt Adele was hypnotizing her with all the sights they would be taking in during the day, and Consuela floated behind her without a backward glance. The two women left the condo, and with a light click of the door, Patricia's lifeline was gone. Their leaving creating a vacuum void of any sound but Patricia's hammering heart, and—unless her lungs lied—totally lacking air.

She squinted at her mother calmly sipping her coffee with her pinkie finger extended.

"What just happened?"

Mama dabbed her lips and resettled her napkin in her lap. "Good morning to you too."

"Yes. Good morning. What's going on?"

"I called Adele last night and asked her to take your friend out so you and I could have a little talk. It's time, don't you think?"

She'd spent the night agonizing over the same idea, but she still wasn't ready for a mother-daughter confrontation. It was a monumental mistake. An error of colossal proportions that could only result in disaster.

"Patricia? Don't you agree?"

Yet, everyone she loved had been pushing her toward this moment. So, okay. She needed to buck up and do this. No time like the present. "Yes. I suppose it is."

Mama rose from the table and swept her hand toward the living room. "Perhaps we should have our coffee in here. More comfortable, don't you think?"

Coffee. That would help. "Good idea. I'll make myself some. Do you need a refill?"

"No, I'm fine."

In the kitchen, Patricia set up the Keurig and drummed her fingers on the granite countertop while she waited. So, Mama wanted to talk. Where to start? What to say? Now faced with the opportunity to clear the air, she wasn't sure she had the nerve. If only Daddy could be here to referee. Since when did creating laws for the United States take precedence over his daughter's traumas? Chef Oscar had already left to shop for the evening meal, his routine for as long as she could remember—nothing but the best and freshest for the senator and his family—so she didn't even have him as a buffer. Not that he would've been much help anyway. He'd always been highly professional, virtually invisible except when serving the family. If not for the occasional *I'm pleased you like it*, she would've been convinced he couldn't speak.

Her mother pushed a button on the remote, and the blinds slid from the windows, letting morning light into the room. If only speaking to her were that simple. Push a button and shed light on whatever it was that kept her from accepting the fact her daughter would not be returning to New York to stay. But there were no buttons. Nothing to push that would make this easier.

The Keurig gurgled and spewed the last of the brew into her mug. She sweetened it, tipping the spoon slightly so the crystals seemed to slip in one at a time. Then she dribbled in a flavored cream and tested the coffee ... a little sweet, but not bad. Then she stirred, slowly swirling the silky liquid around and around, becoming mesmerized by its dark depths ...

She could stir until the spoon melted, but she'd still have to face her mother.

As she slipped her spoon into the sink, she caught a glimpse of the real estate brochure on the counter, featuring in full, glossy color that condo Mama took her to. The one revealing to Patricia that her mother fully supported her marriage to Talon, as long as he changed everything he was and moved to New York so they could both live under her thumb.

She snatched it off the countertop and shoved it into the trash.

The temperature in the living room dropped considerably when she walked in; she herself was the ice floe. She chose a chair with the best view of the Hudson, on the opposite end of the room from where her mother had landed.

Mother eyed her with a bittersweet smile on her lips. She fidgeted with her wedding ring, causing the diamonds to catch the sun. The dancing prisms of color gave away her secret—she wasn't as calm as she appeared. And at this point, Patricia didn't feel generous enough to put her at ease. This was her show. Let her start the opening scene.

"I really do like Talon you know."

No, she didn't know. How was she supposed to tell?

"From everything I've heard about him, he's a fine man."

"Yes, he is."

The diamonds flashed and sparkled, and the little prisms of color danced maniacally along the back of the soft gray sofa.

"It's just that ... "

Patricia didn't shift her gaze from her mother's eyes.

Finally Mother looked away. "You don't intend to make this easy for me, do you?"

Patricia shrugged. Sipped her coffee. Then she set the mug on the table beside her chair. "Sure I will," she said. "Let me finish your sentence for you. *It's just that he's not our kind of people.* He doesn't fit the image you want to share with your friends."

"Patricia! You know I'm not that way."

"Actually, Mother, I've never known you to be any other way. That's why you thought Kent was so perfect for me."

"He was, darling." She leaned forward. "You two had similar backgrounds, similar interests. And he was ambitious. He was going to make something of himself."

"Something you approved of."

"Oh, stop putting words into my mouth." She rose from the sofa and wandered to the window. "It was a good match," she said to the glass, then she turned. "You thought so too at one time."

Patricia retrieved her mug, if for no other reason than to have something to do with her hands. This wasn't the discussion she'd rehearsed under the covers until the wee hours of the morning. In fact, it was old news—over a decade. But that whirlwind courtship had been the biggest mistake of her life, second only to saying *I do*. It had taken all those years to rebuild her heart from the rubble he'd left behind. "When I found out it wasn't such a good match, you did everything in your power to keep us together."

"Yes, baby. You were married such a short time—and every marriage is rough at the first. I just wanted you to give it some time."

"He was cheating on me, Mother. From the very first year. And you knew it, but you still took his side. Still wanted us to stay together."

She wilted into a padded armchair. "I didn't realize how bad it was until later. You never told me—"

"You never listened." Patricia rocketed from her seat and strode to the windows, closer to her mother's chair. "After Kent died, you practically threw me at Vince Hoskins. He had the same ambitions. He was going to make something of himself too—at my expense. Just like Kent. I'm tired of it, Mother. This is my life. You can't control it anymore."

Her jaw slackened for an instant. "I never—"

"Oh, don't even. Let's start with sending Aunt Adele to lure me back to New York, then move to your decision for my color scheme. Green, remember?" She waved her arm toward the window. "What about that condo? You want me to bring Talon here so you can turn him into another Kent or Vince. What's so great about your high society that you want to trap us in it? Do you think you can change a man who has roped cattle for a living since he was a kid? Do you think I want him to change?"

Her mother lowered her head, but not before Patricia caught the tremble in her chin.

Breath left her lungs as if pricked by a knitting needle. What had she done? Who was she to attack her mother like that? She had kept all this bottled up inside for so long, she didn't expect the intensity of the explosion once that bottle was opened. Now Mama's fingers, still fidgeting with her ring, were damp from tears Patricia had caused. She'd never seen her mother cry before, and the sight shattered the ice block encasing her heart.

She knelt at Mama's knee and took her hands. "I'm sorry. I didn't mean—"

"I know." She caressed Patricia's cheek and gave her a watery smile before rising to her feet. "I'm tired. I think I'll lie down for a while."

Patricia remained crouched at the chair as she watched her walk away. She looked older with her head bowed and her shoulders drooping. The dyed hair, the perfect makeup, the trim figure all worked together toward an illusion of youth. But one morning of having her daughter rail at her had aged her—or at least torn away the facade.

"Oh, dear Lord, what did I do?" Patricia lowered her head to the cushioned arm of the chair. "I am so sorry. Help me fix our relationship. I don't want this deep rift between my mother and me."

Chapter Thirteen

Talon pulled on the jersey knit shorts he slept in, then flung his towel to the laundry pile growing in the corner. He hadn't quite lied to Pat when they talked tonight, but the sin of omission was still a sin. And it cranked up his guilt level. Two nights in a row, he skirted telling her the truth. At least he told her he'd talked to the sheriff. That was more than he had told anyone else.

But he hadn't revealed everything, and her own silence during their nightly Skype call indicated she knew it. Her use of silence could echo through a room.

"Got the weight of the world on your shoulders?" Frank drawled.

"Just my corner of it." He stretched out on his bunk with his arm over his eyes.

"Did you talk to Miz Pat about the note?"

"Not yet."

"You'll have to tell her about the connection to Janet eventually."

Talon's response hung in his throat as the bunkhouse door swung open and Chance stepped in.

"Good to see you ladies still awake."

"Yeah, how'd you slip your leash?" Frank quipped. "Ain't the little woman gonna miss ya?"

"Naw." Chance dropped into Buster's recliner. While Buster worked his shift, his favorite chair was up for grabs. "She's at the house boo-hooing over some chick flick. I figured I'd better escape while I could."

Talon moved from his bunk to the couch, clapping Chance on the shoulder as he walked by. "How'd the baby-stuff shopping go today?"

"Spent too much." His grin undercut the complaint. "We went to a maternity store too. Marie got her some pants with that stretchy top. She's been wearing a pair ever since."

"She showing yet?" Frank asked.

He grunted. "Barely more'n me when I'm gassy. But won't be long and she'll fill them out."

Talon propped his bare feet on the coffee table. Pat would look great with a little pooch to her belly. Or a big one, for that matter. An image of his five-foot wife-to-be waddling around with her hand at her back and her stomach extended with their child brought a smile to his face. His wife, their child.

If Janet had lived, their children would've been in school by now. A little girl with a Hello Kitty backpack or a boy in tiny Wranglers and cowboy boots. Maybe they'd have had a third kid at home too, just one year away from kindergarten.

He scowled. How could he think of might-have-beens with Janet when he had a future with Pat? She held his heart now. Janet was gone. He needed to keep his mind in the here and now.

Chance nudged his knee with his foot. "Where's your mind at?"

"Uh ..." The question caught him off guard.

"Tell him," Frank ordered. "He may think of somethin' that makes sense. We outghta tell Buster too. The more heads in this game, the better."

Talon rubbed his neck as he eyed Chance. Might as well tell him about the note. He'd never kept secrets from the guys and had always come out wiser for it. "Keep it to yourself, okay? Don't tell Marie, or she'll tell Pat."

"Something you don't want the boss lady to know?" Chance leaned forward. "This oughta be good."

Frank snorted. "Is it ever good to keep secrets from someone you're gonna marry?"

Talon glared at him—the constant thorn in his conscience—then told Chance about the note.

Chance winced. "Man, someone knows how to hit you where it hurts. Who would do something like that?"

"Colton Royder," Frank mumbled.

"Naw, Brewer already ruled him out." Talon told them about yesterday's failed attempt at sleuthing and his discussion with Sheriff Brewer. "He's going to get the files from Dallas PD."

Chance shook his head. "I could've sworn the potassium chloride would provide a lead. No one I know uses it. I would've put money that Colton ordered it."

"Yeah, but Bart says no one has ordered it. Says the Co-op doesn't get much call for it."

"Pat says you can order it online," Chance said, "so it still could've been Colton Royder."

"He was too young for a romantic interest in Janet." Talon raised a brow. "But Cody wasn't."

"His brother?" Frank grabbed a tube of liniment from the side table and rubbed some of it into his knee. All the horseback riding had gotten to him. "You reckon he had some sort of crush on her?"

He shrugged. "Cody isn't like Colton. I've never had any trouble with him. We get along all right."

"He seems to be a fine young man, but even fine young men have soft spots. Maybe Janet was his."

"Then why kill her?" Chance asked.

"Why would anyone kill her?" Talon blew out his breath. "Still, the way I figure it, whoever did it has to be someone from around here—not someone in Dallas like they originally thought. I mean, think about it. What's happening around here now is related to Janet somehow. So it couldn't be someone from up there. Back then, no one in Dallas would've known about the ranch except her friends and family, and what reason would they have to kill her? No, it has to be somebody from around here."

Talon held up his hand to count off the conclusions he'd reached while mulling all this over throughout the day. "First, he would've had to be old enough for a romantic interest in her—"

"That'd be just about every man who'd ever met her," Chance muttered.

Talon glared at him. "Then, he would've had to know we were getting married in Dallas and where. Finally, he would've had to know the truck I drove back then good enough to follow us to that grocery store."

"That could be anyone anywhere. Hico. Stephenville. The whole local rodeo circuit." Chance went to the mini-fridge and grabbed a bottled water. He offered one to the others, but they declined. As he returned to his chair, he said, "Considering how big the circuit is, that could be anyone in a two hundred mile radius—meaning you still can't rule out Dallas-Fort Worth."

Using a paper towel, Frank rubbed the cream off his hands. "Yeah, but if it is someone local, like Cody, then I don't understand. Why is he coming up against us now? After all this time, why now?"

Talon lowered his chin to his chest. That was the inescapable question. She died in spring, so the timing didn't match the anniversary of her death, and her birthday was still months away. It wasn't a special date between the two of them, but—"Maybe this month is special to him somehow."

"Wouldn't be the first anniversary to go by. Just don't make sense that he'd wait all this time."

"I'm so tired nothing's making sense to me."

Chance took a swig from the water bottle and screwed the cap back on. "Why are you keeping all this secret from Pat? What's the big deal? Haven't you learned your lesson about keeping things from her?"

"He don't want her cuttin' her vacation short and runnin' back home," Frank said. "If whoever's out there is bent on revenge, he may take it out on her."

That possibility alone tightened a fist around Talon's gut, but it was only part of the reason. The way he'd been reacting to thoughts of Janet lately rocked him, and he had to sort all this out before she came home. *After all this time, Father, why is it still so hard?*

Would his heart ever heal?

The early shift of cattle-watching had proven quiet again. The entire night had held no surprises. So why did Talon's hair stand on end at the slightest rustle?

Nothing about the attacks had been foreseeable. No sort of pattern had emerged. The cattle had been killed on different days at different intervals, so he couldn't predict the next hit, if there would be one. And too much time had passed between the last hit and the night the note was delivered. Had he done his worst by delivering it, or was the worst yet to come?

The guy, whoever he was, needed to come out of hiding and face Talon like a man. If he wanted a fight, Talon would be happy to oblige. This cowardly technique of strike-and-hide kept his nerves on edge.

At least the cattle were safe for now, but this pasture wouldn't be able to hold them much longer. The guys would finish the fence dividing Griff's land soon, and they could move the cattle to fresher ground for a while. But they'd still have to keep the herd together and watch over them until that yellow cur causing all this was caught.

A pickup drove down the hill. Buster's turn to feed the cattle. Or was it Chance's? Talon didn't know anymore, could barely keep up with his own schedule. Someday, after the coward was behind bars, Talon would sleep for a week. A month. And if he could talk Pat into marrying him soon, he'd be sleeping with her in his arms.

Assuming she'd forgive him for keeping secrets from her again. And lying to her. And being a sexist cad.

The cattle trotted toward the sound of the hay spool unrolling their morning feed, and Talon followed, counting them in groups of five as they strung out along the hay spread. The truck turned, and after the metallic grate of the hopper opening, range cubes pelted the ground. Once again, Talon counted brawny backs in the headlights.

Chance shouted a number at him from the pickup, and Talon nodded. "Same as I got."

"That's a good thing."

"A mighty good thing."

"I gotta bring out another bale." Chance rested his arm along the window. "Are you heading in for breakfast? Flapjacks and bacon. Chef's in a fine mood this morning."

"I'm glad someone is. I'll see you in a bit. I'm staying out till sunup."

"Okay, but don't ask me to save you any." Chance turned the truck and headed back.

Talon watched the taillights as the pickup rumbled up to the ranch road, then shifted his gaze toward the north. Tall hills surrounded the ranch on three sides; the one to the north held the ranch house and all the outbuildings. From where Talon sat in the basin, all he could see of the house was a soft glow of light in the predawn. Once the sun rose, he wouldn't be able to see that much of the buildings, but he'd get a good view of the rest of the ranch surrounding this pasture. He knew every crag, every scraggly tree. He and Chance had explored the hillsides as kids, probing the crevices, searching for arrowheads or any other kind of artifact left behind by Native Americans.

With his eyes adjusted to the dark, he could make out the bulky shapes of the cattle, but seeing a man among them would be trickier. He'd have to rely on their restlessness if they were disturbed, but even then, a stealthy man could ease through the herd without causing alarm. He could've been there all along, watching the guys. Watching Talon.

Yeah, but why would he do that? Why would he settle for watching when he'd been killing without detection, when he'd eased into Talon's own home and left without being noticed?

Talon needed to keep his head on straight, not give way to the paranoia seeking a foothold. Though it was hard not to see monsters in the shadows when someone was definitely after him.

He'd barely slept, and when he did manage an hour or two, he would wake up in a cold sweat, his hands shaking. Vivid red would blind his eyes until he could blink it away in the darkness of the room. If this kept up, fatigue alone would drive him to an early grave.

When the sun came up, he rode through the pasture—a quick sweep of the land, searching for evidence of an intruder. This had been his routine every morning since before Pat left and would be his routine until the danger passed. So far, he hadn't found anything during his morning sweeps, and this morning turned out to be no different. But the guy's unpredictability kept Talon vigilant.

By the time he got back to the ranch house, Marie had already left for the store—something about an early shipment in the "doggone middle of the night," according to Chance—and the guys had eaten everything on the table. But Chef brought him a plate of flapjacks and bacon from the kitchen. "I saved you some."

Talon clapped him on the shoulder. "You're a good man, Chef."

He glanced out the window. The sheriff's car kicked up a dust cloud on the drive.

"Wonder if he has any news," Frank said. "It'd be good not to have to sit atop a horse every night."

Talon handed his plate back to Chef. "Keep it warm a bit longer. I'll go see what he wants."

Outside, Derrick Brewer unloaded his bulk from his cruiser and set his Stetson on his head. "Mornin', Talon."

"Morning, Sheriff. You're out early."

"Yeah, figured I'd come by in person and talk matters over with you."

Talon's heart jerked. "You've had a breakthrough, then? You know who's doing this?"

Brewer nodded toward the front door. "You got some coffee in there?"

"Oh yeah. Sure. C'mon in."

He led the way through the house and to the dining room where the guys lingered, probably hoping for some news. Talon's nerves were jumpy. He sit still while the sheriff greeted everyone. The guys returned to their places around a table still cluttered with breakfast dishes, with Brewer taking the seat of honor at the head. Chef offered him a mug of steaming coffee.

All these goings-on and useless prattle ramped up Talon's tension. "What have you learned?"

Brewer propped his hat on his knee and sipped the brew, taking his own sweet time to answer. But judging by the squint in his eye, he hadn't quite figured out how to say whatever he'd come to say. Heaven knew why not. He'd had a twenty-minute ride from town to mull it over.

Talon finally sat in the chair to the sheriff's right. "Whatever it is, come out with it. What's going on?"

"Nothing." Brewer fiddled with his hat brim. "That's biggest shame of it. Absolutely nothing is going on."

"I don't understand."

He cradled the mug in his hands and glanced at all the faces staring at him. "Look, we went through the Dallas PD files two or three times. Those guys were thorough. They'd done everything they could and came up empty, just like us."

He focused on Talon. "You were the only decent suspect they had, and when you were cleared, nothing else surfaced. What few leads they did have didn't pan out. Everyone had alibis."

"What about around here?" Chance asked. "You haven't had any leads here either?"

"Nothing, especially now that we've got that note." His lips formed a grim line as he shook his head. "It changes everything. The motive shifted, and along with it, the target. If this really is about Janet, then everything we considered before was a waste of time. Seems like no one here or in

Dallas had a reason to want her dead, but her murder wasn't random, either."

Talon gritted his teeth. None of this sounded good. "What's the plan?"

"The only hope we've got at this point is to catch the guy in the act. We'll continue to ask around. Start patrolling the area at night. Increase our presence."

Didn't seem like much of a plan.

Frank stared out the window and rubbed his jaw until whatever he was thinking finally got to his tongue. "Why is the guy pullin' this stunt now? We was talkin' about this last night, and it just don't make sense. She's been gone near about nine years. What took him so long to act up?"

"Yeah," Chance said. "And if he loved her, why'd he kill her?"

"Or maybe he didn't kill her, but he thinks I did." Talon had been mulling this over since they discussed it last night. "Still doesn't explain why he waited almost a decade to get back at me."

The sheriff set his mug on the table with a light thump. "That's a good question, and sometimes the answer is because the perp was arrested for another crime. And that means ... "

With his brows drawn, Brewer glanced out the same window that had captured Frank's attention. Stared so long, Talon's gut twisted again.

"Don't leave me hanging here, Sheriff," he said. "What does that mean?"

"It means we might have a clue after all." He stood and put his hat back on his head. "If this guy served time, his prints are in the system now. Maybe we can match his prints to the ones on the bullets and get a name for him."

Talon leapt up fast enough to send his chair scooting backward. "That's great! We could finally nail him!"

"And sleep for a full night," Frank drawled, and Buster immediately offered an amen.

But Brewer held up his hand. "Look, we don't know what we'll find. Maybe the prints on the bullet still can't be matched, and we're back to square one. Or maybe they do match someone who's in prison somewhere else by now, and we're still back to square one."

Talon curled his hands into fists. This had to be the clue they needed—it had to be. *Dear God, let it be.* He needed peace again. He needed to leave Janet in the recesses of his mind again, a happy memory, not a daily heartache. Most of all, he needed to know Pat could return and be safe in her own home.

A declaration of faith. A deep belief that God still answered prayer. That was all it took. He believed that. Preached it every Sunday. *If there was ever a time, Father God, make it true now.*

"You'll get a name, Sheriff, and it'll match someone right here in this county."

With an order to the guys to hang around, Talon walked Sheriff Brewer to the door. "Let me know the minute you hear anything."

"I will, but it might take a while."

"That's okay. Just let me know."

The sheriff gave him a two-fingered salute as he walked toward his car. After he revved up his engine and pulled out, Talon returned to the dining room.

Buster scowled at him. "What's all this about a note?"

"Yeah, I wanna know too," Chef said.

After he filled them in about how he got it and what it said, he turned to Chef. "Don't go telling Consuela anything yet. She'll tell Pat, and they'll both hightail it back home."

"And they be mad when they get here too."

"Whatcha holdin' us in here for?" Frank asked. "We're burnin' daylight."

"We're going to do what we should've been doing all along." He set his chair back at the table and shoved away empty mugs and syrup-sticky plates. "We're going to pray."

Everyone returned to their seats and bowed their heads. Talon started. "Father, You say whenever two or more are gathered together in Your name, You'll be right there with them. Each of us here is one of Your own, we're gathered in Your name, and we're in need. You know what's going on around here, and only You know who's doing it. We're asking You to point him out and bring him to justice. We're fine with whatever Your will is, but this time, Father, I'm kinda hoping Your will aligns with ours on this point."

After Talon finished, Frank added a prayer for safety, and each of the others added their own words in a five minute petition that left Talon hopeful and rejuvenated.

"God'll answer our prayers," he said. "Don't know when, but He will."

Chapter Fourteen

As Patricia turned in for the night, Skype pinged for her attention. She grabbed her laptop from the dresser and connected the call.

"Hey, girlfriend, look at this." Marie stepped away from her computer and turned to the side.

Her joy was contagious. The sight of her showing off the tiniest of baby bumps perked Patricia's spirit. She settled back on the bed with her feet tucked under her. "Looking like a regular prego there. Won't be too long and you'll need stretchy pants."

"I'm already wearing them. Most comfortable things God ever created." She returned to her seat in front of the monitor, holding up a pair of baby boots. "Aren't these the cutest?"

"Adorable!"

She lowered the shoes and leaned toward the screen. "I'm calling earlier than usual. Am I cutting in on Talon's time? Have you talked to him yet?"

"Yes. Right after supper. He said everyone but Buster was watching the football game. Can't believe I'm missing it. Can't believe *Buster's* missing it."

"It's his turn for the early shift, and for once, he didn't complain about not seeing the game. He was looking forward to something that resembled a full night's sleep."

Patricia sighed. "I'll be glad when they can quit staying up with the herd. Talon said it's been quiet out there. I was hoping things would return to normal."

"It has been quiet here. Chance says watching the cattle is just a precaution." Marie picked up a towel and began folding it. "So, how's it going with your mother?"

"It's ... tense." She slumped against the pillows. After their discussion, she and Mama had spent the remainder the day being polite and forcing smiles.

"Uh-oh. Did you two fight again?"

"Yes." She massaged her temples. "And I was horrible. I can't believe I made her cry."

"Yikes. That's not good." Marie picked up another towel, then lowered it into her lap. "Will you be able to resolve all this before you come home?"

Patricia shrugged. "Our flight is tomorrow afternoon. If we haven't resolved it in the past few days, one more isn't going to change anything."

"Surely, you're not going to give up."

"No, of course not. But as far as Project Reconciliation is concerned, this trip is a bust. Maybe with a little time and distance, we can try again."

"Not too much time, I hope. I hate this strain between you. If it was my mother—" Marie jerked toward the window. "What was that?"

"What? What's going on?"

"I don't know. I'll call you back."

"Houston's got this game won, boys," Talon said. "I'm gonna call it quits and get some sleep before my shift."

Chance leaned back in the recliner. "Marie's chatting with Pat right now. She won't miss me if I finish watching."

"Make yourself at home. Doesn't look like you'll bother Frank much."

The senior hand's snores about drowned out the game's announcers.

Talon stretched on his bunk and draped his arm over his eyes. He couldn't get too interested in football these days. Besides, sports news was beginning to read like a rap sheet.

Pretty serious charges going around. He'd quit keeping up with—

A shotgun blast jolted him to his feet. Frank startled awake, and for a split second, he, Talon, and Chance stared at each other.

Another blast. What could Buster be shooting at in the dark? A coyote, maybe? Or ...

Pulse racing, Talon dashed outside one step behind Chance.

The porch light flipped on at the main house, and Marie called, "Was that a gun?"

"Get back inside," Chance shouted. "Lock the door!"

They raced to the paddock behind the horse barn—the only place from the hill they could see into the basin below, with the aid of a near-full moon. The cattle bawled in the north pasture, and their hooves thudded against the packed ground. A cloud of dust darkened the night sky, rendering the silver orb weaker than a headlight in a haze. If the herd had stampeded, Buster would never be able to handle them alone.

"This ain't good," Frank said. "I'll get the truck. Meet y'all down there."

Barefoot and still dressed in his sleep shorts, Talon charged to the horse barn, put a bridle on Bodine, and swung onto his bare back.

"Yaw!" he shouted and leaned over the horse's neck. Bodine kicked up gravel on the ranch road. He didn't slow as he galloped down the slope to the pasture.

Talon guided him to the far side of the retreating cattle. Had to turn them right. Had to keep them from the hills.

If Buster headed the herd up front, he could circle them.

If only he could see Buster.

Talon and Bodine passed the stragglers and came up on the main body of the racing herd. "*Yaw! Yaw!*"

Those cows get into the hills, and they'd spend the entire day tomorrow flushing 'em out. But he couldn't let them race to the other pastures, either. No matter how much water the fire department's pump trucks showered over the poisoned acreage, he wouldn't trust it.

"*Yaw! Yaw!*"

His throat clogged with dust. His shouts were coarse. But they were turning. If he could just get ahead of them, maybe he could get them to settle.

Where was Buster?

Headlights glared in the distance. Chance raced the four-wheeler around the horses' paddock and toward the pasture from the west. Another set of headlights shone on Chance from behind. Frank in the truck. With them coming from the west and Talon pushing the cattle around from the east, maybe they could swing them back north again.

Where was Buster?

Chance circled around and came up from the south. Talon bore down from the east, and Frank kept pushing from the west. The cattle became confused, blocked at every turn. They soon stopped yards away from the gate to the poisoned pasture. Their breath fogged in the night air as they milled about, not knowing where to turn.

The men began the slow work of pushing them closer to the northern fence line. Nothing the headlights hit looked like Buster or his horse.

Where was he?

Chapter Fifteen

With her nerves tight and her heart pounding, Patricia marched down the hall to Consuela's room and knocked on the door. "You awake?"

After a moment, she knocked again and entered. Consuela was curled on her side in the bed.

Patricia gently shook her shoulder. "Wake up. We have to go."

She startled, then rolled over. "What's wrong, *chica?*"

"Guard your eyes. I'm going to turn on the lamp." Patricia winced at the light as she sat on the mattress. "Something's happened at the ranch. The cattle stampeded for some reason, and Buster got trampled in the rush."

Consuela bolted upright. "*¡Dios mio!* Is he okay?"

"He's alive, but unconscious. They life-flighted him to Fort Worth." She opened the closet door and retrieved a suitcase. "We need to go home. Mama's making the arrangements now."

Consuela jumped out of bed, grabbed an armful of clothes from a drawer, and shoved it in her suitcase. "We don't have to be neat about it, as long as it closes. Give me five minutes. I'll be ready."

Patricia left her to prepare, then rolled her own luggage to the living room.

Wrapped in a satin robe, her mother took a bag from her and rested it beside the front door. "Anthony is coming. I booked you a first-class flight all the way. You can pick up your tickets at the desk."

"Thank you. That's a tremendous help." Since she couldn't blink her eyes and be instantly transported, at least she could fly in comfort. "I appreciate it."

Mama fluttered her hand in dismissal. "Are you sure you don't want Adele to go with you?"

"There's no reason to bother her. In truth, there's really no reason for her to return. Marie is at the ranch now, lending respectability to our living arrangements there."

"Oh, Patricia, how can you snipe at a time like this?"

"I'm sorry. I didn't mean it that way." She drifted her hand down her mother's arm. "I'm just anxious to get home."

The elevator chimed in the foyer, then someone knocked on the door. Anthony stood on the other side with his chauffeur's hat in his hand.

"Good evening, Miss Patricia." He looked at her luggage. "Is this all?"

"I'm coming!" Consuela had her carry-on over one shoulder and her purse over the other as she rolled her oversized suitcase behind her. "I'm ready. We are going now?"

"Yes, it's time."

"Good." She waved away Anthony's attempt to help her with her luggage and turned to Patricia's mother. "It was real good to meet you, Se ora McAllister. Thank you for your hosp ... your hosp ... for being friendly. I had fun."

"You're certainly wel—"

"C'mon," Consuela ordered Anthony. "We should go now. Get all this loaded up."

He flashed a questioning glance at Mama, who nodded. "They're in a bit of a hurry."

"Yes ma'am." He gathered Patricia's things and led Consuela to the elevator.

Patricia turned to her mother. "I'm sorry we have to rush like this."

"I understand. I just wish we had more time." Mama cupped her cheek with a soft hand. "We didn't finish our discussion. I had hoped ... "

"I know. Soon, okay?" She stepped into her mother's warm hug and relished in it for a moment. Saying goodbye stabbed her with more pain than she'd expected. If only they could have connected again, like when she was younger. Before Kent. But she couldn't think of that now. "I'll call you when I can and let you know we're safe."

"Yes, please."

"Kiss Daddy for me."

"He'll be sorry he missed you."

After another quick hug, she left.

Patricia's and Consuela's footsteps echoed down the almost-empty halls at the hospital. The night staff huddled around the nurses' station. Housekeeping polished the floor. The phlebotomist carried her red tray of tubes and supplies from one room to the next. Why did they always have to show up before the sun crept over the horizon? Didn't the patients deserve a night of needle-free rest?

"There they are." Patricia headed to an alcove near the end of the hall.

Sitting in adjacent padded chairs, Marie snuggled against Chance, whose chin rested on his chest. Frank's head hung low as he sat with his arms crossed over his stomach, and Talon sprawled in his chair with his legs stretched out in front of him. Chef snoozed near a muted television.

"Looks like everyone is here. I wonder who's watching the ranch?"

Consuela hastened her pace. "Who cares? I'm ready to see them."

She had a point.

As they neared the alcove, Patricia used her best stage whisper. "Talon! *Talon!*"

He blinked at her, then rocketed from his seat and closed the space between them. She wilted into his arms. It had been a long six hours from the time she got Marie's call to the time they pulled up to the hospital in a rented car.

Consuela awakened Chef, and they whispered together in Spanish on the other side of the small room.

Patricia asked Talon, "How is Buster?"

"He's still in surgery."

"Still? But it's been hours."

"Yeah, it has been." He ushered her to a chair next to the one he'd occupied. "But that's actually good news. So far, anyway. Means he's still fighting for life."

"How badly was he hurt? Tell me everything."

"It's pretty bad." He stretched his arm across the back of her chair and rubbed her shoulder as he talked. "The medical technicians said he came to on the way over here. X-rays showed three broken ribs, and his collar bone on his right side is broken. And his right forearm and leg."

"They're working on broken bones? Is that what is taking so long?"

"His leg was pretty mangled. That'll take a while, but there's more." He ran his free hand down his thigh. His pained expression amped the ache in Patricia's heart. "Something to do with his spleen. I'm not sure I understood what the doctor said. And he bruised the kidney on the right side."

"Oh, that poor man! I can't imagine how agonizing that was for him. Consuela and I have been praying for him all the way here."

"We've been praying all night too."

She shifted in her seat to rest against him. "What happened? Marie's explanation was rather sketchy."

"We don't know a lot yet." He took her hand and played with her fingers. "Someone fired off two shots, but I don't know who. We thought it was Buster at first, but when we found Pacer back at his stall, the .410 was still in the scabbard."

She raised her head and looked into his eyes. "Buster wouldn't shoot while on Pacer, would he? Pacer is still a high-strung horse. I've worked with him, and he's better, but I haven't tested him near weapons yet." In fact, the idea had never crossed her mind.

"Yeah, that's just it. If Pacer bucked Buster off because he'd fired his shotgun, then how'd the gun get back in the holster?"

"And if Buster wasn't the one shooting, who was?"

"That's the gold buckle question."

She rested against his shoulder again, but only for an instant. "Wait. Do you think this is related to whoever was killing the cattle? I thought you said things have been quiet. Did it just pick up again all of a sudden?"

"It has been quiet for the most part. We haven't lost any more cattle, and everything's fine at the house."

"But?"

With a heavy sigh, Talon pushed to his feet. "Let's take a walk."

The look on his face, one of defeat and resignation, gave her a sinking feeling. He'd been known to keep things from her; maybe he'd done it again while she visited her mother. So what had he not told her?

He kept her hand in his as they strolled toward a window overlooking the parking lot, but as they neared an intersection of two hallways, a man dressed in surgical scrubs and exhaustion approached.

The fatigue on his face eased when he saw them. "You are Talon Carlson, right?"

"Yes sir. This is my fiancée, Patricia Talbert, Buster's employer."

He acknowledged her with a nod. "I have some good news for you."

"Can we talk about it over here?" Patricia gestured to the alcove they'd just left. "Everyone will want to hear."

The doctor walked the short distance with them and waited until they woke the others before sharing his news. "Buster came through just fine."

He'd be okay. Patricia's knees turned to jelly; Consuela sobbed her relief. It seemed everyone expelled a collective breath. Not a one of these people were related to Buster, but the group standing here held tighter bonds than anything Patricia had ever experienced. Her own family didn't seem this close. And she and Marie were now part of it. Even if she were considering it, she could never leave them in favor of New York.

"How long will you have to keep him here?" she asked.

"It's hard to determine that right now. There are too many contingencies. We'll know better after the first couple of days."

"Can we see him?"

"In an hour or so. He'll be in recovery a while longer, then he'll be moved to a room on the surgical floor." He glanced from face to face. "He's going to be out of it for quite some time, and when he comes to, he'll be groggy and disoriented. We've set up a morphine drip to ease his pain, but it won't help his lucidity any."

Consuela sniffed. "I just want a peek at him. Just to see him for myself."

"I understand," the doctor said. "You'll be notified when he's in a room."

He bid them good night and walked away. For a few moments, no one could speak. Suddenly standing seemed to take too much of an effort, and judging from the faces of those around her, the others felt the same. The guys had been pulling shifts watching the cattle. No telling how much sleep they'd had, aside from the naps in these uncomfortable chairs. Marie had worked a full day at her store. No doubt she was tired too. And if Consuela felt anything like Patricia after flying all night, she was lucky to still be standing.

Patricia dropped into the nearest chair. "We should decide some things. I think one of us ought to stay with Buster at all times, but the rest of us need to get back home. If what happened to Buster is any indication, the Circle Bar is still under attack." She shot a glance at Talon. If things hadn't been as calm as he'd indicated, he'd hear plenty from her later.

Frank lifted his hand. "I'll stay with him."

"Okay, good." She shifted her gaze to Marie. "Does Katie know about all this?"

"I didn't think to tell her. Everything happened so fast after the guys found him I couldn't think of anything but calling you and getting to the hospital."

"She'll want to know. She and Frank can take turns staying over—we'll let them decide that—and I can cover for her at the store. Will that work?"

As Marie nodded her agreement, a nurse approached.

"Mr. Milligan is on his way to his room now." She gave them the number. "Give them about fifteen more minutes to get him settled, then you may see him. Only one or two at a time, please. He's still under the influence of the anesthesia, so he's not likely to remember the visits."

"I don't care. I just want to see him." Consuela grabbed Chef's arm and marshalled him toward the elevators.

After the nurse returned to her station, Frank wagged a finger between Chance and Talon. "Y'all need to go in next and hit the road as soon as possible. The cattle're gonna be hungry by the time y'all get back."

"Assuming they're still there," Chance mumbled.

Patricia's nerves jumped. "You think there's a chance they won't be?"

"We don't know anything yet." Talon used his *let's be reasonable* tone. "Let's not get ahead of ourselves."

Chance broadened his stance and propped his fists on his hips. Patricia had never seen him this angry—especially not at Talon. The two were like brothers.

"You know this has got to be related," he said. "Nothing else makes sense."

"Until Buster comes to, I don't know anything. Sheriff Brewer is out investigating now. Let's not go making ourselves crazy until we hear from him."

Chef returned with a visibly shaken Consuela. Marie rushed over to put her arms around the ranch's honorary mother, who wept openly. Buster must look awful for her to carry on so.

Patricia shuddered and returned her attention to Chance, who had lowered his voice. "I'm not making myself crazy. I already am—and probably will be until we catch this guy. I've got a pregnant wife now, and someone's shooting on the property. How could that not make me crazy?"

Marie cooed more soothing words to Consuela, whose tears had finally dried. Patricia wouldn't be able to handle it if anything happened to her best friend and that precious baby she carried. Whatever was going on must stop.

Chapter Sixteen

T alon checked his speed on Pat's rental, then concentrated on the road ahead, which brightened as the sun rose behind them. They'd been out of the city limits for twenty minutes now, and still Pat hadn't said a word. He ventured a glance her way, half expecting her to be asleep after her long flight. Instead, she leaned against her door, gazing out the side window. He didn't know how to read her this time. Usually, her silence while they drove meant he was in some sort of trouble. But this time, it could be because of her fatigue. As a precaution, though, he needed to come clean. The longer she stayed quiet, the bigger the case she'd develop against him in that vivid imagination of hers. Experience had taught him that, left to her own devices, she could come up with some crazy ideas. Well, not all that crazy. His own silences had helped fuel her imagination. This long stretch of nothingness between the metroplex and the next tiny town provided the perfect opportunity to fess up to what he'd been keeping to himself.

"There's something I need to tell you."

Pat shifted her attention to him.

"You need to know what's been going on since you left." He took her hand and entwined their fingers, then told her everything. The note about Janet. The stalled investigation. Even the details about the night Janet died, something he never thought he'd have to share with her. Everything he said was punctuated with her little moans of sympathy. Tears brimmed in her eyes by the time he'd finished, and he'd just given her the bare bones of the story, reporting it as a dispassionate journalist. Her capacity for empathy amazed him.

But there was more. She had to know about his inner conflict, about being torn between her and his first love and feeling as if he'd betrayed both of them.

He kissed the back of her hand. "I love you. I want you to know that and be confident in it, okay?"

Her features softened in the early morning light. The love she felt for him shone from her face, and the look in her eyes reflected the forgiveness he'd been hoping for.

But he hadn't finished, and the rest might erode that forgiveness.

As he considered how to put into words the part that worried him most, she reached across the console and ran her fingers along his jaw. "I know how hard it was for you to tell me all th—"

"There's more." He dried his sweaty palm down his jeans. "The fact that this is apparently about Janet has been getting to me in ways I'd never considered."

He ground his back teeth together. *Lord, give me the words.* He couldn't understand how his love for Janet had flooded him even while he was in love with Pat. How could he explain it to her?

But then she reclaimed his hand, and he discovered he didn't have to.

"Look, Talon. I know I'm not your first love, just as you aren't mine. And if you were half as devoted to her as you are to me, then she was a blessed woman. A love that deep is special. Losing her must've killed you. It hurts me that you had to go through it. Whatever it is you're dealing with, whatever memories or emotions, it's okay. I understand. We can face this together. We can face anything as long as we're together."

A lump bigger than Texas formed in his throat even as his heart swelled to equal size. Most men were lucky to have one great love in their lives. He'd had two. And if it wasn't for this pressing need to get home, he'd pull over and hold this incredible woman until all the emotion drained out of him.

But then she scowled at him. "If you ever again pull another he-man, macho stunt like sending me away to protect your *little woman*, I'll give you a firsthand illustration of how aptly this little woman can take care of herself. You shouldn't have lied to me."

"I know. You're right."

"And you kept lying to me the entire time I was gone."

"Not the entire time. It really was quiet until last night."

She glared at him. "Don't do it again."

"Yes ma'am." He kissed the back of her hand. She was adorable when she was mad, but her short tirade seemed to have sapped the juice out of her. "You look tired. I wish they still made bench seats. You could rest your head on my leg and sleep until we got home."

She offered a feeble smile. If only he could comfortably cuddle her as they drove. His arms had missed her.

Patricia got out of the rental in front of the house, then Talon drove to the shed. They'd have to return it to the agency, but right now, she didn't have the brainpower to figure out how or when. The nearest one was back where they'd come from.

As she drug her feet toward the steps, Marie came out to greet her.

Patricia joined her on the porch. "You just got home. You aren't leaving for work, are you?"

"No, thank goodness. I got off the phone with Katie a minute ago. She's going to cover for me today, then drive up to Fort Worth this evening to be with Buster."

"You think she'd be willing to drive the rental back to the agency? Frank could pick her up."

"Don't see why not."

One problem solved.

Marie held the door open for her and followed her into the house. The smell of sausage frying and biscuits baking reminded Patricia she hadn't eaten since... When had she eaten?

"I'm sorry you had to cut your trip short," Marie said, trailing her through the living room. "This is an awful thing to come home to."

"We didn't cut it that short."

"I know your mother's disappointed." Marie stopped outside the dining room. "I wish you two could've made up."

"One more day wouldn't have made a difference in the standstill we're facing." But it had been difficult to leave her, so who knew what would've happened? She leaned against the doorframe. "But it was cathartic, you know? Telling her everything I'd been holding in was like a huge release, like it's out now and no longer poisoning my system. I just wish I could've been nicer about it."

"I was surprised when you described what you'd done." Marie mimicked her stance against the opposite frame. "I've seen you carve layers of hide off people with such diplomacy they were thankful for the weight loss."

"I seem to have lost that ability since I moved out here." And she'd picked the wrong time to prove that to herself. She'd have to Skype her mom soon and try to make amends.

She gazed out the living room windows. Funny. Wasn't that long ago she thought Talon and Marie were planning her wedding behind her back. She had actually been looking forward to whatever they came up with. There was truth to the notion that ignorance was bliss. Considering the mess she'd made with Mama, and Buster being injured and laid up at the hospital, and the fact that someone was still targeting her ranch—she'd crumble under the load if she didn't have Jesus to hold her up. And it seemed she had to ask Him for support every moment since they'd returned to Texas.

Marie rubbed her arm. "You're tired. Whatever it is you're thinking, you should probably put it off until you've rested."

She nodded.

With her spatula in hand, Consuela peeked out at them. "There you are. Tell the men to come on. Breakfast is almost ready."

Patricia frowned. Talon should have been inside by now. She turned to Marie. "Where's Chance?"

"He said he was going to survey the damage now that the sun's up, but that was almost an hour ago."

"Uh-oh." She stomped through the living room and out the door with Marie on her heels. Saddling Tandy would take too long. Instead, she jumped into the work truck and turned the key they kept in the ignition.

Marie climbed into the passenger seat and tsked. "You're going to get stains that'll never come out."

Patricia glanced down at her travel clothes, not the jeans she'd become accustomed to, but winter-white leggings under a red knit tunic, and shrugged. "Not appropriate for ranch life anyway."

She drove toward the turnoff that led down to the pasture but caught sight of the guys on the opposite side of the road and eased toward them instead. Talon's face was grim, and Chance waved his arms to accent some remark he seemed to be shouting.

As she pulled the truck closer, Patricia lowered her window to catch Chance's remarks.

"How can you say it's not Colton?" Frustration and disbelief percolated in his voice. "Who else would do this?"

Patricia looked in the direction he pointed. "Oh no."

She drove to the new feed bin, now relieved of hundreds of pounds of range cubes. Someone had pulled the lever and drained the bin. They'd have to scoop up the cubes and hand-feed them into the hopper.

Shaking her head, she got out of the truck. "Why would anyone do this?"

The guys strode toward them. Chance wore a scowl deeper than Patricia had ever seen on his face. As Talon walked, he coiled a length of barbed wire.

Her heart sank. "Not the new fence?"

He nodded. "Yards of wire, snipped down to unusable lengths. It's worthless."

"All that work," Marie cried. "All that money wasted. Who hates us this much?"

"Colton." Chance spat the name and faced Talon. "I keep telling you. It has to be Colton. You remember the look on his face when you won. Besides, he was gunning for you long before the competition."

"Yeah, but the sheriff already cleared him. Besides, what does he have to do with Janet?"

"Janet?" Marie looked from one to the other. "What does any of this have to do with Janet?"

So they'd kept her in the dark too. No wonder she never gave Patricia a heads-up about this. Apparently, Talon figured she would and swore everyone to secrecy. Looking at the whole ordeal from his perspective, it made sense. Wasn't right, but it made sense. "I'll tell you later."

"Who knows?" Chance said. "Maybe he had some sort of adolescent crush on her."

"Maybe." Talon tapped the coiled fencing wire against his leg. "But he's known about the bin for a few weeks now—he was the one who filled it. Why didn't he do something sooner?"

"Maybe he was waiting for us to finish the fence so he could get it all at once."

"I don't know. That just doesn't add up."

Chance flung his arm out. "Who else would do it?"

Talon eyed his boots and blew out a breath. "I don't know. I just don't know."

Patricia tucked her balled fists under her arms. Everyone was exhausted, worn to a frazzle with work and worry. She'd never seen Chance this high tempered or Talon at such a loss. Whoever was doing this to them ought to be horsewhipped. And if it was Colton Royder, she'd gladly raise the first welt.

But for now, she needed to pull her wits about her and make some decisions. At least appear like a capable ranch owner, even if that veneer could be blown off by a gentle breeze.

"Consuela has breakfast waiting for us, and she's tired. I want to finish up in the kitchen so she and Chef can go home. I'm giving them the day off." She flipped her hand in the air. "In fact, I'm giving us all the day off. We're all worn out. The cattle are okay, right?"

"Yeah, they're fine," Chance answered. "I fed them."

"Good. Then let's eat and just take it easy today. I'll check in with Sheriff Brewer, then call the insurance company and see if vandalism to the fence is covered." She stalked toward the pickup. "Y'all c'mon. I'll give you a ride to the house."

The truck cab held only two people, so Chance helped Marie up to the passenger side, then he and Talon jumped in the back. Patricia made certain they were settled before driving over the bumpy terrain back to the road.

"That was impressive," Marie said. She clasped the grip over her door with her right hand and held onto her seat with her left. Even then, she bounced and swayed with the motion of the pickup over the rocks Patricia had barely noticed when she'd driven to the feed bin.

"What was?"

"You. Making decisions. Giving orders. Saying *y'all* and *c'mon* as if you're born to it." She chuckled. "Did you say it in front of Natalie? I can just see her being mortified over how redneck you've become."

Had she been mortified? Had Patricia even said it or, for that matter, said anything particularly Texan? She couldn't remember. Although their plane had touched down in Texas in the early morning hours, New York seemed years ago.

The truck tires hit the gravel on the ranch road, and the ride became smoother.

In the rearview mirror, Patricia caught a glimpse of Talon and Chance bickering. Still. "I think the guys are stretched to the limit. I don't know why they haven't collapsed already."

Marie brushed the hair from her eyes. "I know you're exhausted too, but I think I could get by with a short nap. I want to go to the house later and make sure nothing here is affecting the builders."

Patricia's heart skipped a beat. "It hasn't, has it? Is everything okay at your house?"

"It was when I saw it yesterday. I can't believe how quickly it's shaping up. It's going to be beautiful."

"I'd love to see it. Wake me before you leave, and I'll go with you." She pulled to a stop in front of the house. "Besides, I don't think it's a good idea for you to go by yourself right now, or for any of us to be alone. Who knows what this lunatic is likely to do next?"

Chapter Seventeen

P atricia talked to the sheriff and the insurance agent, then climbed into Marie's car and headed down the ranch road. She felt oddly guilty for sneaking off without the guys knowing they'd left, but the feeling passed as she gazed at Chance and Marie's new home. Inside, the light fixtures hung from the ceilings, the walls sported their new colors, and in the great room at least, the hardwood floor struggled to gleam under a soft layer of dust and footprints. The rest of the flooring had yet to be laid and the appliances hadn't found their home in the kitchen, but once these were done and the curtains were up, this place would be move-in ready before she knew it.

And Marie would no longer be her housemate.

"Wait till you see the baby's room." Marie grabbed her wrist and drew her deeper into the house.

A soft shade of pink coated the walls, and the accent wall held paper dotted with rocking horses. The ceiling light, a soft-white dome with translucent pink clouds, gave a gentle glow to the room.

"You've decorated for a girl," Patricia said. "Looks like you and Chance couldn't wait after all."

Marie giggled. "We tried, but we were just too anxious to know." From the windowsill, she grabbed a plastic-covered package containing a valance with rocking horses that matched the accent wall. "As soon as the rods arrive, we'll put up the curtains. Isn't this adorable?"

"It is." She couldn't wait to be decorating rooms for her own children.

"Chance said we needed to start her off early with the idea she'd be more of a country girl than a city girl," Marie continued away in her giddiness. "But I'll make sure she has something of an urban flair."

Justin appeared at the doorway, his torn T-shirt stained with sweat and paint. "I thought I heard your voice." He held up a stirring stick dabbed with a sampling of two colors. "Which did you want for the master?"

As they talked, Patricia studied the pendant dangling from the chain around his neck. From this distance, she could more easily see the details. Fascinating piece, even though she had no clue what it represented. It resembled a grid with what looked like nailheads over the intersections of the bars, all of which was encircled by a trio of woven ivy vines. Or maybe thorns, like the thorny crown placed on Christ's brow. A Christian symbol perhaps?

He caught her staring and dropped the pendant beneath his T-shirt. Whatever the design meant, it was special enough to him to be worn daily next to his heart and private enough that he preferred to keep it from sight.

None of her business anyway. She laid her hand on Marie's arm. "We need to be going soon. I'll wait for you outside."

Their voices grew faint as she meandered through the house. Her own house on the ranch was good enough for her, especially since they updated the lower floor. She wouldn't mind refurbishing the bathrooms, but that would have to wait. With the fiasco going on at the ranch—and the financial peril she'd managed to put it in—any frivolous spending would have to wait.

Marie and Justin joined her in the great room, both still laughing about something she hadn't heard.

"You and your men are doing a great job." Marie turned around in place and took everything in. "I'm excited. I can't wait until it's done."

"Won't be long now." Justin's fondness of her was evident. She charmed everyone she met, and this rough-looking character was no exception.

She turned to Patricia. "Ready to go?"

By the time they returned home, the Garcias had arrived and Chef was toting a large suitcase to the porch.

As Marie parked the car, Patricia lowered her window and called out to him. "Who's here?"

"Just us, *muchacha*." He lugged the thing into the house, letting the screen door slam behind him.

Patricia exchanged glances with Marie, then scrambled from the vehicle. This was not the time to be entertaining guests from out of town. She cringed. Had her mother come?

Inside, they caught Consuela coming down the stairs. "Señora Adele is not here," she said. "We will use her room."

"You don't want to stay in your own home?"

"No. If something else happens, I want to be here."

"She don't want to be alone at home while I'm on cow duty," Chef said. The suitcase clunked over each step as he dragged it upstairs. "I don't blame her."

Consuela slapped her hands together, as if calling an end to the discussion. "You two don't have nothing to do, you can help me in the kitchen."

The meal was a light one, quick to prepare and just as quick to consume. The table wasn't quite the same without Frank and Buster there. Despite the day of rest, everyone seemed tired and despondent.

Patricia wiped her lips, then crumpled the paper napkin. "I talked to the insurance agent today. The fence is covered."

She glanced at Chance and Talon. "Do you want to go to town tomorrow for new wire, or should Marie and I pick it up on the way home from the Quad-B?"

"I reckon we'll spend quite a bit of tomorrow undoing the damage done," Chance said. "We have to salvage what ranch cubes we can and figure out where to store them."

Talon pushed his plate aside. "And we'll have to ride the fence line to see what all's ruined. Have to make sure the posts are still standing. You best go to the Co-op. I'll make a list for you."

"Don't make sense that one person would spend all that time cuttin' the wire into worthless lengths," Chef said. "I bet there's more than one person doing this."

"Probably." Talon turned to Patricia. "Did you talk to the sheriff?"

"Yes. He didn't have much to add. One of the deputies that was here after it happened came back early this morning, I guess before any of us got home. I didn't see him. Did you?" Those around the table shook their heads. Someone probably should've stayed last night, but with Buster in such bad condition, she couldn't blame them for preferring the hospital over the ranch. "Anyway, he surveyed the damage, but there wasn't much evidence anywhere."

"One thing's bugging me." Crossing his forearms on the table, Talon leaned forward. "All this started out in the farthest pasture."

Chance nodded, his lips forming a tight line. "And now it's practically in the backyard. Those fence clippings came from Griff's land behind the house."

Patricia shuddered against the alarm spidering down her back. Although the feed bin and Griff's fence line were hundreds of feet away, they were still too close.

"Do you think they intend to strike here next?" Marie's almond-shaped eyes were wide as she laid a protective hand over her abdomen.

Sitting beside her on the old pine bench, Chance wrapped his arm around her and placed his other hand over hers, as if pulling her into himself could shelter her from harm. "Maybe Katie will let you bunk at her house. It would be safer for you to stay in town."

"I like that idea," Talon said, reaching for Patricia. "Maybe you should too."

She flung off his hand. "No. I'm not going to let him—them—whoever—scare me off my land. It's fine for Marie to go. She has a baby to protect. But I'm not budging. I have too much invested in this place to watch it fall apart."

"There you go, *chica*," Consuela's eyes sparkled with daring and excitement. "Fight for what's yours. I stay here with you. I brought The Judge!"

Patricia stared at her. "The judge?"

"It's a gun, Pat," Talon said.

"It's a good gun to have," Consuela added.

Talon blew out a breath. "She's right. I hate that it may come to this, but she's right. The Judge is manageable. It can shoot .45 caliber bullets or .410 shotgun shells, just like the shotguns we carry in our saddle scabbards. Loaded with .410s, it's great for home protection."

"That's right." Consuela clasped her hands together and pointed both index fingers toward the kitchen as if holding a gun. "If the bad guy's that way, you point that way—don't have to aim, just shoot."

"That's pretty much true. As tight as a .410 scatter pattern is, you'll hit something. Wound the guy if nothing else."

Adrenaline pulsed through Patricia's veins. She'd never shot a gun before. Never needed one in Manhattan. But she lived in Texas now, on a ranch that was under attack. *Her* ranch.

"I want one," she announced.

"Oh, Patty, no!" Marie's voice reflected her astonishment. "I can't believe you'd want a gun."

"Think about it, Marie. The nearest law enforcement is over twenty minutes away. Anything could happen before they got here. I did not come all the way from New York to become a victim in Texas." She turned to Talon. "I want one. Can you teach me to shoot it?"

When Talon hesitated, Consuela waved a dismissive hand. "I teach you. There's nothing to it."

"No, I'll teach her," Talon said. "But are you sure you want to do this?"

For now, she was. Whether she could pull the trigger if she had to, she didn't know. She hoped she'd never have to find out.

When Daddy's face came up on the monitor, Patricia knew she'd have to skirt, sidestep, and outright bat away questions pertaining to the status of the ranch. If he realized what was going on around here, he'd dispatch every policing agency at his disposal. And if he knew that tomorrow she would drive into Stephenville to buy herself a gun, he'd yank her home in a heartbeat. Wouldn't matter that she was over thirty.

"How's Buster?" he asked.

She told him what the doctor had said that morning. The day had been so long it was hard to believe that only yesterday, she'd been in Manhattan. "They're going to keep him several days. He may need a second surgery."

"After hearing all that, I'm amazed he's alive. He's a lucky man." Daddy's brow creased. "His bills are going to run into the tens of thousands. Is he insured?"

"Everyone on the ranch is covered, thanks to the Texas Farm Bureau," she said. "The insurance is high, but it's good."

"Let me know if you need money. Things must be tight there with the loss of all those cows. Did you ever find out what caused it?"

"Yes, and it's not likely to happen again"—she hoped. "Just a couple of isolated problems with their forage. We've taken care of it."

"Okay, but like I said, if you need money, don't hesitate."

"Thanks, Daddy. I love you."

"I love you too, sweetheart." He reached toward his computer to disconnect.

"Wait—where's Mama? Didn't she want to talk tonight?"

"No, she's busy doing something or another in the other room." He leaned toward the monitor and lowered his voice. "What happened between you two? I thought you were going to make amends."

She twisted her hands in her lap, unable to look him in the eyes. "What did she say to you?"

"Nothing, which is why I'm asking you. When I talked to her earlier this week, she was all excited about you coming. She's barely cracked a smile or strung two sentences together since I got back from DC."

"I guess one of those two sentences was about Buster." She didn't want to guess what the other was.

"That was the bulk of the conversation, yes. I was looking forward to seeing you when I got home. She explained why you had to leave." He delivered a stern look over his glasses, and she felt five years old again. "Now it's your turn. Explain her mood."

She resisted the urge to squirm, though she still found it difficult to look into his eyes, and focused instead on the framed photo of her and Talon to the right of her monitor. "Things didn't go as well as we'd hoped."

"Because ... "

Her father was on a number of investigative committees in Congress, and if he looked at the witnesses the way he was looking at her right now—brows drawn, eyes piercing—the poor souls would probably wither away. She didn't see this side of him often, and under his intense gaze, she could feel her backbone crumbling.

"Because I botched it up and let my temper get the best of me."

His brown eyes widened a fraction. "That's not like you."

"I don't know what came over me. One minute I was all ready for our discussion, and the next I couldn't wait to bite her head off." She slumped in her chair. During her nap, she'd dreamed of the scene, watched herself acting like a spoiled brat and hated it. That was the old Patricia Talbert, the one before she'd accepted Christ as her savior. She didn't want to be like that anymore. "Believe me, I'm not proud of myself."

"Good. Fix it." He gave her a final nod and disappeared from the screen.

Fix it. How could she if Mama wouldn't talk to her? Not that she could blame her mother after the tongue-lashing she'd received.

Patricia flopped against the back of the chair. So ... this was what walking a mile in Mama's shoes felt like. All this time, Patricia had been the one unavailable for conversation. The receiving end of the snub treatment chilled her to the core. If she ever could fix this, she'd be careful not to allow it to happen again. For either of them.

Chapter Eighteen

The next day, while the man at Co-op packaged her purchase, Patricia slipped her checkbook back into her purse and caught sight of Griff Griffith nearby, watching her. He gave her a cautious tip of the hat. The look in his eyes confused her, but she offered a smile.

He strolled toward her, not speaking until he was a whisper away. "Saw you bought a gun. Things that bad at your place?"

"Well, you know..." Caught off guard, she wasn't certain how to respond. By now, half the town probably knew she'd bought a gun.

"Don't mean to pry, but since your trouble started with my cattle and all, I just wondered if y'all ever got all that straightened out."

"Here ya go, Miz Pat." Bart handed her the package. "We'll load the rest of your things in the truck for you."

"Thanks. I'm in the blue Ford up front."

"I know which one."

When he turned to summon help with her order, she took Griff by the arm and walked with him away from the counter. Keeping her voice low, she asked, "What have you heard?"

"Nothing more'n things bein' rough out your way. Heard about Buster for sure. Word gets around."

They strolled single file past a crowded display of weatherproofing supplies and headed toward the front doors.

"In truth, Griff, no, we haven't straightened things out. Can I talk to you?" Talon or even the sheriff might have covered this with him already, but she'd never heard about it. Maybe he would have a fresh perspective.

Outside, the wintery November breeze caught her hair and made her eyes sting. Griff shrugged deeper into his coat. They probably should find a place inside to talk, but he seemed okay with braving the cold. She shifted him away from a rancher and his wife approaching the store and guided him to a quiet corner near the supply of fencing panels and squeeze chutes.

"It seems all of this has something to do with Janet Parsons," she said. "Did you know her?"

He shoved his hands in his jacket pockets. "Everyone around here did. Talon brought her home from college a few times. She'd stay at the main house with Jake and Loretta for spring break, or maybe a week or two in the summer and go with him to his rodeo events."

"Did anyone seem to take a particular interest in her?"

"Yes and no." She shot him a *that's a lot of help* glower, and he chuckled. "You have to understand, everyone loved Janet. She had that type of personality. Knew how to draw people and make 'em feel special. She was perfect for Talon—forgive me for sayin'—and it was apparent she only had eyes for him. 'Course, there were a few young bucks wantin' to change that dynamic."

"Like who?"

"Aw, Miz Pat, there were so many, and I don't remember that far back. But like I said, she drew 'em in like a magnet. She was a sweet person."

"What about Cody Royder? Was he drawn to her? Or Colton?"

He rubbed the stubble growing gray and thick along his jaw. "Come to think of it, Cody was mighty smitten with her. Took it hard when Talon proposed to her. Even harder when he found out she'd been killed." His eyes brightened with a sudden revelation. "I bet Talon don't even know about this, since he spent time in jail under that silly notion he'd murdered his own fiancée, but Cody drank himself cross-eyed after he found out. Ben nearly booted him off the Flying K."

"You don't think ... "

"You askin' if he's the one behind all the trouble out at your place?" He lowered his brows, considering, but ultimately shook his head. "Naw, I just can't see it. I've known him and Colton since they were young'uns ridin' on their mama's hip. They may get a wild hair now and then, but this kind of thing ... Naw. Especially not Cody. It's just not in his disposition."

The wind kicked up, and Griff shuddered. Patricia squeezed his forearm. "Okay. Thanks for talking to me. At least we can rule him out."

"Wish I could be of more help." He shifted so the wind hit him from behind. "Did y'all set a date yet?"

She winced. Just what she needed—someone else wanting to know their wedding date. "Not yet. Hoping we get all this settled first."

"Well, I'm looking forward to performing the ceremony when you do. I like seein' Talon happy again. Janet was good for him, but you are too. I think y'all are a good match."

His words warmed her. How special that he and the others in her adopted town accepted her.

Marie closed the Quad-B and took her place in the passenger seat of Patricia's pickup. "Did you get it?"

She wasn't asking about the fencing wire, visible in the bed of the truck, or anything else from Talon's list she'd purchased.

"Yes." Patricia patted the lid of the center console. "I'm surprised how easy it was."

"I'm surprised you didn't have a waiting period."

She was too. The crime statistics in larger cities like New York, Chicago, and DC—and Houston and Dallas—had kept her firmly planted in the gun-control camp of the debate. But the change of locale gave her a change in perspective. Considering the probable response rate from the sheriff's department, a little insurance wouldn't hurt.

"I did have to fill out some paperwork and wait through a background check. I guess that's something." She pulled out of the parking place and drove away from the store. "Have you decided whether you want to stay in town?"

"I talked to Katie, and she said it would be okay. She even told me where to find the spare key. But I can't imagine being here without Chance, and he'd want to stay out there to help protect the ranch."

"We're shorthanded. We can't afford to spare him." Patricia glanced at her. "Does that mean you're staying with us?"

"I guess so." Her eyes drifted toward the center console. "But if you're going to have that thing, you'd better learn how to use it."

"Talon's going to teach me as soon as we get home. Between Consuela and the guy who sold it to me, it seems pretty easy. As long as I use the shotgun shells, all I have to do is point and shoot." Although the man in the store had used terms like *kill shot* and *center mass* and other words that made her shudder.

Marie huffed. "It doesn't seem right for Christians to carry firearms. What does that say about our faith? What would Jesus say about this?"

"He wasn't a fool, Marie. He knew the perils of the times He lived in, and He knows them now. Even back then, He sent His disciples out armed that second time. Don't commit murder doesn't mean we can't defend ourselves." She'd studied that in her Bible just last night as she tried to reconcile faith and gun ownership, and she felt more comfortable about buying the pistol today. But she'd prayed she would never need it.

She turned onto the highway. "Did Katie mention how Buster's doing?"

"She says he sleeps a lot, and when he's awake, he's groggy and on the ornery side. She's so glad he's going to be okay, she doesn't care."

"I never considered those two would be a match. Can you imagine?"

"You know what they say about opposites. Just like Adele and Frank. Do you think those two will ever get together?"

"That one really does stretch the imagination, though I could've sworn she was learning to be happy on the ranch." After Aunt Adele landed in Texas last year, Frank had taken quite a liking to her. The feeling had seemed mutual, but as a New Yorker, the City's pulse was her lifeline.

"Is she coming back?"

"Who knows. She said with you and Chance home, I didn't need a chaperone anymore—as if I'd fallen for that excuse to begin with—and after the wedding, we won't need her at all. She seems happy to be home."

"Yes, but it's not like she'd never lived in the country. Remember her mountain home? The horse farm?"

"Neither were as far from Manhattan as we are." As she turned down the ranch road, she said, "I don't really think she'd come here to live, and I know Frank won't go up there. Whatever little romance started to blossom between them while she was here isn't likely to grow now that she's back in New York."

"That's a shame. It would be nice to pair Frank with someone special." Marie nodded toward the walkway to the house. "Let me off here. I swear, this little one is already messing with my bladder, and she's no bigger than a bump."

With a laugh, Patricia pulled over. "I'll leave the fencing for the guys to unload and be right in."

As she drove toward the shed, she caught a glimpse of late-afternoon sun reflecting off the feed bin. No telling how the guys got all those range cubes up, but thank goodness they had. She veered off the road and bumped over the rocks to greet them. Chance waved as he straddled the four-wheeler. He cranked up the vehicle and drove past her.

Talon strode over and gave her a kiss through the open window. "Got everything?"

"Yes. That was the easiest shopping trip I've ever had."

"That's man-style shopping. No mess, no bother. In and out, buying only what you need."

"Right. Like you never overspend."

"I plead the fifth."

"I also got the ...you know..." She tipped her head toward the console.

"The gun," he said. "You can say it. There's no shame in being a gun owner out here. We shoot snakes and other varmints—anything that would endanger us or our animals."

"Have you ever shot a man?"

"No, and I hope that I never do. But it doesn't hurt to be prepared, just in case." He glanced around for a few moments and finally nodded toward the pens. "Let's park the truck in the shed. Then, we can set up a target near the security lights and shoot a few rounds."

With a one-armed jump over the back of the truck, he landed in the bed and slapped the cab roof as a signal for her to drive. He jumped out again at the truck shed and headed off as she backed in. By the time she joined him, he'd braced a sturdy piece of plywood against the pen rails.

"Where's the gun?"

She handed him the store sack, which held little orange earplugs, the pistol case, and the ammunition. "I got .45s too. I guess it wouldn't hurt for me to learn how to shoot it both ways."

"Probably not, but let's try the .410s first." He drew the pistol from its case, loaded the two-inch-long shotgun shells into each of the revolver's five chambers, then clicked the cylinder closed. "What do you know about guns?"

"Barrel, cylinder"—she pointed at each part, identifying them as the salesman had taught her—"trigger, hammer, grip. Aim the barrel, cock the hammer, pull the trigger."

"That's basically right. Quick safety tips: Treat every gun like it's loaded, whether it is or not, and never point it at anyone unless you intend to shoot. Got it?"

"Got it." She felt like a ten-year-old learning shooting basics from her daddy, but when it came to firearms, she was definitely an innocent.

They put their earplugs in, then he handed her the gun. It was heavy, but not too, and the grip felt awkward in her hand. He turned her toward the board against the fence, showed her how to hold the pistol and how to stand—all the same instructions she'd received in the store—then stepped back. "Fire when ready."

She pointed at the board, cocked the trigger, and with a deep breath, squeezed off a round. Then she opened her eyes to see what she'd hit. A tight pattern of pellet holes mangled the top left of the board.

"You injured his shoulder," Talon said. "That'll stop him long enough for you to run."

"So I did good?"

"We'll have to work on your aim if you ever want to kill a snake, and for that, you'll have to keep your eyes open. But for the purpose at hand, that's good." He kissed her forehead, then stepped away. "Do it again."

She'd expected the blast to knock her off her feet, but it just jerked her wrist a bit. She took another shot, then another and another until the cylinder was empty. Talon had her reload and shoot again. After another five rounds, they put in the .45 bullets. The blast was louder and the kick was stronger, but the bullet never hit the board.

"Try again," Talon ordered. "Keep your eyes open this time."

She clenched her teeth. With the shotgun shells, she'd been able to at least squint at the board, but she'd definitely kept them shut tight with the bullet round. She raised the gun and tried again. And again. She fired all five rounds and reloaded. Out of the ten shots, she'd hit three times. If a man's silhouette had been painted on the board, it would have shown a nick in his right ear. The other two shots would have whizzed past him.

"I think I'll stay with the shotgun shells for a while."

"Good plan," he agreed. "Let's put this away and go in. I'm starving."

He began picking up the empty casings and cartridges, and after she had the gun safely back in its case, she joined him.

"Talon, you said you've never shot anyone. Do you think you ever could?"

"I've been thinking about that ever since you decided you wanted a gun." He squatted to put the discards in the store bag. With his forearms resting on his knees, he looked up at her. "Like I said, I never want to be put to the test. I never want to have to use a gun against another human being.

But heaven help the guy who threatens you. Who puts you in danger. I wouldn't think twice."

The intensity of his answer stunned her, though it shouldn't have. He'd already lost one fiancée to violence, and if he'd had a moment's notice, he would've killed the assailant to protect her. He'd do no less for Patricia. And she'd do no less for him.

Talon groaned at the buzz of the alarm, too loud a noise in an otherwise quiet and empty room. Two thirty a.m., and he felt like he'd just fallen asleep. He couldn't get used to having the bunkhouse to himself, so he'd slept on the couch with the TV on low. Not the snores and snorts of the other guys, but it helped. Sometime during the night, he must've turned it off. If he could get enough quality sleep, his three-to-seven shift wouldn't be too bad. But with the guys gone, he hadn't gotten enough quality sleep.

The alarm clock continued its annoying racket. He walked groggily to his bunk where it was plugged in and slapped it off. The eerie silence permeated the place again, sending shivers down his spine. Or maybe he was just cold. The temperature had dropped during the night.

He started the coffee and strode in for a shower. Hot water helped ease his muscles, and a cold finish guaranteed his wakefulness. With a towel wrapped around his waist, he returned to the kitchenette, slapped a couple of blueberry Pop-Tarts into the toaster, and went to his chest of drawers to dress. Same thing every day since he was a kid, minus the Pop-Tarts. He'd thrown those into his routine recently to tide him over until breakfast. Something he didn't need to do when they worked regular hours. He sure looked forward to working regular hours again.

Almost as much as he looked forward to getting married.

Pat wasn't quite the Yankee she'd been when she first moved here, but she could still make a flannel shirt and blue jeans look stylish. Learning to shoot was just another step toward her transformation from a city girl to a country girl. Probably thanks to her dad—Dale—she didn't have the big city attitudes her aunt held, or even Marie for that matter. Getting her countrified hadn't taken too much effort. She already knew how to ride and wasn't shy with a pitchfork in the barn. Going from horses to cattle hadn't been that much of a shift.

Still, considering the way she looked in those spring dresses she'd worn earlier this year, back when Adele was bent on fetching her back to the nation's fashion center, he'd be happy if a little of the City remained in her. She filled them out quite nice. Had great legs ...

The sooner he bought that marriage license, the better. If he got his way, and she'd consider eloping, he'd be sleeping in the main house before the month's end, with her arms to fend the cold winter away.

He downed his quick breakfast, poured the rest of the coffee into a thermos, then shrugged on his warmest coat and grabbed the shotgun. The thermometer at the window showed the temperature hovering just below forty. He'd spend the next four hours shivering in his saddle.

As he headed out, the dim glow from the mercury light at the pens reflected off a scrap of white paper taped to the door. For an instant, his heart stopped. Then he snatched it and flicked on the reading light by Frank's chair.

> Heard you shooting today. Target practice, not that it would do you any good. You think you'll ever get a shot at me? You don't even know when I'm coming. Could be anytime. Tonight. Tomorrow. Did you even try to help her, or did you just stand there and watch her die?

Talon slapped the note down on the coffee table, then with a wild sweep of his arm, sent everything else on the table's surface flying through the room and skittering across the floor. Who was this guy—this coward who came in the dark of night? Why couldn't he show himself like a man? If he wanted a fight with Talon, *bring it on!* Stop hiding in the shadows!

He tipped his head back and released a feral roar that echoed in the room. Then, he folded into Frank's chair and held his head in both hands.

What was going on? Why couldn't someone catch this guy? Why couldn't he?

No telling how long the note had been there. The only reason it was taped on the door this time was because Talon had started locking it after the last time.

But had Chef remembered to lock the doors of the main house after his shift? Had Chance when he went out?

Talon grabbed his shotgun and headed across the gravel road to where Pat slept. He couldn't bear it if she wasn't safe, if anything happened to her. He couldn't take another such loss. Not again. *Dear God, not again.*

Gulping deep breaths, he tried to control his jittering nerves and hammering heart. If the house was locked, he wouldn't need to bother those inside who slept so trustingly. He'd check the doors and windows, then relieve Chance. Make him aware of what had happened. Make sure he locked the doors when he entered and maybe checked the inside rooms before going to bed.

He made a full circle around the house. Everyone was safe. All was quiet.

Relief drained his strength. He collapsed on the porch steps, laying the shotgun across his knees, and bowed his head. *Dear Father, I don't know how long I can take this. You know who's doing it. Please direct the sheriff's and deputies' steps so they can catch him.*

This had gone on long enough. The ranch couldn't take any more losses, and he couldn't take any more nights of seeing Janet in his dreams and worrying about Pat in his wakefulness. Brewer and his deputies needed to track this guy down.

He shot to his feet, gripping his gun. *They'd better catch him before I do.*

Chapter Nineteen

Patricia's stomach tightened as she read the note again. Whoever had penned it possessed a mean, evil spirit to believe that Talon wouldn't have done everything in his power to save Janet. Even worse, to believe he'd killed her.

"He must have been close by to have heard us shooting," she said.

Talon shook his head. "Sound carries around here. Bounces off the hills. You can hear a gunshot a mile away."

Consuela gathered the breakfast dishes. "Maybe he needs to hear more gunshots. Maybe he'd think twice about coming around here."

"He heard them yesterday, didn't he?" Chef wasn't really asking. "Didn't stop him from coming around last night."

"Still, we should shoot." She bustled toward the kitchen with her hands loaded, tossing her words over her shoulder. "We all should carry a gun."

Chance nodded. "I've got my Colt and shoulder holster upstairs. I intend to strap it on before I start my watch tonight."

Marie gaped at him. "What are you going to do? Kill someone for leaving a note?"

"Not if I can help it. But what if leaving notes isn't what he has in mind next time?"

She wrapped her arms around her middle, and Patricia hurt for her. With her riotous hormones, all this talk about guns and shooting probably didn't set right with her.

Patricia pushed back from the table. "Let's get to the store and surround ourselves with pretty things and forget about this awhile."

"That's a good idea," Chance said to Marie. "You need to get out of here for a while. Take your mind off things."

Whatever else he said disappeared as Patricia studied Talon's face. "Are you okay?"

"Yeah." He rubbed the back of his neck. "Yeah, I'm all right. I just wish they'd catch this guy."

"Me too." She laid her hand on his cheek. He looked tired, worried. No doubt his faith was being tested down to its very roots. "Come with me."

She took his hand and drew him through the kitchen and out to the back porch. There, she faced him and took both of his hands, then she bowed her head. She hadn't been in the praying business for long, but they both needed to get in touch with their Father before they started this day.

"Dear Lord, please watch over this man I love and keep him safe in Your grace and strength. Grant him wisdom to know what to do and the ability to do it. Please bring this horrible ordeal to a close so we can move forward, with Buster healthy and everyone home and safe. We ask this in Your name—"

"And, Father"— Talon drew her closer so her cheek rested on his chest and she could hear his heart beat—"please watch over this woman that I love and keep her safe. I don't know how to thank You for bringing her into my life, but I want to dedicate our future, our lives together, to You. We love You, and we trust You to keep us and those we love safe from further harm. Amen."

She pulled back from him and bobbed her head in affirmation of the optimism their prayer had enlivened in her. "We'll be all right. Somehow, dumping all this into stronger hands than ours helps."

"Yeah, it does." He gave her a little squeeze, a light kiss, then released her. "You'd better get going. Marie's customers are probably lined up around the block by now."

Marie glared at her through the window, jamming a forefinger at her watch. Patricia gave Talon one more kiss. "See you later. Maybe we can finally discuss wedding plans."

Halfway to the store, Marie was still scowling behind the wheel of her car. The anger roiling off her rendered the heater pointless, but she hadn't said a word since they left.

Patricia slanted her eyes toward her. "Don't you think you ought to get it off your chest before you face your customers?"

"What good would it do me? You're on his side."

"About him carrying a gun? If it means he'll be safe, then yes. I'm all for it."

Marie huffed. "I can't believe we lived in the City for over thirty years without ever needing a weapon, and now we're in the middle of nowhere, and everybody's armed to the teeth!"

"You're exaggerating. Besides, what happened to Buster has us on edge."

"All the more reason not to have guns. If everyone's on edge, they're too jumpy to be wise. No telling what he'll shoot at. Or what you'll shoot at for that matter. Have you told your parents about all this?"

"Oh, not on your life! If Mama hated the idea of me moving to Texas before, she'd really hate it now. Aunt Adele wouldn't try to lure me back to Manhattan. She'd yank me by the collar and haul me back! Have you told your parents?"

"No. And for the same reason, though they'd probably send one of my brothers to wrestle me away from Chance."

She parked behind the store, but before they left the car, Patricia said, "I know it seems awful for the guys to be carrying weapons. Everything that has happened these past few weeks has been awful. But I know it will all turn out right, and none of our men will have to fire a shot at anyone. Surely, Sheriff Brewer has some clues to follow. Maybe this will be settled soon."

"Let's hope so."

"Let's pray so."

Inside, Marie set up the register, while Patricia got the espresso machine and coffee maker started in the coffee bar. Marie hadn't known when the bar was installed what a success it would be, but it had become the gossip hub of the downtown area. There had even been talk of holding a Bible study there before store hours. Once everything settled down at the ranch, Patricia would ask about it. The idea was a good one, but with the holidays coming, maybe spring would be best.

Abby Jackson knocked on the storefront window and rubbed her arms as if she were about to freeze. Fiftyish and on the pleasantly plump side, Abby worked at the courthouse, clerking for Judge Sawyer. She made it a habit to grab a coffee from the Quad-B before facing her day, but today she was early. They had ten more minutes before opening. Still, her pleading eyes and pitiful expression wore Patricia down. She glanced at Marie.

"Sure. Let her in before she turns into an ice sculpture."

The temperature outside was nowhere near freezing, but the low humidity and the nippy breeze could send a chill to anyone's bones.

Patricia unlocked the door and flipped over the closed sign before letting Abby in. "Good morning. You're early. The coffee's not quite through brewing yet."

"Oh, that's fine. I'm just glad to get out of that wind. Felt like it was going right through me." She strolled to the counter where Marie flicked a feather duster over the merchandise. "And how's the little mama doing today? You and Chance about to have your new nest ready?"

Marie's expression brightened at the mention of her favorite subject. "Won't be long now. I can hardly wait."

"You know, Keith and I drove by the other day. I was surprised to see Justin Anthony working there. You'd think Chance would know better than to hire him."

"Why's that?"

The coffee maker wheezed out its last drop, keeping Patricia from hearing the conversation. She filled a ceramic mug and prepared the brew the way Abby liked it—two sugar cubes and a dollop of cream.

By the time she joined them at the counter, Marie's eyes were wide. "Chance never said a word."

Patricia handed Abby the mug. "What did I miss?"

Abby blew on her coffee, then ventured a sip. "Perfect, as always." After another sip, she said, "I was just saying that Justin is a troublemaker. Always getting into fights. He and your guys were on the circuit together, but he quit a while back for some reason."

"I can't imagine why Chance didn't mention it," Marie said. "Even if they never witnessed a fight, I bet they knew about it. Those guys gossip like women in a beauty shop."

"They do," Abbie agreed. "But Justin and Chance ran in different circles. Justin favored the drinking and partying crowd, and Chance—"

"—didn't." Marie flashed a grin that showed how deeply her pride ran. "I knew I got myself a good man."

"One of the best," Abby said. "How's Buster? Do you have any word on him?"

"He's going to be fine," Patricia said. "May take a while, but he'll be okay."

"Whole town's just worried sick about him." She drank her last sip, then said, "I think I'll go to the office and see if I can get a jump on the day. Judge is mighty persnickety in his old age."As she talked, she hurried to the coffee bar and left her mug by the little sink. On her way out, she paused with her hand on the door and looked back at Patricia. "You know, the whole town's just worried sick about what's going on over at your ranch. All of y'all are so very loved and appreciated we're just sick this is happening to you."

"Thank you, Abby."

She pulled open the door and tucked her chin low as she walked out into the cold.

Marie nudged Patricia. "The whole town's just worried sick."

She snorted. "Apparently. I wonder how much they know."

"Probably everything. It's been in the paper."

"Everything except the notes left for Talon. I wonder who knows about them."

Chapter Twenty

Sitting on the window seat in her bedroom, Patricia drew the lap quilt tighter around her shoulders and brought her knees to her chest. She needed a cup of coffee. Or cocoa. Something to keep her warm and awake while she kept watch over the bunkhouse across the road. During the shift change, as Chef came in to shower and Chance left to watch the cattle, Patricia had brought Marie and Consuela together for a girl-power rally. With the three of them taking shifts watching the bunkhouse, maybe they could catch whoever was leaving messages for Talon. Considering Chef and Consuela had to make breakfast in the morning, it made sense for her to take the first shift, which was already over by the time Patricia told them of her plan. After that, the logical schedule was for each woman to work the same shift her man did. Which left Patricia the three-to-seven. She'd settled into place fifteen minutes early.

The lights at the pens offered just enough glow on the bunkhouse and horse barn to make movement noticeable. She'd seen Talon go from one to the other when his shift began. Even this early in the morning, he walked with long, purposeful strides. If he yawned, she hadn't seen it. No telling how much caffeine he consumed in the thirty minutes he'd been awake.

She rubbed her eyes, then surveyed the shadows around all the outbuildings, craning her neck to see as far as the tractor barn. Nothing seemed unusual or out of place. Only Talon and Bodine moved in the darkness. Since he hadn't already found anything tacked to the door, the night might be a quiet one.

Funny how the culprit always managed it so that Talon was alone and would be sure to find the note, as if he'd had the house under surveillance and knew everyone's schedules.

Had the house under surveillance.

The thought sent chills racing down her spine. She peered through the window toward the hills. Everything seemed too far away for someone to spy on them, then have enough time to arrive, deliver the note, and disappear without a trace. If someone really was watching them, he'd have to be doing it from somewhere closer . . .

Griff's pasture. That would be the perfect place.

She slipped downstairs to the dining room and studied the hill beyond the window there. While the right side of the house benefitted from the pens' lights like the rest of the outbuildings, there were no mercury lights on this side of the house. The moon's glow only made the shadows creepy.

She shuddered again—either from being freaked out or from traipsing around the cold house barefooted—and padded to the kitchen window overlooking the back porch. The roof blocked most of the view of the hill beyond the house. Maybe she could ease outside without being noticed. If anyone hid on the hill to notice her. Best bet would be to dress in black—

Light burned her eyes, and she snapped them shut.

"What are you doing up?" Chance's voice.

"She's on duty," Marie said.

Patricia squinted at them in time to see the quizzical look Chance gave his wife.

Marie shrugged. "While you guys keep watch over the herd, we decided to keep watch over you."

"Great idea, but you're looking out the wrong window." He peered inside the refrigerator. "I'm hungry. Anything good in here?"

"Here, let me." Marie nudged him away, then pulled out a platter of leftover roast. "This'll make a good sandwich. Does that work for you?"

"Like a charm." He sat to wait at the tiny kitchen table and addressed Patricia. "What do you expect to see on the back porch?"

"Not the porch," she said. "Beyond it."

She told him what she'd been thinking, and he nodded. "That makes a lot of sense. With him being above us like that, we wouldn't hear his truck, and with all the grass between there and the bunkhouse, we wouldn't hear him walking. He could sneak in and out without anyone knowing."

"He does sneak in and out without anyone knowing," Marie grumbled. "And the idea that he may be this close to the house gives me the heebie-jeebies."

He frowned as he watched her make his sandwich. "Maybe Talon is right. Maybe I should teach you to shoot too."

"Oh no. You know how I feel about guns. I don't even want to touch one."

"But if it would make you feel safe—"

"No. I don't want to hear another word about it." She pointed at him with the knife she used to slice the roast. "When our baby starts walking, that gun of yours had better be unloaded and locked away."

"I'm good with that. But I'll teach her gun safety and how to shoot. She'll be a Texas girl. She'll need to know."

Marie turned back to her sandwich preparations, shaking her head and muttering, "Not going to happen. She will never handle a gun."

Chance opened his mouth to say something, but Patricia stopped him with a hand on his shoulder. "No use trying. The more you argue, the more she'll dig in her heels."

Marie pointed with the knife again. "Listen to the one knows me best."

"Anyway"—Patricia snagged a slice of the roast and sat across from Chance—"I don't know what I expected to see out there. Moonbeams bouncing off binoculars or something, I guess. But I'm not comfortable with the fact there are so few lights around the house. We should get another mercury light installed."

"There's a practical idea. One we should consider for our house too." Marie placed a plate holding the sandwich before Chance, then returned to the fridge where she grabbed the milk jug. "If we had more light, I'd feel more secure."

"That's not a bad idea," he said. "But light casts shadows somewhere. And a bad guy can always find the shadows."

Marie thunked the milk glass in front of him a bit harder than necessary. "You're just a bright ray of sunshine and optimism, aren't you?"

"What? I was just sayin'—"

"I'm going to bed."

He gaped at her as she stalked out of the room, then turned to Patricia. "Hormones?"

She lifted a shoulder. "Could be. Or it could be that she's more scared than she lets on. Carrying life inside her could do that." She assumed. She had no way of knowing, but couldn't wait for her own turn at expecting a baby.

"The light's a good idea," Chance said. "But it's important for her to learn how to defend herself. If not against a two-legged enemy, at least a four-legged one. We live on hundreds of acres and have all kinds of wildlife. Snakes. Coyotes. Bobcats. Feral hogs have moved into the area too, and they're dangerous. She should learn how to use a gun."

"I'm not arguing the point. Just give her time." She glanced toward the window. With the light on inside, the glass showed nothing but black, and that man could be out there watching. She rose from the table and closed the shades. "First light, I think we should go to Griff's pasture and look for signs that someone's been out there."

"You know someone has been. The new fence was cut up."

"Yes, but I mean signs that someone stayed there for a while, waiting to make his move. Doesn't hurt to ease our minds about it."

At sunup, Talon reined his horse from the pasture and aimed for the barn. With the exception of a pack of coyotes howling and making the cattle edgy, it had been a quiet night.

Chance drove to the slope in the feed truck, and Talon rode toward him.

"How was the night?" Chance asked.

"Quiet and good. Not much going on."

"That's a good thing."

"That's a mighty good thing."

"Pat's waiting for you up at the barn. She's got an idea worth listening to."

"What would that be?"

"I'll let her tell you." He lifted his foot from the brake, and the truck started to roll. "See ya in a bit."

Talon clicked his tongue at Bodine, urging him to trot. Pat spotted him from the horse barn and mounted Tandy. She loped toward him with that blond hair flying out behind her like a glorious flag. A sight he loved seeing first thing in the morning. If he could just get her to ride that fast to the altar, she'd be the last thing he saw at night too.

She caught up with him and slowed Tandy to match Bodine's gait. "Feel up to a little investigating?"

"Investigating what?"

She told him, and Chance was right. The idea held merit. He turned his buckskin to take a detour behind the house.

They rode through the pasture he and the guys were fencing —again—then started up the steady incline of the hill.

"I don't know exactly what we're looking for," he said. "Tracks, I guess. Depressions in the grass where he sat awhile or something."

"I don't suppose we'll get lucky and find a pyramid of beer cans to mark the spot."

He laughed. "I think we would've already noticed that."

They rode high enough to see the entire layout of the Circle Bar, about midway up the hill. This area would be perfect. A man could watch their activity without being silhouetted against the sky.

"Should I go left and you go right?" Pat asked.

Talon looked off to the right. Didn't make sense for the guy to hunker down so far from the bunkhouse. "No, ride with me. I don't think he would've gone any farther out than this. Besides, this'll give us a chance to talk."

She gave him a flirty look. "What do you want to talk about?"

As if she didn't know. "Weddings, of course. Do you still want to get married?"

"The sooner, the better."

"Whew." He made a show of drawing his forearm across his brow in exaggerated relief, and she giggled. Her laughter could drain away all his fatigue in a heartbeat. "Have you given any more thought to the wedding itself?"

"Since we returned from New York, I haven't had time." She studied the grass and the uneven terrain as she rode, something he'd be doing if he could take his eyes off her. She cut a glance his way. "Do you have something in mind?"

"What do you think of eloping?"

Her shoulders relaxed as if relieved from a burden. "That's been my wish since you proposed. I've been dreading this. I've already had a big wedding. They're not all they're cracked up to be. Do you think we could still have Griff?"

"I'll ask, but I imagine so."

"I love that idea. I'd be honored to have a man who knew love that deeply perform the ceremony."

"Good. It's settled then. All we need is a date."

"That's the problem. I'd really like to wait... " She squinted at something in the near distance. "Talon—look!"

He stopped Bodine and scanned the area where she pointed. Half hidden by shrub brush was an indentation in the grass, as if someone had been sitting there awhile. "C'mon."

They walked the horses a little higher up the hill. His initial guess was right. The skewed circle of crushed vegetation would match the size of a grown man's backside. He dismounted and surveyed the surrounding area, finding the trail leading up higher and back toward the west.

"Here's something," Pat said. She pulled a wool glove from her coat pocket, then picked something up from the ground. The corner edge of a wrapper off a candy bar. Fairly new. "I don't know that it'll do any good. Is it big enough to get a fingerprint from?"

Shrugging, he said, "Worth a try, I guess. Don't touch it. Just keep it in your glove." He stooped over, searching for the rest of the wrapper, but whoever had left that small piece hadn't been careless enough to leave more.

He straightened and gazed down toward the ranch. "Man, he could see whatever he wanted to from here."

"Right into the house." She shivered. "That's just creepy."

"I don't see tracks leading from here down to the pasture. He probably didn't use the same route to the bunkhouse both times. Didn't create a trail." He shifted and studied the grass uphill. "These tracks are pretty obvious though, once you know what to look for. I wonder how many times he's been here."

She took Tandy's reins and swung up on his back. "Let's see where they lead."

They lost the trail, but over the rise, they found tire tracks instead, leading out toward leveler ground. The tires had landed deep in a couple of patches of sandy soil, leaving some clear tread marks, but who knew whether Sheriff Brewer could discern anything from them.

Pat raised a hand to her brow and stared off toward the east. "The trail leads to the highway to Griff's house, right?"

"The blacktop's that way, but Griff's house is more that way." Talon pointed north-northwest.

"What else is on that road?"

He dismounted, pulled his pocket knife from his jeans, and flipped open the blade. In the dirt, he drew a map. "Here's where we are now. Here's Griff's house, and here's the road. It dead ends at Griff's property one way, and the other goes down here and intersects the highway leading to Chance and Marie's place. Their road circles around and intersects the one leading to our place. One huge square of about five or six miles." He put his knife back in his pocket. "Of course, once he gets on our ranch road, he could go on into town or head out the other way, toward the cemetery and beyond. No telling."

Still in the saddle, she studied his sketch with her lips in a tight line.

"What's wrong?" he asked.

"I'm not sure, but I think I have an idea."

"Going to let me in on it?"

"Not yet. Let's just say that if I'm right, Marie's going to have my head mounted on the wall."

Patricia had no valid reason for her suspicions—everything she'd been thinking could be circumstantial. Still, she couldn't shake the images of the map Talon had drawn in the dirt and of the proximity of Chance and Marie's house to the hill behind her own.

And Abby had said the guy was a troublemaker.

Supper had ended an hour ago, and Talon had already left for the bunkhouse to get some sleep before his shift. Chance and Marie were upstairs in the room they'd been calling home since they returned from their honeymoon, and Consuela watched TV in the living room while she waited for Chef's shift to end. With everyone else preoccupied, Patricia fired up the computer and entered "Justin Anthony" in the search line.

Most of what came up was from his rodeo days, though she did find a website for his father's construction business in Stephenville. She clicked on the link and scrolled through it. One image showed Justin and the team that was currently working on Marie's house. All the guys sported good-natured grins designed to invoke trust. If she didn't already suspect him of making their lives miserable the past several weeks, she would've believed them worthy of hire.

She took a closer look at him, then right-clicked on the image and saved it to her computer. In the picture, his medallion lay outside his T-shirt, and if she could isolate it ... and make it larger ... *there*.

Now she could see it more easily. What she had mistaken for nailheads earlier now looked like hearts welded onto the intersection of the grid lines. She'd also been wrong about the ivy encircling the entire piece. It more resembled barbed wire.

She uploaded the image into a search function. None of the results matched it completely, but all the ones that came closest were prison symbols. Why would he have made a prison medallion?

She returned to the search page featuring his name and scanned the entries. One newspaper article caught her attention, and she clicked on it.

Just as Abby said, he'd gotten himself into trouble. He'd unleashed some serious fury on a poor guy he didn't know for bumping into his pool cue as he was trying to shoot. She let out a low whistle. And they thought Colton had a temper. He'd been sentenced to prison for assault and battery.

She looked back at the top of the article. The journalist who wrote it didn't include the date the incident occurred, but the date of the article itself was a year after Janet died.

According to Justin's sentence term, he must be out on parole now—but when was he released?

Nothing matched, but she couldn't stop the nagging feeling in the pit of her stomach. Could there be a connection? It seemed strange that the guy who had hung rocking-horse wallpaper and pink globe light fixtures in a cozy little nursery could be Janet's killer. Marie was totally comfortable with him, and he did seem friendly enough. Polite. Easy natured. Could he have been in love with Janet? Could she have ever been in love with him?

Not likely. Anyone who could exhibit such fury over a bumped pool cue probably wouldn't catch the eye of someone like Janet.

Unrequited love, maybe?

She shook her head. For all she knew, they might not have even known each other. Still, what could it hurt to follow a hunch? She looked up the number to Judge Sawyer's office at the courthouse and dialed.

After their greetings, Abby asked, "How's Buster doing? Any news about him?"

"Frank and Katie are bringing him home today. He's still pretty beat up, but the doctors can't do anything more for him until he mends better, and he can do that here."

"That's good. We've been just worried sick about him."

"We have been too."

"I've been wondering about that man building Marie's house too. Just don't know why Chance wouldn't have done a background check before asking such a man to work for him. Did she ever talk to Chance about it?"

"Actually, he's why I'm calling. Marie said they knew each other from the circuit and that Justin had quit for some reason. Same as what you said the other day. Chance didn't check him out because, like he said, they knew each other." She clicked her mouse to wake her computer again, bringing up the report of Justin's sentence. "He confirmed what you said, that Justin was a troublemaker."

"Yes. When he was younger, he was in a number of brawls."

"Did you know he'd been to prison?"

"Prison?" Judging by the surprise in her voice, the answer was no. "What did he do?"

"I found an article that said he got drunk in Dallas one night and beat a man almost to death."

Abby tsked. "How long ago was that?"

"I don't know. That's what I need you for. I found a newspaper article about the event, but it came out after he was already sentenced. The reporting is really shoddy. I don't know how long he had to wait for his trial, so it's hard to pinpoint exactly when he was arrested."

"I'm surprised I hadn't heard. But why are you calling about it today? Has something happened? He didn't do anything to the house, did he?"

"No, nothing like that," Patricia answered. "But I'd like to know more about what happened and when. I'm also wondering how long he's been paroled. I couldn't find anything that would give me a time line of events."

"Oh, you think he has something to do with the awful events at the ranch." The woman was sharp. "Let me see what I can find out. It's all a matter of public record now, if you know where to look. I can get the particulars for you."

Just the answer Patricia needed to hear. "I'd appreciate it."

"The judge's schedule is full, and it's a little crazy around here right now, but I'll get it to you as soon as I can."

"That would be great. Thank you." She hesitated. "You don't mind keeping this quiet, do you? It may turn out to be nothing, and I don't want to cause trouble if I can help it."

Abby chuckled. "You mean you don't want to get Marie mad at you about her builder."

"Something like that." But if this did turn out to be something, Marie would need to know. Hopefully, her house would be finished soon.

Chapter Twenty-One

Sunday morning, Talon buttoned his shirt and kept an eye on Buster, who was having a hard time trying to get back to his bed from the bathroom with a broken arm and a broken leg. Frank hovered at his elbow, in case Buster needed him. What with work and sleeping odd hours and his two roommates being back in the bunkhouse, Talon hadn't had a lot of time to work on his sermon for the morning. Fortunately, he'd had plenty of time during his three-to-seven shift to commune with the Lord and at least come up with ideas. He hadn't written them down to turn them into a more formal speech, but he could wing it.

Buster grappled with his crutch and muttered his frustration.

"You going to make it?" Talon asked.

"Yeah, yeah. Just a little challengin' right now."

Said the king of understatement.

Frank shook his head. "I guess you'll get used to that thing eventually."

"Guess I'll have to." Buster plopped onto his mattress with a groan. "I'm gonna need it awhile. But doc says my arm'll heal before my leg does. Arm should be out of the cast before too long, then I can use two crutches. Might be easier."

Someone knocked on the door, and Frank peeked out the window. "Your breakfast is here."

Talon helped Buster settle in the bed and made sure he was covered before Frank opened the door.

Consuela bustled in and settled the breakfast tray over Buster's lap, one set of the tray's legs on either side.

Buster lifted the dish towel from a plate of scrambled eggs, bacon, and cat-head biscuits. "I been hankerin' for this, 'Suela. Thank you."

She stared at the fingers of his right hand dangling from his cast and sniffled. "It hurts just to look at you."

"Aw, it ain't bad, long as I got my pain meds." He fumbled his fork with his left hand, trying to scoop up some eggs. "I practiced this at the hospital. You'd think I'd have it figured out by now."

"Here, let me." Consuela opened a biscuit, put some eggs on it, topped them with a slice of bacon, then handed the sandwich back to Buster—all the while eyeing Frank, who looked on in his undershirt and jeans. "Why aren't you ready for church? You should hurry. You should be going soon."

"Reckon I'll hang round here and give you a hand with that ol' codger. He ain't fit to be left alone yet."

"All I'm gonna do is sleep," Buster mumbled over his breakfast.

"Who says I'm gonna do differ'nt?"

Talon chuckled to himself. Good to have those two home again. Place didn't feel quite so lonesome.

Later, after his sermon in the rodeo arena, he figured it good that Frank, Buster, and Consuela hadn't come. The Lord had given him some ideas and key points, and he'd raced through them, finishing fifteen minutes early and probably not making a lick of sense. But those who greeted him after he stepped down from the podium didn't seem to mind.

As he tried to spot Pat in the crowd, Ben and Sadie Kilgore, from the Flying K Ranch, stepped up to greet him. Ben stood with his legs shoulder-width apart and his hands on his hips. "Heard Buster's back now. How's he doing?"

"He's a bit banged up, but he's happy to be home."

"I reckon him being all broken up makes you a bit short-handed. How about I send over some of my men to help you rebuild that fence?"

"Takes a mean spirit to cut a man's fence like that." Sadie scowled. Talon hadn't seen her angry too often, but she seemed mighty ticked off now. "Ought to be horsewhipped, that's what I think. Horsewhipped."

"I've had similar thoughts," Talon agreed. With Buster in such a bad way, he couldn't be left alone for long. And there were some things Frank would be better help with than Consuela, which would knock him out of work awhile. Their summer hands were away in college, so Ben's offer was solid gold. "If you think you could spare a few guys, we'd sure like the help."

Ben nodded. "I'll send 'em out there first thing in the morning."

Talon shook his hand. "Appreciate it."

As they turned to go, Sadie said, "You tell Buster we're praying for him."

"Sure will. He'll appreciate it." He watched them walk away to mill about the crowd. Good people, good friends.

He scanned faces for Pat again. Seemed with his short sermon, people were more willing to hang around longer and visit. A rancher's nearest neighbor could be a few miles away, so church served as both a spiritual and a social center.

Marc Travis and his little girl, Madison, approached him—more like Madison was dragging Marc with her. She had a tight grasp on two of his fingers and was leaning forward with him in tow as if he were a hard load to haul.

Marc grinned at him. "She's got something she wants to ask you."

Madison looked up at him and bobbed her head in solemn agreement. She was one sweet-looking girl, a little heart thief in a purple dress and those pink cowboy boots she loved.

He scooped her up. "What is it you want to ask?"

She clamped her index finger between her teeth and turned a charming shade of red.

"It's okay. You can ask me."

Without removing her finger, she looked at him with serious, mournful eyes. "Are you gonna buy Chewwy Bewwy?"

"Cherry Berry? Your horse?"

"Uh-huh."

"I was thinking about it. Reckon you and I can strike up a deal?"

Patricia didn't know that little cutie currently wrapping Talon around her pinkie, but she looked as if she belonged in his arms, just as he seemed perfectly happy holding her.

"Looks right natural, don't he?"

She offered a smile to Griff, then returned her gaze to Talon. "Yes, he does. Perfectly natural."

"He's gonna make a good daddy."

"He'll make a great daddy."

"Beth wanted young'uns real bad, and it got to her for years that she couldn't ever have them. After a while, she found Isaiah fifty-four. Stopped her short. 'Sing, O barren,' it says and talks about extending the tent stakes. She latched hold of those first two verses and never looked back." He stared off into the distance. "That's when we started having the Cowboy Poetry Campfire. Everyone came, bringing children who loved on her and treated her like a favorite aunt. Many of them are grown now, and they still come around, some with their own little'uns."

It was true. The number of people who'd come to her funeral was astonishing. All ages, all races. And everyone spoke highly of her.

Patricia slipped an arm around his waist and gave him a little squeeze. "I'm honored that I got to meet her. More honored that you're willing to perform our wedding ceremony for us."

Griff gave her a hug and a sympathetic smile. "Y'all are having a pretty rough ride to the altar, what with everything happening at your ranch. You two are facing challenges most young couples don't have to worry about. If you can weather this storm, I'd say you'll be all right. I think you two are a good match."

Talon strode toward them, wearing a relaxed smile she hadn't seen since her return from New York. He'd carried a lot of weight on his shoulders the past several weeks, and the strain had begun to show. Her heart went out to him.

"You're right," she said to Griff. "We're a God-made match."

She gave him a final smile, then walked to meet Talon halfway. "Ready to go home?"

"Ready." He snugged her against his side and started off toward the parking lot. "What were you and Preacher Griff talking about? You backing out of the ceremony or giving him particulars."

"Neither," she said. "We were talking about you and what a great daddy you're going to be."

"I'm ready, just waiting on you." He stole a kiss from her as he helped her into the truck, then he circled the hood, climbed up to the driver's seat, and grinned. "When do you want to get married?"

"Look at everything going on." She flipped her hands in the air. "Who has time to think of wedding dates? Buster has a long way to go before he's healed and can work again, and taking care of him will be a full-time job for Frank and Consuela, not to mention having to drive him back to Fort Worth for doctor appointments. And the ranch is short-handed, and the pasture's too small for the number of cattle on it, and we can't move them because we need a new fence, and there's a guy out there who hates us—"

Talon grabbed her hand and kissed it. "Breathe."

She blinked at him and sucked in a breath. It didn't help her feel calmer, it made her want to cry. "I don't know when we're going to get married." She couldn't help the whine in her voice.

He cupped her face; his own shone with sympathy and understanding. Not to mention a little humor. "I promise, before the end of this year, you will become Mrs. Talon Carlson."

She looked at him sideways. "We're on the downhill slope of November now. December isn't going to see much improvement in our situation. How can we get married this year?"

"It'll happen." He started the truck and pulled out of the parking place. "Besides, things are already looking up. Ben's sending a crew out to repair the fence."

"That's kind of him." But it solved only one of their problems. She glanced out the side window and sighed. After watching Talon with that sweet little one in his arms, she'd begun to hear her biological clock echoing in her ears. But planning a wedding—even if they intended to elope— seemed impossible right now.

As if reading her thoughts, he gave her a wink and repeated, "It'll happen."

Something in his expression—was it the wink? The I've-got-a-secret grin?—made her believe. By the end of the year, she'd be Mrs. Talon Carlson.

He was right. Things were looking up.

When they got back to the ranch, he pulled over in front of the house. "I want to check on the guys. I'll be back in a minute."

Inside the house, the ringing phone made her quicken her pace to office. She snatched up the receiver. "Circle Bar Ranch."

"Hello, dear." Mama greeted her with a professional tone. A distant, icy tone. "Do you have a moment?"

Patricia sighed inwardly. The cold-shoulder treatment landed in the *cruel and unusual punishment* side of argument techniques. Once she and her mother had mended their relationship, she'd never use it again. "Sure I do. How are you?"

"I am fine, thank you." After a heartbeat's pause, she said, "Adele left her things there, and she'd like to come get them."

"Of course. She's welcome anytime."

"I hope that welcome extends to your father and me. We were thinking of coming with her."

Patricia hesitated. So much for things looking up. With everything happening at the ranch, this was not a good idea. But denying the request would open an entire case of worms. She'd have to explain why they couldn't come, or Mama would believe it was because of their fight. Just thinking of it made Patricia want to apologize for the argument again. But explaining everything would cause alarm and perhaps bring them to the ranch sooner.

No, turning them down was out of the question.

She squeezed her eyes shut and pinched the bridge of her nose. "I think that's a great idea. We can show you around the ranch, let you meet some of the people I've talked about all this time." Yes, maybe it wasn't such a bad idea. Maybe all this mess would be cleared up before they came. "When are you coming?"

"Congress breaks at Thanksgiving, and we thought we'd fly down then. Would that be too much trouble?"

Thanksgiving? So soon? She gulped. "That would be great. Consuela usually makes enough to feed the entire county, so you wouldn't be any trouble at all."

Please, Father, let all of this be over by then.

Chapter Twenty-Two

Marie's baby bump was getting larger, and Patricia couldn't help the wistfulness sweeping through her soul. She was getting a bad case of baby envy. She had no clue how Talon intended to make it happen, but he'd promised to marry her by the end of the year, and she intended to hold him to it.

A cold breeze brought Katie through the back door of the Quad-B. "G'morning, y'all. It's downright blustery outside."

Marie grinned. "Just like home."

"You can have it." She slipped out of her coat and hung it up. "But it's good to be back. How's Buster doing this morning?"

"I didn't get to see him," Patricia answered. "Until he gets the cast off his arm, he doesn't venture out much. Consuela took his breakfast to him as we were leaving to come here."

"That late?" She giggled. "With him sleeping in and getting breakfast in bed, he's going to get downright lazy."

"Probably, but I think we can afford to coddle him a little. For now anyway." Someone rapped on the glass at the front door, and Patricia said, "I bet that's Abby. She's earlier than usual. I'll let her in."

Sporting a huge grin, Abby waved a file folder at her through the window. Patricia quickened her step and unlocked the door.

"I have it all here," Abby said. "The information you wanted."

Patricia had to restrain herself from snatching it out of the woman's hands. When Abby handed it to her, she forced herself to accept it politely. Then, instead of whisking it away so she could study it, she said, "The coffee's ready. Help yourself."

Marie and Katie came out of the office, and Patricia held the file up. "It's here."

"What's here?" Katie asked. She greeted Abby with a hug, then joined Patricia and Marie at a bistro table.

"Justin Anthony's arrest record."

"Arrest record? When was he arrested?" Marie's eyes narrowed. "And why are you investigating him?"

"Just a hunch I had based on something I read." Patricia opened the file and searched for the date.

"He was always getting into trouble, but that was years ago." Katie stood over Patricia's left shoulder, and Marie sat to her right. Katie asked, "Why is it important now?"

Patricia found the date and pointed it out to her. "Does this mean anything to you?"

"No. Should it?" She looked again, squinting at the page. "Wait. That's the night Janet was killed. You don't think..."

"I don't know. It could be a coincidence. Did he know Janet?"

"Does this have something to do with her?"

"Talon's been getting notes that mention her."

She winced. "I hate that. It took him years to get over her."

"I know. I've heard."

"But you've been good for him." Katie gave her an apologetic look. "I didn't mean—"

Patricia smiled. "I know."

"Did he know Janet?" Marie asked.

Katie shrugged. "Sure. He even had a crush on her. Everyone did."

Even if he had, that didn't put him in Dallas at the right time, unless ... "Had he been invited to the wedding?"

"Oh good heavens, no. He was a nice guy and all when he was sober. But he was a mean drunk, and all he wanted to do was get drunk. After the rodeos, he'd head to whatever bar he could find. The guys from the Circle Bar didn't have much to do with him."

"That's true. Nice enough until he got drunk." Abby nudged Patricia. "But until you told me, I didn't realize he'd been in prison. I thought he'd finally straightened up."

"Maybe he has straightened up," Marie said. "He's building our house."

Katie nodded. "He was always a good carpenter. Good with his hands like his father. And when he was sober, he could be pretty artistic too."

"Look at his release date." Abby blew on her coffee and took a sip. "He hasn't been out quite a year."

Marie studied the document. "About a month after Chance and I got married."

Patricia turned to her. "How did he know you two were going to build a house?"

"I don't know. Chance handled all that."

"Your house is almost finished. In the three months he's been working on it, he's had plenty of time to watch us and learn our routines."

Katie shook her head. "I've known him almost as long as I've known Chance and Talon. This is beyond what he does. Fights are spontaneous. What's going on at the ranch requires planning."

"So, you don't think it could be him?" Patricia asked.

"I don't know. It's been a long time since I've seen him—but, of course, he's been in prison, hasn't he?" She glanced at the file. "Who knows how much he's changed because of that."

Marie dismissed the discussion with a wave of her hand. "I've never had a moment's trouble with him. He's always been polite, except when he cuts up with me, but then—like I said—he's cutting up with me. I can't believe he's the one doing all this."

"Still, it makes for an interesting coincidence." But a coincidence just the same. He lived in Stephenville, and Dallas was too far away for a casual night out. So why was he in Dallas? If only she had more to go on. "Why don't we go out to the house after closing today? Maybe he'll still be there."

"Oh no you don't." Marie scowled. "What are you going to do? Interrogate him? Get him angry enough to quit when he's close to finishing? No way. Leave the sleuthing to the sheriff's office."

"No, I'm not going to interrogate him. I wouldn't know how. But I wouldn't mind seeing the house again. Is the baby's room finished now?"

Marie's smile came complete with a new-mother glow. "The curtains are up, and we've even moved some of the furniture in. We couldn't wait ..."

While Abby and Katie kept Marie talking about the baby and the house, Patricia slipped into the back, claiming a need for the lady's room, and rummaged through Marie's desk. She might not interrogate Justin, but she could take a picture of his tires and measure their width. All she needed were her cell phone and a tailor's measuring tape.

That evening, the house smelled like beef stew and cornbread. And chili. And ... pumpkin pie? While Marie headed upstairs to change into more comfortable clothes than what she'd worn to work, Patricia followed her nose into the kitchen. Consuela was mixing the batter for a chocolate cake.

Using her finger, Patricia scraped batter from the edge of the bowl and popped it in her mouth. "Are we expecting company?"

"No." She nodded toward the cabinets. "Get the cake pans, would you? I forgot to get them ready."

Patricia dropped Justin Anthony's file on a counter cluttered with dishes and pots before digging out the aluminum cake pans. Consuela held the mixing bowl against herself with her left hand and beat its contents into submission with her right, all the while scowling as if the chocolate had committed some offense.

After spraying some oil on the pans, Patricia dusted them with flour and set them beside her.

Consuela kept whipping the batter.

"I have the pans ready."

When she didn't respond, Patricia touched her shoulder. She jumped.

"I have the pans ready for you," she said again. "Are you all right?"

"Si," Consuela answered, then she plunked the mixing bowl down on the countertop. "No. I am not all right. Nothing is all right."

She focused on Patricia, and her eyes filled with tears. "Buster is in much pain. The boys—they don't sleep. They fuss with each other all day. Mr. Ben and his men came over to help, and if it wasn't for them, nothing would get done. And I can't fix anything," she wailed. "I can't help. I can't make anything better for anyone. All I can do is cook. So I cook."

"Oh, Consuela, I'm sorry. This is overwhelming for all of us."

"And that's not the worst part." She waved toward the windows. Even though it was still daylight, the shade was drawn. "Somebody is out there watching us!"

For as long as Patricia had known her—admittedly, only a year—Consuela had always been rock solid. To see the old woman like this tore through her. "We're all on edge now, but maybe the sheriff will catch the guy soon."

"Him? Huh." She flapped her hand as if shooing a fly. "He and his men were here again today, looking over that hill. They didn't find anything that you and Talon didn't already know about."

"Did he say anything about that candy wrapper Talon gave him? Or the prints on the bullets?"

"No, not that I heard." Consuela drew a hand across her brow. She looked worn out with work and worry.

Patricia guided her to a chair in the little kitchenette. "You rest. I'll take over here."

"You don't know how to cook."

"I know enough to pour batter into a couple of pans and to wash dishes. You've cooked all you're going to today." She glanced around at the steam rising from pots and bowls and platters. "And probably tomorrow and the day after."

"No. We feed Ben and his men tonight before they leave. They put in a hard day's work."

"Oh. Good idea." She hadn't thought about that, though she should have. A hot meal was the only payment the ranching community would accept for helping a neighbor. "Let me fill the dishwasher, then I'll get Marie to help with the extra tables and chairs."

Once she finished in the kitchen, she tucked Justin's file away in her office and headed out in search of Marie.

So the guys had been bickering enough to upset Consuela. She couldn't say they never sniped at each other, but for the most part, hers was a harmonious ranch. Everyone treated each other like family. The tension that had settled over them like some demonic spirit was wearing everyone's patience thin, and she wanted it to stop.

Please, Father.

After everyone ate and said their thank-yous, complimenting Consuela on her cooking, the guys filtered out to visit with Buster in the bunkhouse. Patricia shooed Consuela and Marie from the kitchen and spent an hour cleaning it. By the time she'd given everything a satisfied nod, Talon came in.

"Been wondering where you were."

She wrapped her arms around his neck and basked in the warm glow emanating from his eyes. "I'm glad you found me. Consuela had such a rough day I thought I'd give her a break."

"Yeah, she didn't seem quite herself tonight. Everyone seemed a bit on edge today."

"So I heard. But I found something that may help settle all this." She crooked her finger for him to follow her, then led the way to the office.

She went to the desk to retrieve the file on Justin. "I think I'm building a case. I mean, this is totally outside my expertise. I've never investigated anything like this before. But I've found out a few things, and I think you should see them." She handed him the file. "Look at the dates."

As he studied the documents, he felt behind him for a chair, then dropped into it. "Justin Anthony? You think he's the one behind all this?"

"I don't know, but it's looking that way." She thumbed through the photos on her cell phone and found the best one of Justin's tire tread. "See this? It may match those tracks we found on the rise, and I think the width matches too. I measured his tires and took these pictures."

"You what?" Talon's voice rang with alarm. "Pat, what if you had gotten caught? How would you explain your actions?"

"Don't worry about that. I didn't get caught." She pointed at the picture. "What do you think? Does it match?"

"I don't know. I can't tell. Tons of trucks have that same tire, the same tread. They're not like fingerprints and snowflakes, all different. All the tires of a particular brand have the same width and tread. Maybe the wear is different, but I wouldn't be able to tell."

"Okay, maybe that doesn't prove anything, but what about the file? Aren't the dates a little suspicious to you?"

He rubbed his neck as he studied the file again. "Yeah, and it would explain why nothing like this has happened in all this time. But it's coincidence, Pat. I don't know how he ties in to Janet." He looked at her. "What made you ask for this file, anyway? What has you suspicious of him?"

She sat down beside him. "When Abby Jackson from the courthouse said she was surprised Chance would let him build the house, I just got curious. I mean, think about it. Their house is right adjacent to the pasture where we found the first dead cows, and you said yourself that he could just circle around from the construction site to Griff's land."

"Yes, but anyone could."

"But why would they?"

"Why would he?" He shook his head. "The one thing we know for certain right now is motive, and that motive centers around Janet. As far as I know, they never met."

"Griff said you used to take her to the rodeos. They could have met then. Katie figured they had anyway. She said he probably had a crush on her like everyone else in town."

"Yeah, everyone loved her. She was that kind of person." He rubbed his neck, kept his brows drawn while he thought, then shook his head. "I just don't see it. The reason she was at the rodeos is because we were together. Everyone knew that. If anyone had made an unwanted move on her in any way, I would've heard. She would've told me. If Justin had more than a crush on her—and if he'd acted on it—I would've known."

"Well, that's it, then." She took the file from him and tossed it on her desk. He'd effectively shot down all her ideas. She'd been grasping at straws anyway. "There was a lot of tension between Chance and Cody during dinner. What does he think?"

"He's still arguing that Colton's the only logical suspect." He pushed up from the chair and walked toward the window.

The sun had gone down, and Chef would soon take his shift with the cattle. Talon probably needed to get his rest before his turn, but Patricia still wanted to hear about Chance's suspicion.

"So, if he thinks Colton is the culprit, why was he glaring at Cody all night?"

"He says Cody and Janet knew each other somehow in Dallas. Maybe they met at a rodeo or something, I don't know, but apparently they hit it off and dated awhile. It wasn't too long after they broke up that I met her, and we started dating."

"That's motive for Cody, not Colton. And you said Colton was too young for Janet."

He shrugged. "As Chance said, blood's thicker'n water. Maybe the idea that Janet and I were going to get married hurt Cody pretty bad, and Colton got even with me for it."

She walked over to him. "I guess that would make sense, but it would be hard to prove."

"Sheriff Brewer has already eliminated Colton as a suspect, so I guess Chance is just doing what you're doing—trying to figure this out." He pulled her to his side. "At least you two have ideas who might be doing it. I don't even have a clue. Neither one of the guys makes sense to me, but no one else does either."

She slipped her arm around his waist. "You may be too close to the situation to see clearly."

"Maybe so."

"Wait a minute. You said Cody knew her from Dallas?"

"That's what Chance said."

"Did Cody and Justin ever run together?"

"Sure. Colton too. He'd always tag along with them until he started hanging with the guys from the Rocking T."

"Then it's possible Justin knew her before you started dating her too." She jabbed her finger on the file. "He was playing pool in Dallas when he got into his fight. There are pool tables in Stephenville, closer to where he lives. I bet that wasn't the first time he'd played there. I just wonder if Cody or Colton were with him."

"I have no clue."

He released a sigh that reminded her how tired he was, and suddenly guilt squirreled its way through her head. She'd kept him too long.

"You need to turn in," she said. "You must be beat."

"I am," he admitted. "It's been a long day. A good one, since the guys got the fence rebuilt in half the time Chance and I could've done it alone, but a long one just the same. Walk me out?"

As they strolled to the front door, he said, "Once Chef leaves, make sure all the doors are locked and the curtains are closed."

"Oh, don't worry, I will. Still gives me the creeps how vulnerable we've been."

"The sheriff said he found the break in Griff's fence up there where the guy's been cutting through to the rise over our house. He said he would set some deputies there to keep watch, see if he comes again. That should make you feel a little better."

"A little, but I still intended to close the curtains and lock the doors."

"Good girl." He kissed her again, then headed out into the sunset.

As she watched him walk away, she hugged herself, rubbing her arms against the chill. Some show on the TV sounded from the living room, and from the kitchen, the dishwasher hummed. Chance's and Marie's voices murmured from upstairs, and the furnace rattled heat through the vents. All normal, homey sounds she heard every night.

But somewhere out there, someone had been watching the house with a heart full of hate.

Chapter Twenty-Three

After working in a stuffy store all the past week, sitting astride Tandy in the crisp morning air felt heavenly, but today's task made Patricia uncomfortable—and not because she was riding drag.

She sneezed as the cattle in front of her kicked up dust and residue from dead grass. Talon had talked her into wearing a bandana around her neck before they left this morning, and now she knew why. Though how she managed to get herself in the position of riding behind the herd still mystified her. Chance rode point, and Talon and Chef flanked the herd. All she had to do was bring up the rear and sneeze. Having the bandana over her nose didn't help that much, but it beat being without it.

Talon dropped back and reined Bodine alongside Tandy. He stared at her like he was investigating some strange phenomenon. "You in there somewhere?"

With her hat brought low over her eyes and the bandana covering her nose, he probably couldn't see much of her face at all—and what he could see was probably grimy.

Whether he could see her glare at him was answered when he said, "Sorry about you're winding up back here. It's just the way everyone landed. Want to ride flank?"

"No, I'm fine," she said around the grit in her throat. At breakfast, when Talon announced that they'd move the herd up to Griff's land today, red flags had flashed in her head. She hadn't argued with him in front of the men, but now she needed to understand his logic. "Is this really smart? We're putting the cows where we know the bad guy's been. It's like we're handing them over to him."

"I know it sounds crazy, but this pasture is about done in." He kept an eye out for strays as he answered. "We have too many cattle for what's left of the forage here to sustain. And I'm not comfortable moving them down to either of the other pastures where the grass near the ponds has been poisoned."

He was right. And besides, the jerk had already proven he could go anywhere he wanted. "Did Ben and his crew help you guys divide out the range?"

"No. We'll just try to keep the herd together while we put a fence between the pastures."

"That could take days."

He shrugged. "We don't have much of a choice right now."

She eased behind a cow and ushered it back to the herd stringing along the trail ahead of them, then trotted to Talon. "So, do you think we'll have to double up on the guard?"

"I've been thinking about that. If Frank and Chef could team up from sundown to midnight or so, that would leave Chance to keep an eye on everyone in the main house and me to keep an eye on Buster. Then we could switch places, and Chance and I would ride guard until sunup."

"It gets dark early this time of year. You guys would be pulling five-hour shifts." She shook her head. "To pull those hours, then work a full day—that's too much."

Talon rose up on his stirrups and watched the cattle in the distance. "They're bottlenecking at the gate. We'll have to talk about this later."

He tore out after a few cattle that strayed away, then started yelling, keeping the herd moving through the gate and across the road. Patricia kept them moving from behind at a nice, easy pace. Since beef cattle were sold by the pound, she didn't want any of them to lose an ounce from being trotted from pasture to pasture.

According to what the Ag Extension guys had said, the other pastures were probably safe by now, if the firemen had done a good job of flooding the affected areas. But Talon was right to be skeptical about whether the cyanide had been completely eliminated. They'd already lost too many cattle to risk—

Potassium cyanide. That was the missing link between everything that had happened and Justin Anthony. She'd bet the ranch on it.

Talon had been skeptical when Pat told him about her evidence against Justin, but as she laid everything out for Sheriff Brewer, he could see her point. It was all circumstantial, but it fit.

"He was in Dallas the night Janet was murdered," she told the sheriff. She pulled out the arrest report from her file and turned it so he could see. "Compare the date and time to what's on her report."

Sheriff Brewer rubbed his jaw. "His sentence would explain why he took this long to retaliate if he thought Talon killed her."

"Yes, and look at this." She showed him the picture of Justin's necklace. "He told me he made this himself. I've seen him wear it—actually, I don't think he ever takes it off—and guess what?"

The sheriff lifted his gaze from the photo to her. "Can't guess."

"It's gold-plated."

She gave him a final nod as if she figured that explained everything. Frankly, Talon hadn't caught the connection either until she told him. Looked like he wasn't the only one who was ignorant of jewelry-making techniques. Sheriff Brewer gave her a puzzled look.

"Don't you get it?" she asked. "Potassium cyanide is used for gold plating. And the first pasture where it was found is right next to Marie's house—the one he's working on."

"Yeah, but you have to have a commercial address to receive a shipment of it. Feds don't allow it to go just anywhere."

For a moment, she looked defeated. That was one tidbit of information neither of them had known. But her disappointment lasted only a second. She whipped out the photo of Justin and his team she'd printed from his website and stabbed it with her finger. "Look in the background. Anthony Construction and Renovation."

"That would work." The sheriff nodded, but then reversed the movement of his head, shaking it in skepticism. "But what connection did he have to Janet?"

"That's something we haven't figured out yet," Talon said.

"Would've helped if you could. Might be just what we need to call it a wrap." Brewer studied the photos and file pages Pat had provided and shook his head again. "Pretty flimsy evidence."

"Yes, but it's all we have," she said. "Unless you were able to lift fingerprints from that piece of candy wrapper."

"Or the notes he left me," Talon added.

"Haven't heard back on those yet, or about the prints on the bullets. Janet's case is cold, so it doesn't have a high priority. And the felony mischief going on at your place doesn't rank at all. It would help if we had our own lab and equipment, but low-population areas like ours have to rely on the state or the larger cities to fit us in. Right now, we don't fit in." Sheriff Brewer leaned back in his chair with the photo of Justin's necklace in his hand. "The potassium cyanide's got me curious. He wouldn't need much for electroplating, would he?"

Pat shrugged. "I didn't research it that closely, but I wouldn't think so."

"He poured a good amount of it around those ponds, so he must have some other use for it."

"It's an insecticide too," she said. "Maybe he uses it as a prep for building sites like Marie's house."

"Could be. Seems like that'd be dangerous though." He eyed the paperwork in front of him, then slapped his desk as if he'd made a decision. "All right. Looks like you've given me something to think about. I reckon we'll look into this.

See what we can come up with. Like I said, I can sure see how you're connecting the dots. I wish we had a clear connection to Janet's murder, but it'll be interesting to see where this leads."

"Great. Thanks, Sheriff." Talon all but jumped from his chair to shake the man's hand. Maybe at last they'd make some progress on this, and life could return to normal.

As they left the office and headed for the truck, Talon squeezed Pat's hand. "This is good. This is real good. I feel like celebrating."

Pat slanted a glance his way. "For someone who was hesitant to bring me down here, you sure are excited now."

"I've had time to mull it over. It makes perfect sense to me now."

"Let's just hope it makes perfect sense to him. Maybe he can fill in some gaps." They gave way to a bundle of giggling teenage girls strolling toward them, then she asked, "Have you said anything to Chance about this?"

"Not the specifics the way you've laid them out. He shakes his head every time I bring it up. Doesn't think it's Justin. Says he's been doing a great job on the house and Marie feels safe with him. The guy's never done anything to make Chance suspicious, so he won't hear anything I have to say about it."

"I'm glad he's been doing a good job. If it is him—and I think it is—I hope he can finish the house before Sheriff Brewer gets him."

Talon chuckled. "Maybe we should put a hold on the investigation until it's done."

"No. I just want everything to work out right. A happy ending all around. Except for him, of course. I hope the deputies are there to arrest him the moment he hammers in the last nail."

When they got to the pickup, Talon opened her door for her. But before he helped her in, he pulled her into his arms. "You're amazing, you know that?"

Her sweet lips lifted in a sly smile. "Good of you to finally notice."

"Finally? I've noticed from day one." He pointed across the street. "We're right here at the courthouse, and the offices aren't closed yet. Let's go get our marriage license."

"Right now?"

"Why not?"

The skepticism in her eyes shifted to excitement. "Let's do it!"

He locked the truck again, then grabbed her hand and ran with her, crossing the street as soon as traffic allowed. He could've run to the moon and back as long as she ran with him. Other than the actual proposal, this marked their first positive movement toward getting married. Finally! Enough of the negative distractions and bad memories and painful dreams. He was ready to move on. He needed to move on.

At the top of the courthouse steps, he turned her toward him and held her by the shoulders. "Why don't we just get married while we're here?"

She released a happy laugh as she shook her head. "I think there's a waiting period. Besides, even if we do elope, I'd still want Marie with me."

He huffed out his breath. So much for being spontaneous. But she was right. "I'd want Chance too. Can't blame a guy for trying."

Her laughter lifted his heart and sent it floating like a hot air balloon. He'd promised they'd be married this year. He'd make it happen.

Chapter Twenty-Four

A strange car sat in front of the house when they returned, and Patricia's heart lodged in her throat. What now? The vehicle didn't bear any identification that she could see from the entry gate—no side-door emblem marking it as a squad car or Ag agent's vehicle, and the vet always drove a pickup, so it wasn't likely to be his.

"I wonder who's here?" Patricia muttered.

"No telling."

Other than riding drag this morning, she'd had a good day. The sheriff would follow up on her lead. Her purse held the newly acquired marriage license, evidence that Talon did not intend to wait, bless him. Her hand felt safe and warm in his. With the exception of some idiot targeting her ranch and ruining their harmony, things were going well. Strange cars gave her the jitters.

As they drew closer, Chef came out of the house. He popped open the car's trunk with the key fob and started pulling out luggage. Aunt Adele's luggage. Undoubtedly, the mismatched cosmetic case Chef pulled out with it belonged to Mama.

Patricia groaned. "My family is here."

This was Monday, three days before Thanksgiving. She thought she would have at least until Wednesday before she had to deal with family issues. Had Congress let out early?

Talon eased on the brake. "Do you want me to let you out here?"

"I guess so."

He studied her. "You look like a scared calf. It can't be all that bad."

"Oh, it can be. I dread this." She shifted her eyes from Chef and the luggage back to Talon and flicked her fingers toward the windshield. "Keep driving. We can put the truck in the shed."

"Not much of a delay tactic."

She bit back a remark about the humor in his voice. This wasn't funny. "Daddy wanted—no, *ordered*—me to fix the rift between Mama and me. And I want to. But I can't because she won't talk to me." She sighed and stared out the glass. "When I think about how I acted that last day, the way I lashed out at her, I just cringe. I can't believe how vicious I was. And I hate it. Coming face to face with the old Patricia shames me and makes me realize how much I've changed since accepting Jesus."

Talon backed into the shed and turned off the motor. "She's here. She can't avoid you during the entire visit. Now's your chance to apologize."

"I know, and I'm going to. But, Talon, I swear I meant every word I said. I can't allow her to continue to control my life. And I certainly can't allow her judgmental attitudes toward this ranch to affect me. I love it here. She'll simply have to deal with that fact."

"You can apologize for your argument without apologizing for the content. But you'll need to find a nicer way to tell her."

"I know."

She hung her head, and while it was bowed, Talon prayed for her. "Father, You know what's in both Pat's and her mother's hearts, and I pray You'll guide them back to love and forgiveness for each other. Help them to mend their fences, Father. Amen."

"And give me courage, Father," Patricia added. "Amen."

By the time she got into the house, Consuela was telling Chef to put the luggage in Patricia's room.

Aunt Adele frowned. "I thought we would stay in my room."

"Chef and me—we stay in that room right now. I moved your things."

Patricia cringed inwardly. She hadn't thought of the sleeping arrangements. Since Marie's house wasn't finished, she and Chance had taken over one of the smaller bedrooms, and Chef and Consuela had taken over the other. That left her room, the master. She shifted her eyes to the living room. A pillow and some blankets occupied a sofa cushion, and a small overnight bag had been propped on the floor in front of it. At least Consuela seemed to have figured everything out.

"You and Chef are staying here?" Aunt Adele looked at Patricia, then back at Consuela. "I thought you two had your own home."

Consuela explained as she and Aunt Adele followed Chef up the stairs.

Patricia gave her mother a hug. "I'm glad you're finally here, but I didn't expect you until Wednesday." She looked through the windows. "Where's Daddy?"

"He's coming later in the week. Congress isn't on break yet."

Talon came in and gave her mother a one-armed hug and a kiss on the cheek. "Hi, Mom. How was the flight?"

Hi, Mom? He'd been a nervous wreck talking to her dad on Skype, but for her, he said *hi, Mom*? One would think they were old friends.

"It is good to finally meet you in person," Mama said with a sparkle in her eye. She actually gave him one of her genuine smiles—not the one reserved for politicians and polite society, but one containing true affection. Patricia hadn't seen that one much lately.

Talon grinned. "It's great to meet you too."

She took him by the shoulders as if measuring the width of them—the impressive width of them. To Patricia, he had always looked like he could carry the weight of the world. Mama finished looking him over and met his gaze. "I understand what my daughter sees in you. You're not only a nice-looking young man, you have kind eyes."

"I told you so," Aunt Adele said as she came back down the stairs with Consuela on her heels. "You had nothing to worry about."

Talon tipped his hat. "It was fun talking to you, but I have to get back out there while there's some daylight left. Good to see you, Miz Adele." When Chef joined them, Talon clapped him on the shoulder. "Ready?"

As they walked out the door, Patricia's heart sank. She needed Talon's fortifying presence. But she brought her chin up and offered her mother a smile. "Why don't I show you the house? Marie and I had it remodeled last year. Texas chic, we call it."

"Si," Consuela said. "I have a new stove and everything."

Patricia put her nose to the air. "Is that enchiladas I smell? Mama, you'll love her enchiladas. They're a ranch favorite."

"They are good," Aunt Adele said. High compliment, considering she'd flown in her own personal chef earlier in the year.

For some reason, the polite um-hmms Mama made as Patricia showed her from room to room got on her nerves. Why did she need her mother's approval anyway? This was her house—actually, it was everyone's house. Where they ate and visited and gathered to watch sports. Where they prayed together and teased each other and showed how much they cared. They'd never entertain diplomats and high society, so the homeyness of it suited her—

"I just love this," her mother said. "It's perfect! I don't believe I'd change a thing. It suits you. The new you. You've done a wonderful job."

Patricia clamped her jaw tight to keep it from hanging open, then managed to squeak out a thank you. "You really like it?"

Mama put an arm around her. "I really do."

Elation gave way to guilt—again. She'd been feeling that an awful lot lately.

Maybe this Thanksgiving week, she and her mother would have something to truly be thankful for.

"You're lookin' right fine, Dellie," Frank said as he passed the platter of enchiladas to her. "A little break from ranch life must've been good for you."

Patricia missed the response as she shifted her eyes from Frank and her aunt to Mama, who had reacted exactly as she had expected. No one but Frank dared call Aunt Adele "Dellie." Despite Mama's upbringing and social graces, her eyebrows traveled up her forehead. When Aunt Adele thanked him with a blush flowering her cheeks, Mama's brows disappeared into her hairline.

"It's good to be back and see everyone once again," Aunt Adele said. "A girl could get used to this place."

"It gets in your blood, don't it?" Consuela brought a casserole dish in each hand. She'd made double the enchiladas as if she'd expected these extra appetites to feed.

Aunt Adele rubbed her hands together. "Just wait until you taste these, Natalie. No one makes them like Consuela. Even Chef Gregory can't quite get it right. He keeps wanting to improve upon them. Now I ask you—how can you improve perfection?"

Consuela turned bright red and tittered like a school girl all the way back into the kitchen.

After she returned with the rest of the side dishes, everyone bowed for Talon's prayer, then Aunt Adele turned her attention toward Patricia. "Now, about the wedding. Have you at least picked out a dress?"

"Not yet." This was it. The dreaded interrogation. She'd expected this question ever since the guys had slapped Talon's back and congratulated him about getting the license. At least this time she could say something encouraging. "But I have flipped through a few of the catalogs Marie gets at the Quad-B. I've narrowed it down to three."

She didn't care to admit she couldn't afford any of them.

Her aunt nodded. "That's a start. Have you considered a Christmas wedding? You said you wanted a small, informal ceremony. That shouldn't take too long to arrange."

"I'm sure it would take longer than a few days. Actually, Talon and I—"

"A Christmas wedding would be great," he said with his full fork hovering over his plate.

She glowered at him. He popped the bite into his mouth and winked at her.

"Oh, good. I was hoping you'd like the idea," Aunt Adele said. "I found a perfect venue in your area that could hold a cozy group of a hundred or so, and it's available on Christmas eve, but we have to act quickly. After supper we'll fire up the computer, and I'll show you—"

"Now, Adele," Mama scolded lightly. "We agreed we wouldn't try to influence Patricia in her decisions."

"I agreed to no such thing," Aunt Adele replied. "Now, Patricia, you just say the word, and we'll put a deposit down for you."

"Won't hurt to look," Talon said.

"No, I guess it won't." Once again, Patricia felt outnumbered, and it wasn't even her mother leading the pack.

Mama had seemed uneasy, not really speaking except when something was expected of her. Patricia had tried to make her feel more welcome, more at ease, but now that the conversation had shifted to the wedding, she felt ill at ease herself.

She glanced from Chance and Marie to Frank, who occasionally eyed Aunt Adele. She watched Chef stealing bites of cheese from Consuela's plate and Consuela's teasing swats. How she'd learned to love these people. She missed Buster, but his arm would be out of the cast soon, and he'd be better able to maneuver on his crutches so he could join them. Chance would witness their wedding regardless of the plans, but she couldn't imagine the other guys not being there. Or Chef and Consuela. How could she get married without Consuela there? Maybe eloping wasn't that great of an idea.

Consuela turned to Aunt Adele. "Why can't they get married at the church? It's a cowboy church. A nice arena. And it would hold a hundred or more."

Marie shook her head. "The arena is definitely out. I know it doubles as our church home, but no woman's going to want all that sand in her shoes."

Patricia had wondered when those two would enter the debate. The guys kept their heads down and cleaned their plates of second servings.

"Sand?" Her mother looked appalled, her first unveiled response to anything that had happened since they arrived. Aside from Frank calling Aunt Adele *Dellie*. "I can't imagine—"

Consuela waved the comment away. "Women around here know better than to wear sandals out there anyway."

"But sandals go with wedding attire," Marie argued. "Besides, who says the invitation list is going to be restricted to the women around here?"

Patricia sipped her tea and listened to the women in her life plan her wedding. The only person of true importance who wasn't at the ranch right this moment was Daddy. And she'd want him at the wedding too. When it came right down to it, she didn't care where they got married, or when, as long as everyone she loved could be there.

Talon leaned toward her and whispered, "What's on your mind?"

"I was just thinking, I don't want to elope. I want everyone here to share in this with us. But I don't want a big production, either." She nodded toward Marie and Consuela, who were still arguing over venues. "Those two are almost as bad as Mama and Aunt Adele. We can start with a small gathering, but the more they talk, the bigger this thing will get."

"Hey, it's your wedding. You make the final decisions."

"Are you okay with a small ceremony instead of eloping?"

"Sure, and I'm certain Griff won't care one way or the other, but you'd better speak up."

She glanced again at the women, each talking over the other, discussing plans that no longer mattered to Patricia as long as they resulted in her getting married. "I think I'll wait until they get this out of their systems."

He leaned toward her and whispered, "Don't let them get too carried away. And don't forget to pick a date."

Frank got up from the table and went to the kitchen to retrieve a plate. When he returned, he began to fill it with enchiladas.

Consuela rose and swatted at him. "Let me do that."

"Naw, you go ahead and plan the weddin' with the ladies. I can fix Buster up." He finished loading the plate, then raised a brow at Talon. "You comin'? Ain't much time to rest tonight if you stay too long."

"Yeah, I'm comin'." He kissed Patricia's cheek as he rose. "Love you. See you in the morning."

"I best get out there. It's already dark." Chef fell in line between Frank and Talon, and after saying good night and thanking Consuela for the "good grub," filed out.

Soon, Chance was the only man left in the dining room.

"What's going on?" Aunt Adele sent a quizzical look to Chance, then shifted her eyes to Patricia. "Where are they going? I don't remember this being part of the nighttime routine."

The question caught her off guard. "They're ... umm ..."

Chance jumped in and rescued her. "We've moved the herd to a new pasture. Gotta take turns watching over them during the night to make sure they stay safe. You know, until they figure out their boundaries."

A flush crept up his neck and reddened his ears, a sure sign he was lying. But Aunt Adele and Mama didn't know it. Aunt Adele nodded as if understanding the logic behind the practice. Marie rolled her lips between her teeth to stifle a giggle, but her amusement revealed itself in her eyes. Patricia shot her a warning glare.

Consuela started collecting the dishes. "I better get started. These won't wash themselves."

"Let me help," Mama offered. She stacked together the plates around her, but Consuela took them from her.

"Tonight, you're a guest. You're probably tired after your long trip."

"Oh, it's early yet," Aunt Adele said.

"Yes, but I'm still on New York time, and I do feel a bit tired." Mama turned to Consuela. "If you're sure it's all right, I may go up and soak in the tub for a while."

"It's fine." With an arched brow, Consuela nodded toward Patricia and Marie. "I have all the help I need right here."

Mama rested her hand on Patricia's arm. "Actually, I was hoping to have a few moments alone with my daughter. Can you spare her?"

Consuela gave her a knowing look. "I can spare her. You two talk."

Patricia lowered a casserole of leftover enchiladas to the table before the dread weakening her limbs made her drop it. She really hadn't planned on a confrontation between the two of them just yet. *Give me wisdom, Lord.*

Patricia perched on the edge of the bed as Mama put away the clothes from her luggage. Apparently, Consuela had thought to clear drawers and closet space for both Mama and Aunt Adele, but when did she have the time? The woman truly was a wonder.

"This is a nice house." Mama deposited a stack of sweaters in the top drawer of Patricia's dresser. "I don't know what it looked like before you and Marie worked your magic, but it's truly appealing now."

"I was afraid you'd find it too rustic." Patricia sat on her hands to keep from fidgeting. She'd offered to help unpack, but Mama waved her away.

"It is rustic, but in a good way." Mama looked at her with eyes that held understanding and a hint of admiration. "It suits you, and I should have realized that it would."

"I don't know how you'd realize it. There's nothing in my life's history that indicates I'd prefer ranch life over the City."

"Oh, but there is. When you started riding, you preferred the stables over the stores, and in college you never allowed a groom to put your horse away. You could take days to train a horse, but get impatient and snippy with a senator's aide within minutes."

"I never had much tolerance for their bloated egos."

"Me either," Mama confessed, then sat beside her and took her hand, tracing the calluses in her palm without a glimmer of judgment in her features. "Honey, I've been thinking about what you said ..."

Patricia cringed. "Oh, I am sorry. I don't know what got into me. I was horrible."

Mama raised her hand to stop her flow of words. "No. You were right. It's never pretty taking a barefaced look in the mirror, but you made me see myself, and I'm ashamed."

"But you were only doing what you thought was right."

"Yes, but my concept of right and wrong was skewed, wasn't it? The right thing would have been to support you against Kent. To recognize that you were an adult and needed to make your own decisions." She shook her head, her face sad, her spirit broken. Seeing her this way was almost impossible to bear. "Instead, I worried about the scandal and about your father's career and, worse, about my own place in society." Her pain and penitence reflected in her eyes, and Patricia's heart clutched. "I just hope you can forgive me."

"No, you're right too. I am an adult. As much as I love and appreciate your opinion and counsel, I need to take responsibility for the major decisions in my life." She sighed. "But I was so indecisive at that time, so unsure of myself, that it just seemed easier to take your advice, then blame you when things didn't go right."

Mama offered a sympathetic smile. "We've both made mistakes. I love you, sweetheart. Can we put all this behind us?"

Patricia nodded and swallowed the lump in her throat. "I'd like that."

She rushed into her mother's open arms. "I'm sorry I talked to you like that. I didn't mean to hurt you. I don't know what got into me."

"It's over now, baby, and you were right." She smoothed Patricia's hair, then cupped her face with tender hands. "One thing I know for certain. The way Talon looks at you, I can tell—he's very much in love. You'll never have the trouble with him that you did with Kent. And I'm happy for you."

"I'm happy for me too." She grinned, feeling almost giddy with the joy bubbling inside. Maybe now they could develop that mother-daughter friendship Consuela had talked about.

Chapter Twenty-Five

C onsuela sprinkled cinnamon into two mugs of hot chocolate, then set one of the mugs in front of Patricia on the old dinette table in the kitchen. "As late as your mama stays up in New York, I'm surprised she's already asleep now."

"It's nine o'clock back east, but still, you're right. It's early for her and Aunt Adele both. They must've been tired." Patricia stirred the cinnamon into her cocoa. Chef and Frank were taking the early shift with the herd. And since Chance would take over, partnering with Talon at midnight, he and Marie were also in bed. Patricia should've been asleep by now, since her watch began when Talon's did, but her talk with her mother had her wired.

"So, you and your mama are good now?" Consuela hadn't actually read her mind. She'd probably been itching to hear a detailed account since Patricia came down from her mother's room.

"I think so." She sipped from the mug, then cradled it in her hands. "And I think you were right. She doesn't like the distance between here and Manhattan. But being here, seeing the house, and meeting the people have helped. Now when she thinks of me living in Texas, she won't have an image of the wild West."

"What about the fight you two had? Is that all better too?"

"Believe it or not, *she* apologized to *me*. I wasn't expecting that." The phone rang while she spoke. She got up and picked up the receiver on the wall phone by the kitchen window. "Circle Bar Ranch."

"Miz Pat? Sheriff Brewer here. Looks like you were right about ... "

An orange glow brightened the window, distracting her from whatever the sheriff had to say. She brushed the curtain aside for a better look.

"*Fire!*" The new pasture blazed, pinning the cattle between the flames and the barbed wire fence. She dropped the receiver and turned to Consuela. "Go get Chance up. We have to save the cattle!"

Consuela stared out the window with her mouth agape. "*¡Dios mio!*"

Patricia darted into the living room and nabbed her boots. As she yanked the first on, Chance and Marie scrambled down the stairs.

"Pat! Fire!" Chance shouted.

"I know. I know. I saw it." She reached for her other boot. "Get out there!"

On his way out, he grabbed his coat and hat from the hook by the door. "Call the sheriff."

Patricia could've smacked her head. "The sheriff! He was just on the phone."

"Is okay," Consuela shouted. "I told him. He comes."

Marie's eyes were wide and her face pale. "How do you think it happened?"

"I don't know, but I have my suspicions." Patricia grabbed her gun and checked to make sure it was loaded.

"*Patricia!*" Mama gawked at her from the stairs. Aunt Adele watched from over Mama's shoulder with her fingers splayed over parted lips. This was not a good time to explain her new firearm, especially not if that maniac was still out there.

"Stay inside and lock the door," she ordered. "It'll be all right."

Her mother stared at the gun, then back at her. "What are you going to do with that thing?"

"I'm going to protect my ranch."

As she strode out the front door, she tucked the gun into the back of her waistband and looked up the hill behind the house. With the pasture grass being as dry as it was, the glow from the fire devoured more land by the instant, trapping the herd. She felt sick. All the cattle were up there. All of them. The ranch's entire livelihood.

The only thing the men could do was to cut the new fence line and let them out.

And they must've done just that. Soon, the cattle began racing around either side of the house, charging ahead in different directions. Those going to the left could be out on the highway in a matter of moments. She had to get out in front of them and turn them before they followed the ranch road right off the property.

She sprinted to the barn and saddled Tandy in record time. The cattle's hooves thundered outside, their bawls reverberated through her nerves and amped up her tension. The herd could go anywhere. It would take forever to round them up again.

Grabbing the reins, she raised up in the stirrup, ready to sling her leg over Tandy's back. Then saw the soft gleam of the barn light on the barrel of a shotgun leveled at her middle.

"Uh-uh, missy," Justin said. "Step down from there."

She eased down, keeping the reins in her hand. "You can't get away with this. The sheriff's coming."

"We won't be here. We'll be long gone." He twitched his gun toward his left. "Drop the reins and let's go."

With her heart pounding, she took a step forward, reaching to her back for her pistol.

The click of the hammer cocking on the shotgun paralyzed her. She darted a nervous glance from his gun to his hard, cold eyes. He'd kill her. Put her down like a nuisance cat and not think twice about it.

Holding the weapon in one hand, he waggled the fingers of his other. "Hand it over, real slow."

She stretched her pistol out to him, grasping it between her thumb and forefinger like she'd seen on TV. Her voice shook as she asked, "Why are you doing this?"

"Quid pro quo," he said as he walked toward her, reaching for her firearm. "Talon took my girl, now I'm taking his."

She dropped the gun with a thud on the packed dirt and slapped her horse. *"Hee-yah!"*

Tandy charged, knocking Justin to the ground as he galloped away. The shotgun fell from Justin's hand, discharging one of its shells in a deafening blast. She grabbed her pistol, then kicked his weapon toward the alfalfa bales behind her.

As she stood over him with her gun trained on his heart, he studied her in the dim light. Calculated whether she'd shoot. Whether she had the nerve. She could see it in his eyes, discern it in his calm regulated breathing.

If she hadn't spent years masking her emotions in the political arena, he would've been able to read her. He would've realized she'd locked her knees to keep them from shaking, that she couldn't peel her cramped fingers from the gun's grip if she tried, that her panting breath wasn't from adrenaline.

Gaining the advantage over him had been sheer instinct. Now she needed to think. But only one thought echoed in her head—she'd never wanted to point a gun at another human being.

Then, in the briefest instant between inhale and exhale, the image of Buster's broken and bruised body crossed her mind.

"Buster's injuries are your fault." Her voice was low, controlled. "And you're the one who has been killing our cattle and destroying our property. Why? Because of Janet? What was she to you?"

"You think I'm gonna talk with that gun aimed at my chest?" His velvety tone sent anger roiling through her veins. His voice was too smooth, too confident. The gun didn't scare him because a woman was holding it. The man had been in prison. Very little was likely to scare him.

He raised up to his knees, keeping one hand palm-forward. She eased backward a step, not knowing whether to shoot, but afraid to pull the trigger.

He got up and raised both hands. *See? I'm harmless*, his motions said. But his eyes sought a weakness in her. An opportunity to attack.

She shifted her finger from the trigger guard to the trigger itself. If he took one step ...

"Janet must've meant something to you," she said. "Why else would you risk violating your parole? Returning to prison? Who was she to you?"

"Put the gun down, and we'll talk about it."

Outside, men shouted orders at each other and at the stampeding cattle. The smell of dead, burning grass permeated the barn, dominating the scents of hay and horsehide. Too much happened outside for anyone to notice them in here.

Testing her resolve, Justin took a step.

She blasted the ground in front of him.

He jumped back, raising his arms again.

"Did you kill her?" she demanded.

"You wanna know? Put the gun down."

"You think I'm stupid?"

"I think you're curious. I think you really want to know so you can tell your precious boyfriend out there."

"My bet is the sheriff will get it out of you."

Justin shook his head. "I won't be here. You'll either kill me, or I'll be gone. You know how long it takes the sheriff to get here."

At least twenty minutes. How much time had already elapsed? Where was Brewer when he called? She needed to keep Justin here until he arrived. If only he'd hurry.

"Fine." She stretched her arms out to either side but didn't drop the gun. "Who killed her?"

"Talon did."

"The authorities have already proven he didn't."

"He didn't pull the trigger, but he's to blame."

She shook her head. "I don't understand."

"He moved. I was aiming at him, but he moved. He's supposed to be dead—not her. I didn't mean to kill her." He reached his right hand behind his back. "You, on the other hand ..."

She swung the gun around, holding it with both hands. "Stop! Don't move!"

The steel blade of a four-inch knife glinted in the light as Justin covered half the space between them in one step.

"No!" She shouted.

And fired.

Blood spread on the shoulder of his white T-shirt. He glanced at it without so much as a wince, then laughed. "All that target practice, and you can't kill me from this distance?"

"No," Sheriff Brewer growled behind him, "but I can."

Chapter Twenty-Six

B y sunup, the Circle Bar Ranch looked like a parking lot. A smoky, smoldering parking lot full of official-looking sedans and pickups. The fire trucks stayed on the hill behind the house, where the men kept an eye open for any flare-ups. The sheriff's and deputies' vehicles were parked helter-skelter at the barn; those khaki-clad guys were all over the place. Sheriff Brewer had shoved Justin in the back of one of the vehicles.

Flying K trucks and trailers lined the side of the ranch road beyond the barn. Someone must've called Ben during the night, and he'd arrived with his crew early this morning. They helped round up the cattle and herd them into the same pasture Patricia and the guys had moved them from not twenty-four hours ago.

Staying out of their way, she sat on the porch of the bunkhouse, wrapped in a heavy saddle blanket. During all the excitement last night, she'd forgotten to throw on a coat.

Buster hobbled out to join her and flopped awkwardly onto a chair with his casted leg stretched out in front of him. "Reckon it's over now?"

"I sure hope so."

He eyed her. "I know it's taken a lot out of you."

"Yeah." It had changed her a lot too. The weight of a loaded pistol at her waistband was something she'd never expected to feel. She patted his hand. "It's taken a lot out of you too."

"All of us."

"Yep." She laughed to herself, realizing how very Texan she sounded. She belonged here.

Down the road, Talon and the others trotted their horses toward the barn, but when he saw her, he nudged Bodine to lope to her direction. She threw off the blanket and left the porch to meet him. As he neared, she could see the fatigue on his grimy face. He needed a full day of rest. They all did. At least one day.

He dismounted between her and the barn, then gave Bodine a swat, sending him back to join the other horses. She hastened her step, opening her arms to him and clutching him when he enfolded her in his.

"It's over," she said.

"Yes. Finally." He took and released a deep breath as if it were the first in days. "Has anyone pieced it all together yet?"

"It was Justin. It was all Justin. He killed Janet too. Sheriff Brewer heard him say it. But I still don't know how they knew each other or what she meant to him, though he called her *his* girl." She leaned back and looked Talon over. "Are you okay? Not hurt anywhere?"

"No, I'm all right. Everyone else seems to be okay too."

One of the deputies drove away with Justin, who glowered at her and Talon from the back seat. Sheriff Brewer watched from the porch with his fists on his hips. He caught a glimpse of Patricia and Talon and waved them over.

Talon wrapped his arm around her shoulders and guided her toward the house, but Frank called from behind them. "Don't walk too fast. I want to hear this too."

Inside, Marie hovered near the stairs with Mama and Aunt Adele. Each wore an expression of fear, concern, confusion. Especially her mother and aunt. Patricia had a lot of explaining to do.

She pulled the pistol from her waistband to return it to its case and caught Talon gaping at her.

"You used your gun?"

"We had an intruder."

"That's right," the sheriff said. He pulled a small notepad and pen from his pocket. "And all y'all have to fill me in on what went on overnight."

"This is going to take a while," Patricia said as she strode toward the kitchen. "I'll put some coffee on."

But Consuela already had the coffee brewing.

Patricia put her arm around her. "Let's get some sort of breakfast made for everyone, okay?"

"Si. That would be good."

Aunt Adele entered with Marie and Mama in tow and stopped Patricia as she went to the refrigerator.

"You need to be in there." Aunt Adele grabbed an apron. "I'll help in the kitchen."

"Are you sure?"

"I've been here a few months now. It's not like I've never cooked for a crowd before." She made shooing motions with her hands. "Go on. We've got this."

Mama gawked at her, then at Patricia. "What has happened to you two? This—all of this—is this what life is like out here? Is this what you have to live with? I don't understand."

"I know I owe you an explanation, Mama. It isn't like this all the time." She rubbed her forehead. "I'll tell you everything later."

In the living room, the sheriff sat on the edge of an armchair and listened to Chef and Frank as they described finding the fire during their shift. There wasn't much to tell about it; no one had seen how it started. Chef had raced to get Chance and Talon—probably about the same time Patricia and those in the house had noticed the flames.

"Consuela must've called the fire department," Patricia said.

"And me," Ben added.

"I'm glad she did." Talon seemed tired, overwhelmed after a night of chasing cattle. "We never would've saved the herd without you and your crew."

Patricia turned to the sheriff. "You called last night. What were you saying?"

"That you were right." Sheriff Brewer twisted his hat in his hands. "Based on the evidence you provided, we were able to get a search warrant for the office and grounds of Justin's construction company. Turned up a large supply of cyanide—more than enough to make a whole store worth of jewelry."

"I can't imagine what he'd need it for," she said. "Unless he bought it with the intent of poisoning our pasture."

"We intend to question him about that." He shifted his gaze to Talon, barely suppressing a grin. "But the big news is, his prints matched the ones on the bullets."

Talon straightened in his seat. "You mean ..."

Sheriff Brewer nodded. "We've got him."

As if the wind had been knocked out of him, Talon slumped against the back of the chair. "After all this time, it's over. It's finally over."

Chance let out a *whoop* that brought the women scurrying from the kitchen. Despite the riotous chatter of voices that followed, Patricia heard a timid knock on the front door, then a triple rap with a firmer fist.

Before she could answer, her father stepped inside. "What's going on out here?"

"You're here!" She threw her arms around him, her anchor, her safety net for the bulk of her life. For a few minutes, she could afford to be a little girl again, wrapping herself in her daddy's protective arms. "I didn't know you were coming."

"Your mother called last night. I got here as fast as I could."

In the chill and drizzle of the late afternoon, the Flying K and the Circle Bar crews stretched barbed wire from post to post—again. Third time for this fence. At least this time, the repairs weren't quite so severe. Unlike Justin, snipping wires helter-skelter in his mischief, Talon and Chance had been a little more careful about how and where they'd cut the fence to save the cows. Along with Ben and his crew's help, they'd have it repaired in no time.

Using the wire stretcher, Talon pulled the last line tight while Pat's dad wrapped its tail around a cross brace and secured it. Every time Talon glanced down the slope toward the house and realized how close that fire had come to the back porch, he felt sick at his stomach. Fifty yards. Half a football field. When Dale first saw it, his lips had drawn tight and fury smoldered in his eyes. But he never said a word.

Still hadn't said much, and Talon didn't want to push him. After Pat filled her parents in on all the events she'd kept from them over the past month or so—including her new status as a gun owner—he needed some time to digest it. When he joined the men to help repair the fence, wearing a pair of jeans and a denim jacket, he'd shown his Western roots. Best way to work through a problem was to work on the land. Talon had always believed it, and he was right proud to see Dale did too. No wonder Pat hadn't been afraid to dive in.

That she had defended herself against Justin put her on top of Talon's hero list, despite the fact she was still rattled from shooting the man. He could certainly understand. He'd never had to aim a gun at another human—though after hearing what she'd gone through as she reported it to the sheriff, he would have. And judging from Dale's reaction as she recounted the event, he would've had to stand in line.

Ben approached as Talon freed the wire stretcher. Cody and the others from the Flying K were filing down the hill toward their pickups. Chance caught up with Cody, and the two stood apart from the rest. Chance was probably apologizing for his behavior of late, but if Cody hadn't already forgiven him, he wouldn't've come to help. Unlike his brother, he was a good man. And though Colton was a hothead, he wasn't so bad. Just needed to grow up and lay off the booze.

"That's the last of it." Ben said. "And I hope it's the last time you have to work this fence."

"That makes two of us." Talon yanked his gloves off. "You stayin' for supper?"

"Not tonight, but Consuela invited us out for Thanksgiving tomorrow." His grin widened. "I know I'll have no trouble getting Sadie to agree."

Dale stepped up, joining the conversation. "It's going to be a good day."

The affirmation made Talon's chest swell. In the few hours he'd been on the ranch, Dale seemed have to accepted him and the other folks here. Considering the timing of his arrival, that said a lot. Thanksgiving day promised to be truly special all the way around.

"Really good to meet you, Senator." Ben shook Dale's hand, then turned and shook Talon's. "See you tomorrow."

"Can't thank you enough, Ben."

As he left, Talon began to retrieve his gear and stow it in the toolbox. He tossed the wire snips in and caught a glimpse of Dale surveying the land. From here, he could see the layout of the house and other structures and beyond to the distant hills forming the horseshoe around the pastures. Only the charred land they stood on ruined the peace of the scene, and it would be healed by spring.

"This is a beautiful place," Dale said, not taking his eyes from the scene. "I can see why Patty loves it here."

"She took to it right quick like she was born to it. She never ceases to amaze me."

Dale smiled at that. "During her entire life, she's never ceased to amaze me either."

The moment suddenly felt awkward, as if Dale were holding something back. Talon rapped the tack hammer against his palm and regarded his future father-in-law from beneath the brim of his hat. "You figure Pat should've told you what was happening around here?"

He gave Talon a pointed stare. "I figure someone should have."

"Maybe," he said. "And what could you have done?"

Dale blew out a breath. "I don't know." He shifted his gaze to the house as if he could see inside and watch over her from here. "I really don't know. But finding out she doesn't need me anymore after all these years ..."

Talon considered arguing the point, but he wouldn't have been convincing. Dale needed to hear it from her. Still, he couldn't leave it like that, either.

"I reckon she'll always need you. You're her dad." That a daughter always needed her daddy had better be true, because he wanted at least one girl in their passel of kids.

He clapped Dale on the shoulder. "C'mon. Supper's probably ready, and I bet the guys are hungry enough not to leave us any."

Patricia snuggled up to Talon in front of the hearth and gazed lazily into the fire. The clock ticked its way toward eleven, the latest they'd stayed up since they started babysitting the herd. Now that everything could return to normal, the household had shifted. Consuela and Chef went back to their own home, and Aunt Adele had reclaimed her room, leaving the master to Daddy and Mama.

Despite her long nap that afternoon, Patricia was tired. Tomorrow promised to be crazy with everyone here and those from the Flying K coming for Thanksgiving dinner, so she should go to bed. Talon needed to rest too, but she wasn't ready to let him go yet.

He rubbed his thumb along the back of her hand, watching the motion as he traced her veins. "I don't know that I could've done what you did, facing Justin like that."

"It wasn't me. I believe God gave me His strength and courage. I don't think I could've faced him without God there with me."

"Amen." He stayed quiet a few moments, still rubbing her hand, then he raised his eyes to meet hers. "Are you sorry you came out here? You know, the wild West. Cowboys and outlaws. Guns and shooting. Do you want to go back to civilization?"

She barked out a laugh. "You mean back to my old world, my old work, where the good guys and bad guys dress the same and shoot ammunition of innuendo and deceit? Where knives are plunged into backs, and character assassination is far more likely than physical death?" She returned her gaze to the flames. "No thank you. I'll take my chances here."

"When you put it like that, I don't blame you." He nuzzled her hair. "Your aunt's back at the ranch now—and your mother. Does that mean we have to start dressing up for dinner again?"

"Oh, I don't know. That's such a silly rule. I can't believe it went on as long as it did."

"Yeah, but let's humor her. At least for Thanksgiving. Besides, everyone's going to be here."

"Right. Everyone's going to be here in jeans and Western shirts and boots. Do you really think anyone's going to dress up for Thanksgiving?"

He shrugged. "You never know. Maybe it's our tradition to get all gussied up for a special occasion."

"If it is, it's a new one. I don't remember anyone wearing anything other than the usual last year."

"Adele wasn't with us at Thanksgiving last year. She's got us all cultured now."

Patricia met his eyes. "You *want* to put on your Sunday best?"

"Maybe. What would it hurt?"

She sighed. "I guess we could. At least it will keep the peace. Heaven forbid that Aunt Adele delay dinner while everyone changed clothes to meet her whim."

Her first night at the ranch, she'd done just that.

Chapter Twenty-Seven

C onsuela chased Patricia out of the kitchen. Again. Considering it was Thanksgiving day, and they'd intended to feed a hoard much larger than usual, Patricia thought she'd appreciate the help. But with Marie, Katie, and Sadie Kilgore coming to her aid with far more experience and expertise, Consuela had shooed Patricia away.

"Your parents are here. Go. Visit. We've got this."

She sighed and wandered into the living room. Ben and Daddy, each dressed in their best suits, swapped tales with the guys, while Aunt Adele and Mama, also fancied up, glanced through *Brides Magazine*.

Apparently, they had gone shopping yesterday while Patricia slept the day away and the guys worked on the fence. This morning, Marie had decked out the living room with huge sunflowers as if she'd always decorated for Thanksgiving. A wreath of them adorned the fireplace mantel, and bouquets of them sat in ribbon-wrapped vases throughout the room. One bundle, tied with a chocolate-brown and teal ribbon, lay across the coffee table.

She shot a glance at Talon, who leaned toward her father as if hanging on to every word he uttered. He must have felt her staring at him; he looked up and offered an innocent smile. He looked all scrubbed and ready for church. In fact, everyone and everything seemed overly fancy for such a casual feast.

"Patricia, dear, come look at this."

She wandered to the table set up near the window. Magazines and venue brochures shared space with pens, paper, and coffee mugs. Mama held up a picture of an amphitheater created in the hills. Descending the hill, bench seats on either side of a center aisle faced a simple stage with an acoustic covering. The surrounding landscape was lovely. It would be a perfect place for a play or concert. Or a wedding.

"What do you think?" Mama asked.

"It's gorgeous."

"Yes, but remember," Aunt Adele warned, "this is a winter wedding. Having an outdoor wedding in December is inviting disaster." She handed Patricia a different brochure. "This one seems best and definitely more your style. More your *new* style anyway."

She was right. A simple high-beamed barn with a concrete floor, all decked out with candles and garlands.

Aunt Adele pointed at a paragraph on the brochure. "After the wedding, the chairs can be stacked to clear the floor for a huge dance. Wouldn't that be nice?"

"It would, though I don't know about huge. Keep in mind I want a small, intimate wedding. Just a few friends."

Someone knocked on the door, but before she turned to answer it, she raised a brow at her mother and aunt. "Just a few of *my* friends, okay? Anyone I'd want from New York is right here in this house."

She opened the door to Griff's smiling face. He shifted his Bible from one hand to the other and gave her a side-arm hug. "Am I late?"

"Of course not. Come on in." Inwardly, she cringed. She hadn't invited him but would have, had the thought crossed her mind. Thankfully, it had crossed someone else's— someone who had invited him to offer the Thanksgiving prayer or something. Why else would he bring his Bible?

His pickup sat in front of the barn with a trailer attached.

"What do you have out there?" she asked.

"I brought a mare for you to look at." He waved a dismissive hand toward it. "No rush. She'll be fine."

She craned her neck, trying to see inside the trailer's small window opening. "Is she causing you problems? Something wrong with her?"

"Leaving that for you to say." He gave her a sly grin. "Reckon I can come in now?"

"Oh! Yes, of course." She ushered him into the living room and introduced him to her parents. "And you remember my aunt, Adele Cameron."

"Sure I do." He shifted his Bible from his right hand to his left and shook hands with everyone.

Talon's handshake seemed especially exuberant. His face glowed with excitement.

"Everyone's here," he announced, then looked at Chance. "You ready?"

Chance nodded, flashing his own broad grin. "Just let me get the women out of the kitchen."

Patricia looked from one to the other. "What's going on?"

Only a happy squeal from the kitchen responded, leaving her more confused than ever. Soon, Mama, Aunt Adele, Marie, and Consuela surrounded her and hustled her up the stairs to the master bedroom.

"It's time," Marie declared with a giggle.

"I can't believe we kept it a secret that long," Mama said.

"We played our roles perfectly." Aunt Adele fussed with Patricia's hair, while Consuela brought Patricia's makeup kit from the bathroom. "You didn't guess, did you?"

"Guess what? I have no idea what you're talking about!"

"You're getting married," Mama said. She pulled a simple tea-length dress from the closet. Holding it with the hanger in one hand and the bulk of the skirt over the other arm, she said, "Something new."

Patricia caught her breath. "It's beautiful. It's perfect."

The gown was a satin ivory with an embroidered sweetheart neckline.

"Something borrowed." Marie held out a pair of white cowboy boots with gold stitch work, the ones she'd worn for her wedding.

Aunt Adele opened a gift box from Tiffany's, revealing a small, tear-drop sapphire on a simple silver chain. "Something blue."

Consuela sidled up to them, tears glistening in her eyes. "Something old." In her hand sat a pair of ornate, antique Mexican earrings. "My mother gave me these when Chef and I married. I want you to have them."

Patricia fingered the silver scroll work and couldn't keep the tears from welling in her own eyes. "These are lovely. So special. Thank you." She gave them all a watery smile, still trying to take in what was happening. "I'm getting married."

"Yes, you are." Mama hugged her quickly, then released her. "And you need to get ready."

Patricia stepped out of the bedroom and found Daddy waiting for her at the head of the stairs. He opened his arms, and she rushed into them.

He held her close and whispered into her ear, "He's a good man. I like him. And I think you'll be happy here in this new life you're carving out."

Katie and Marie joined them, and Marie asked, "Ready?"

It took a moment for Patricia's head to stop spinning. "All this was Talon's idea, wasn't it? He arranged it?"

"Not entirely by himself," Marie said with a proud grin. "Perfect, isn't it?"

"Absolutely."

Marie and Katie had changed into teal dresses with dark, chocolate-brown sashes, matching the ribbons wrapped around the sunflowers each of them held. Marie shoved the bridal bouquet into Patricia's hands.

Downstairs, Talon and Frank escorted Mama and Aunt Adele to the sofa that faced the podium in front of the fireplace. The rest of the living room chairs and benches from the dining room made up the seating arrangement for the ceremony. After the women were seated, Chance strolled with Marie down the makeshift aisle, followed by Buster, hobbling along with Katie. They took their places on either side of the podium and looked up at her expectantly.

Patricia glanced around the room. Everyone who mattered to her was there, witnessing her step into a new life. A new chapter. Different from the one she'd left behind, yet perfect.

Her father squeezed her hand. "Are you ready?"

"Oh, yes," she whispered and took his arm. "I'm ready."

Marie signaled Chance, who grabbed his guitar and plucked out a rendition of Mendelssohn's "Wedding March."

As they walked down the stairs, Daddy patted her hand. His voice sounded strained as he said, "I'm going to miss you all the way down here."

She smiled. "That's why God made planes."

He laughed. "That's why indeed."

When they reached the front, her father coupled a handshake with a clap on Talon's shoulder. "I believe I'm giving her to a good man, son. Welcome to the family."

Daddy stepped back, and Griff took over, clearing his throat and glancing at the small group of friends and family. "It's been a long time since I performed a wedding, but I'm honored to do this one."

He shifted his gaze from Talon to Patricia. "You know, my Beth figured this was about to happen, and she was excited about it. Wish she was here to see it." He gave his head a quick shake, then cleared his throat again. "But this is about you two, so let's get to it."

Addressing those assembled, he said, "Talon and Pat have had a rough road to the altar this year, given everything that's been goin' on around here. But I think God was testin' their mettle. Trials build character. They strengthen our faith and bring us closer to Him. But they also prove to ourselves and to each other what we're made of. These two are made of powerful stuff. Their bond is solid, and their union will be strong. Based on what we've seen of them as they've endured this test, we can be assured they'll face whatever lies before them with the same faith, strength, and character they've faced these past few weeks.

"Now these two are released from the burdens of the past and ready to take on the future. I know God's going to bless their union." He looked at Talon. "Y'all have the rings?"

Patricia's heart skipped a beat. She'd bought Talon's ring but didn't have it with her—she didn't even know she was getting married today.

But Marie did, and with a wink, she pressed the ring into her hand.

The vows, the I dos, the exchange of rings, all faded into memory with their first kiss as a married couple.

Thank you, Father, for this remarkable man.

How Consuela and the others had managed to pull off such an amazing Thanksgiving feast in such a short period of time was puzzling. But after the meal, she rolled a cart holding a three-tiered wedding cake from the kitchen to the dining room, and Patricia was floored. When had that happened?

Camera phones snapped pictures as she and Talon cut the first slice. She held a warning finger up at the idea he'd smash the piece in her face. "I'm not that traditional, so don't you dare."

He laughed and smudged her nose with a fingertip full of icing. Her scowl faded when he kissed it off, then kissed her lips.

"Okay, enough of that," Griff chided. "When are you going to give her her present?"

Talon flashed a grin. "Is it time?"

"It's going to be dark soon. Reckon you'd better give it to her now."

"You have a present for me?" Patricia's heart sank. "I don't have a gift for you."

At that, Talon shifted his gaze to her parents and Aunt Adele and offered a smile. "You've given me a family. I'd say that's something."

His words touched her, and she could tell they touched them too. The people at the ranch had been Talon's family for years, and now he could add her own to the list of those he loved.

Outside, in the golden haze of the sunset, Talon presented her with the sweetest strawberry roan she'd ever seen, a Quarter Horse with flowers braided in her mane and tail. The mare had been saddled and stood with one hoof resting, calmly waiting for them.

"Her name is Cherry Berry," Talon said. "I think she'd be a good horse for you to start your riding school."

"She's beautiful." As Patricia stroked Cherry Berry's cheek, the horse breathed in her scent, then bobbed her head as if approving of her new owner. "Why is she saddled?"

"Griff is loaning us a cabin out at his place." Talon rubbed his hands together nervously. "I know it's not much, but it's a pretty area, and it gives us a chance to ... you know, be alone for a while."

A few chuckles sounded from behind them, and heat rose to Patricia's cheeks.

Frank brought Bodine out for Talon. "You two best be movin' along, or you'll be pickin' your way there in the dark."

With a little help from Talon and Marie, Patricia mounted Cherry Berry, draping her skirt across the horse's rump. Her beautiful dress would probably be ruined, but at the moment, she didn't care.

As they walked the horses toward the hill behind the house, she waved at everyone, feeling like she would explode with all the love built up inside of her. This incredible man had arranged everything, and she'd never had a clue. They turned their horses at the top of the hill and headed east. Patricia nudged Cherry Berry closer to Bodine and reached for Talon's hand.

"You amaze me," she said.

He gave her fingers a kiss. "You're the one who's amazing."

"Everything is much like a fairy-tale romance." She glanced at him from the corner of her eye. "But there is one small thing ..."

"What's that?"

She shifted around in the saddle and gazed behind them at the flaming ball dropping lower in a gold- and-crimson sky. "Aren't we supposed to ride *into* the sunset in the last scene?"

The End

Also by Linda W. Yezak

Fiction

The Circle Bar Ranch Series:
Give the Lady a Ride
The Final Ride

The Cat Lady's Secret

Skydiving to Love
a novella

The Simulacrum
(with Brad Seggie)

Nonfiction

Writing in Obedience
(with Terry Burns)

About the Author

Over twenty-five years ago, after a decade of life as a "single-again," author Linda W. Yezak rediscovered God's love and forgiveness when He allowed her a second chance at marital happiness. She is now living her greatest romance with her husband in a forest in East Texas. After such an amazing blessing, she chooses to trumpet God's gift of second chances in the books she writes. Linda's novels are heart-warming hallmarks of love, forgiveness, and new beginnings.

Special note from the author

Authors live for reviews—and reviews keep authors alive and working. If you enjoyed this, or any of my novels, please let others know. And, if you'd like to get first notice of my newest releases, sign up for my "Coffee with Linda" newsletter! You can find the link on my website, lindawyezak.com.

Acknowledgments

This was one of the hardest manuscripts I've ever written. Thanks to several readers, I gained some insight as to what I should present in this, the third of the Circle Bar Ranch series. It took two years to figure out how to do it, and the results are a mixed-genre hybrid of women's fiction and mystery. So my first note of thanks goes to Donald Maass, who unknowingly gave me permission to create such a beast in his how-to book, Writing 21st Century Fiction.

Next note of appreciation goes to award-winning mystery author, C. Hope Clark, who let me know that I am not a mystery writer. But her comments and early direction helped me develop the mystery in this novel, despite its blended-genre state.

Aside from these two, I must thank my Caffeine Dream Team. Every author has a group of amazing people who encourage, support, offer professional help and personal opinion, and make the work in progress as perfect as it can possible get. My team never ceases to amaze me. Their insights are always spot-on and always help guide me as I write and edit.

Among those on my team are Cathy Reuter and Kimberli Buffalo, each of whom had to put up with the fact that for the longest time, they only got to read the first half of the novel. In the early stages of writing, they helped to keep me aimed in the right direction, a service I desperately need when I'm writing by the seat of my pants. Thank you both!

Kimberli served double duty by reading the completed manuscript and making sure I was on point. Her comments and encouragement got me through some tough times. Special thanks and love, sweet /k, for all you do for me. I'd be in a mess without you!

If it wasn't for my critique partner, award winning blogger and author, K.M. Weiland, most of what I publish would be a mess. Very few things go from my computer to public eye without her stamp of approval. She guides me in some of the more technical aspects of novel development, and I don't know what I'd do without her. Thanks, Katie, for all the years you've been there for me.

To Janet, my comma mama and over-used word spotter. You are such a vital part of my team. Thank you for taking me on and helping me polish my work. You are indespensible!

As always, love and appreciation to those who have to put up with me as I work—Mom and Billy. I can't possibly express how much I love you two.

To my Lord and Savior: my heart belongs to You.

www.ingramcontent.com/pod-product-compliance
Lightning Source LLC
Chambersburg PA
CBHW031150120726
47905CB00006B/1884